"Have you ever
she asked.

He laughed. "Do I look like it?"

"That's what I thought."

"What—that no woman would have me?"

"I'm sure plenty of women would have you—
and probably regret it later," Sienna replied.

Brodie grinned down at her, not insulted. "You
could be right. I'm probably not great husband
material. Have *you* ever been married?"

"No." Why had she started this conversation? It
was becoming too personal for her. Reaching the
hotel, Sienna said hastily, "Thank you for seeing
me back." She swung away, stepping into the
road as headlights suddenly swept over her. A
car engine roared, and the vehicle she hadn't
seen or heard leapt out of the darkness.

Just in time, a hard hand grabbed her arm,
hauling her back onto the grass and clamping
her against an equally hard male body.

Dear Reader,

Welcome to another month of excitement and romance. Start your reading by letting Ruth Langan be your guide to DEVIL'S COVE in *Cover-Up,* the first title in her new miniseries set in a small town where secrets, scandal and seduction go hand in hand. The next three books will be coming out back to back, so be sure to catch every one of them.

Virginia Kantra tells a tale of *Guilty Secrets* as opposites Joe Reilly, a cynical reporter, and Nell Dolan, a softhearted do-gooder, can't help but attract each other—with wonderfully romantic results. Jenna Mills will send *Shock Waves* through you as psychic Brenna Scott tries to convince federal prosecutor Ethan Carrington that he's in danger. If she can't get him to listen to her, his life—and her heart—will be lost.

Finish the month with a trip to the lands down under, Australia and New Zealand, as three of your favorite writers mix romance and suspense in equal—and irresistible—portions. Melissa James features another of her tough (and wonderful!) Nighthawk heroes in *Dangerous Illusion,* while Frances Housden's heroine has to face down the *Shadows of the Past* in order to find her happily-ever-after. Finally, get set for high-seas adventure as Sienna Rivers meets *Her Passionate Protector* in Laurey Bright's latest.

Don't miss a single one—and be sure to come back next month for more of the best and most exciting romantic reading around, right here in Silhouette Intimate Moments.

Yours,

Leslie J. Wainger
Executive Editor

Please address questions and book requests to:
Silhouette Reader Service
U.S.: 3010 Walden Ave., P.O. Box 1325, Buffalo, NY 14269
Canadian: P.O. Box 609, Fort Erie, Ont. L2A 5X3

Her Passionate Protector
LAUREY BRIGHT

INTIMATE MOMENTS™

Published by Silhouette Books

America's Publisher of Contemporary Romance

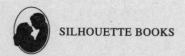 SILHOUETTE BOOKS

ISBN 0-373-27360-6

HER PASSIONATE PROTECTOR

Copyright © 2004 by Daphne Clair de Jong

This edition published by arrangement with Harlequin Books S.A.

® and TM are trademarks of Harlequin Books S.A., used under license.
Trademarks indicated with ® are registered in the United States Patent
and Trademark Office, the Canadian Trade Marks Office and in other
countries.

Visit Silhouette at www.eHarlequin.com

Printed in U.S.A.

LAUREY BRIGHT

has held a number of different jobs but has never wanted to be anything but a writer. She lives in New Zealand, where she creates the stories of contemporary people in love that have won her a following all over the world. Visit her at her Web site, www.laureybright.com.

Prologue

A skeleton isn't an unexpected thing to find under the sea near a sunken ship, and this wasn't the first one Brodie Stanner had come upon. But when he saw the whitened rib cage rising from the sand and a small, gleaming fish shooting out of one of the shadowy eyeholes of the skull, he felt a chill of instant gooseflesh inside his wet suit. The sound of his breath, amplified by the air valve of his scuba tank, was suddenly louder.

Twenty minutes ago, with his diving buddy Rogan Broderick, he'd stepped from the deck of the *Sea-Rogue* into the warm embrace of the Pacific Ocean, emptied air from his buoyancy compensator, and began to glide down in the tropical water, the tank on his back becoming weightless. Some distance away the uneven wall of the reef shimmered with color—purple, blue, orange, green, red—corals and sponges and layered sea fans crowded together in fantastic shapes; seaweeds and giant anemones weaving gently in the current while iridescent jewel-like fish darted in and out among them. Rogan was at his side, a stream of tiny glittering air bubbles from his breathing apparatus expanding as they floated upward.

The water became almost opaque, then cleared. The divers swam up an incline toward the reef, skimming above white sand littered with dead pieces of coral, shells and less recognizable objects encrusted with marine growths. Huge crabs danced daintily over the seafloor, and a bright orange starfish stirred its arms, raising a small puff of sand.

A low curve arched from the seabed, and even before Rogan pointed, Brodie recognized part of a ship's side, studded with barnacles and festooned with seaweed, the rest of the wreck covered in a blanket of soft sand.

They tried with gloved hands to sweep away some of the sand, perhaps identify the bow where there was a slim chance the ship's name might still be visible, but in the time they could safely stay underwater they hadn't made much progress before Rogan indicated they should surface.

The current was stronger than Brodie had realized, carrying them to the reef and some way along it. Then he'd seen the unmistakably human bones huddled by the coral wall.

The lower part of the skeleton was either buried in sand or missing, but the rib cage seemed intact, as was the skull with its huge, empty eye and nose-holes and macabre death-grin. When he paused and waved a hand over the pathetic remains, disturbing the sand, a gleam of white arm bone showed before the cloud of grains started settling again.

One last look, then he finned upward to join Rogan at the first decompression level on their buoy line. They made the remainder of the ascent, taking a couple more decompression stops on the way to clear nitrogen from their systems and prevent the dreaded bends—which could cripple or kill a diver—from attacking them when they surfaced.

Back on board, Brodie took his mouthpiece out and said, "Did you see the skeleton down there?"

Rogan lowered his air tank to the deck and fastened it into a storage clip. "The *Maiden's Prayer* went down with all hands. We might find a few more skeletons, even after a hundred and fifty years.''

''It doesn't look right.''

''Someone died.'' Unzipping his wet suit, Rogan gave him a quizzical look. ''That never looks right. Of course your skeleton might not be from our particular wreck. This reef would have caught quite a few ships over the centuries, specially before it was properly charted.''

The clippers carrying nineteenth-century miners and their newly acquired wealth from the Australian gold fields home to America hadn't had modern navigation instruments and satellite systems to guide them. The *Maiden's Prayer* wasn't the only one reported sunk without a trace, taking a fortune in gold and goods to the bottom of the sea.

Brodie and Rogan finished mapping the site of the wreck as far as they could define it with their sonar and magnometer supplemented by visual inspection, and noted the exact locations of the few artifacts they'd recovered. Rogan's initial survey had been interrupted when he'd discovered the sunken ship some months ago, and they hoped on this trip to find conclusive evidence that it was, as Rogan believed, the *Maiden's Prayer*.

Eating fresh-caught crab on the deck of the *Sea-Rogue*, Rogan said, ''I didn't have time for a thorough inspection when I was here before, but we picked up coins and ship fittings and pieces of jewelry. There just doesn't seem to be as much here now as I would have expected.'' He stared at the three palm trees on a strip of white sand that marked the edge of the reef.

''Maybe you found all there was on the surface. And things shift and get reburied in storms—you know that.''

''Yeah,'' Rogan agreed halfheartedly. ''I hope we haven't had poachers on the site while we've been busy confirming our legal claim to the wreck and organizing a proper recovery operation.''

''We haven't seen any other boats around since we got here. And if some fisherman or recreational diver did get lucky enough to find a few bits and pieces scattered about, they haven't broached the wreck. They'd need proper equipment and a professional team of divers, and you know how long it's taking to set that up yourself."

Rogan cracked open a crab leg and removed a morsel of white flesh. "Right. Even if the location of the site has leaked out somehow, probably the worst that can happen before we get to the real treasure is a bit of pilfering." He popped the bit of crabmeat into his mouth. "Well, our last dive is tomorrow."

"Yeah." Brodie grinned. Rogan had to be back in port for his wedding. "Better get you to the church on time."

They dived early, found a couple of coins and some glass bottles that might help date the wreck, and then Brodie spotted a few inches of something curved. Something metal and man-made—green, and almost invisible under the sand. Maybe Rogan's porthole, he thought, digging his fingers into the seabed to clear the object.

He signaled Rogan and they excavated it and took it to the surface, hauling it on board. It was a ship's bell, tarnished and half covered in corals and sponges. But after scraping those away, faintly the two men could discern some letters just above the rim.

"Eureka!" Rogan exclaimed softly, turning the bell to read the inscription. "*Maiden's Prayer.* My dad was right. He found his gold-ship. Let's go home. But we don't mention this to anyone."

Brodie looked up from his awed contemplation of their find. Abruptly he said, "I want to have another look at that skeleton."

Rogan gave him a curious look but said, "Sure, okay."

He stowed the bell in the master's cabin, and when they'd been out of the water long enough for a second safe dive, they donned their gear again and swam to the reef wall.

It took a while to find again the place where the skeleton lay, apparently undisturbed, and by then their time was nearly up. Brodie looked down at the empty eye sockets—almost accusing with their blank, black stare—and peered inside the skull.

There was sand in there, not unexpectedly. But…dimly he discerned a faint raised lump. A brief hesitation, then he stripped off one glove, gingerly poked two fingers into an eyehole, and withdrew a small, dully gleaming object.

A bullet.

Chapter 1

Sunlight slanted through a small high window in the seamen's chapel at Mokohina. The insistent sound of the sea washing onto the beach backgrounded the bride and groom's voices as they recited their vows.

In the second row of the pews, Brodie watched the golden light burnish the bridesmaid's piled curls, inside a coronet of flowers, and turn a wayward strand lying on her graceful neck to an almost ruby red. Something about that slim, pale neck, contrasting with the rich auburn glow of her hair, hinted at vulnerability. A stirring of curiosity kept his gaze focused lazily on her.

He hadn't seen her face when she'd preceded Camille down the aisle—he'd been riveted by the sudden blaze in Rogan's eyes as the other man turned to watch his bride approach. The raw emotion of that look had shaken Brodie, waking complicated feelings of awe coupled with a surprising shaft of something remarkably like envy.

Marriage wasn't something he'd ever thought seriously about, himself. He was pretty sure Rogue hadn't either until he met Camille, who was gorgeous enough to weaken any man's resolve, with her green eyes and thick, glossy brown hair, a face that turned men's heads in the street, and a figure any model might envy.

When the bridal party turned toward the door and the best man—Rogan's brother, Granger—offered his arm to the bridesmaid, Brodie got his first real look at her.

An almost translucent complexion that reminded him of pearl-shell, delicately arched eyebrows, eyes that were more gold than brown framed by dark, gold-tipped lashes. Which meant their color must be natural, surely. And a mouth made for kissing, with a decided bow on the upper lip, a delicious fullness in the lower one, firmly set together. For a moment he thought he caught a hint of sadness in the golden eyes, and extra sheen. But then, women always cried at weddings, didn't they? By all accounts they quite enjoyed a good weep.

Even as he watched, the luscious mouth trembled into a smile. Not quite as radiant as the bride's, but bewitching. He let his gaze slide over her figure—on the thin side, he thought critically. But subtly curved in the right places, her breasts surprisingly well-rounded. Maybe Mother Nature was getting some help there. A man could never tell for sure.

Because her bronze silk dress was quite short, worn with matching high-heeled shoes, he could see she had great legs, the ankles so slim they looked breakable. He reckoned he could easily put a hand around one of them. Picturing it, something more than simple curiosity stirred his blood— something much more carnal. And unsuitable for a church.

Then she swept past with the bridal party and he followed the rest of the congregation outside.

The reception was held in the private lounge of the nearby Imperial Hotel, a two-story white wooden leftover of New Zealand's colonial past. After the meal and toasts were completed, the cake was cut and the bridesmaid offered pieces to the fifty or so guests now mingling around the room. He followed her progress, having covertly watched her ever since she'd sat down at the bridal table with Camille and Rogan.

Apart from the bride, she was, he'd decided after a quick check, the most watchable woman in sight, intriguing and somewhat perplexing. Most of the time she wore a pleasant but slightly cool expression that only kindled into warmth when she spoke to Camille and now, when she bent to offer a piece of cake to a small, shy boy, giving him an encouraging, full-on smile as he took his time over choosing.

Her position also gave Brodie a chance to check that the temptingly rounded breasts encased in a low-cut cream lace bra were nature's work alone.

As she straightened, he hastily shifted his gaze to her face. Her smile abruptly faded when she met his eyes, and she blinked before turning to allow a couple of people to take their share of cake.

Finally reaching Brodie, she gave him a quick smile but her eyes seemed to look through him before she lowered her gaze to the platter she offered.

He took a piece of cake with a thick layer of white icing and said, "We haven't met. I'm Brodie—Brodie Stanner. And you're Sienna Rivers, the archaeologist who assessed some of the pieces Rogan salvaged."

She seemed surprised that he knew that, the dark pupils of her eyes almost obscuring the amber glow when she looked up at him. "I did look at some stuff for Camille," she acknowledged rather warily.

Brodie nodded. "You work with her at the university."

"Camille's in the history department at Rusden, but at the end of the semester she's joining Rogan's treasure-hunting company." Her voice sounded disapproving, or perhaps disappointed. Turning away from him, she murmured, "Excuse me."

She went on wending through the crowd, giving the same nice but impersonal smile to everyone as she dispensed her slices of cake.

Ruefully, Brodie stared after her.

Most women found something at least superficially attractive in his tanned, fit body, his clear blue eyes, the squared-off jaw with its hint of a cleft, and even his thick, naturally sun-streaked hair.

Sienna's patent disinterest, and the fact that it annoyed him more than was reasonable, made him wonder if he was guilty of having an overinflated ego.

Across the room she tilted her head to the best man as Granger relieved her of the empty platter and handed her a glass of wine, his perfectly groomed dark head bent and aquamarine eyes fixed on her as they talked, the expression on his undeniably good-looking face attentive.

For the second time that day Brodie envied one of the Broderick brothers.

Tearing his gaze away, he found it caught by a sweet-faced little blonde. She gave him a come-hither smile and did that bashful, fluttering thing with her eyelashes that women sometimes used to signal interest. After a peculiar instant of something that couldn't possibly have been boredom, he smiled back and began to make his way toward her.

Granger Broderick offered to take away Sienna's empty cake platter, and as he left her side, she turned and surveyed the room.

The glass in her hand was something to hold and an excuse to stop smiling for a while, giving her aching facial muscles a rest. She took a sip of the wine Granger had poured for her.

Rogan's brother was carrying out his duties with impeccable courtesy and a certain aloofness that was infinitely reassuring. Quite unlike the unabashed interest of the man with the brazen summer-sky eyes.

She'd thought, before he gave his surname, that "Brodie" might be short for Broderick. But according to Camille, Rogan had only one brother.

Besides, he looked nothing like the Brodericks, who both met the classic definition of tall, dark and handsome—where he scored two out of three. Not that his blond-streaked brown hair was any handicap. She wondered if the streaks were artificial. Although he didn't give an impression of vanity, his confident manner and assumption that she'd be pleased to stand talking with him argued that he was well aware of his own male appeal.

Men with such obvious sexual self-possession made her uncomfortable, sending out signals that she found too overt, taking for granted that she—or any woman—would be only too happy to return them.

Which most women would, she supposed, being fair. She'd learned the hard way that she wanted—needed—more from a man than good looks and sexual prowess, real or imagined.

Her glance idly passed over the guests. Camille and Rogan were circulating among them, and Brodie had moved to another part of the room, his head interestedly cocked to an animated blonde who was surely delighted to have his attention.

Sienna drank some more wine and reminded herself not to overdo it, especially as she'd only picked at the food laid out on the table. Her appetite hadn't yet recovered after a virulent bout of food poisoning that had landed her in hospital only weeks ago, followed by an attack of some nasty superbug that had taken advantage of her weakened state and prolonged her stay. It had been doubtful whether she would make it to the wedding at all.

The big room seemed suddenly stuffy. Perhaps the wine wasn't a wise idea after all, and she'd been on her feet too long.

There were no unoccupied chairs nearby. Cursing the continuing weakness that she'd hoped had passed for good, she turned to put down the glass on the nearest table and experienced a wave of dizzy nausea.

A quick visual search for an escape route revealed a pair of closed French doors leading to the hotel garden and an umbrella-shaded table with canvas chairs set on the grass. She started toward the doors.

They wouldn't open, and wrestling with the catch she ex-

perienced a moment's panic. Black spots were beginning to
float before her eyes. The last thing she wanted was to cause
a sensation by passing out at her friend's wedding.

Then a suit-sleeved arm reached around her and pulled
down a recalcitrant bolt, a masculine hand pushed the door
open and a blessed wave of fresh, salty air stirred her hair
and cooled her face. The hand circled her arm as she stumbled
onto the grass, and a rough-timbred, urgent voice said in her
ear, "Are you all right?"

"Yes," she lied, but her voice was almost inaudible, and
she was infinitely grateful for the chair the man thrust her
into. She rested her elbows on the table and let her head fall
onto her raised hands until the dancing spots disappeared and
the breeze cleared her swimming head.

Looking up, she saw Brodie Stanner had seated himself and
was watching her, his eyes darkened to cobalt with concern.
"Can I get you anything?"

"No, I'm fine." She would be in a minute or two. "Thank
you."

"Fine, huh?" Concern changed to patent disbelief. "You
look like death."

"It was hot inside. I'll be all right now."

Ignoring the hint, he ran a disparaging glance over her.
"Are you dieting or something?"

"I don't diet!"

"You didn't eat much in there."

"I'm not very hungry." He'd taken note of how much she
ate?

"Why not?"

The look on his handsome face didn't encourage her to
think he'd let the subject go until he was satisfied. She finally
said, "I've been sick recently, but it wasn't life-threatening
and I'm perfectly all right now, only I haven't got much appetite yet."

"I thought you were going to faint."

So had she, but fortunately that hadn't happened, mainly
thanks to him. Recognizing a fatal tendency to gratitude, she

said distantly, "It was kind of you to open the door for me, but don't you want to go back to your…companion?"

For a moment he looked blank. Then he said, "I only just met her—she's not likely to miss me."

Sienna might have disputed that. No woman could be immune to so much blatant masculinity, and the blonde had been quite clearly smitten.

She looked down at her hands, clasped tightly on the table, and deliberately loosened them. "I'm all right now," she reiterated. "Really."

He reached out and touched the back of his fingers to her cheek, bringing a quick, unexpected heat flaring under the skin, a tiny shock of pleasure setting warning bells off in her mind. "You've got a bit more color," he said, "but you're still pale."

"I'm naturally pale," Sienna argued. "It comes with my hair."

"It's fantastic," Brodie said. "The color, I mean."

"Thank you." The words came out clipped, and she pretended not to see the curious look he cast her. "Excuse me, Camille might need me." He was altogether too attractive. Sienna knew to her cost how easily she could fall victim to compliments and concern. Especially when allied with such a good-looking face and a calendar-hunk body that even a formal suit couldn't hide. She began to rise from her chair.

Brodie's hand immediately pinned hers to the table, his palm warm, slightly roughened and very firm. He glanced past her to the hotel. "Camille doesn't need anyone but Rogue right now. They're still talking to people. You should rest a while. You don't want to go all woozy again."

He was actually right. Even her sudden movement had made her head spin a little.

Despising the alarming melting sensation in her midriff evoked by his clasp on her hand, she tried to pull away, but he retained his grip and held her gaze until she stopped resisting, though her eyes showed her resentment.

Brodie slid his hand from hers and said calmly, "Just relax, and tell me if there's anything you want. A glass of water or something?''

''Nothing, really.'' Unsettled by his steady regard, she carefully turned her head to admire the blue-green water across the road and the boats riding at anchor in the harbor. Making conversation, she said, ''Mokohina's a pretty little town.''

''I like it.''

''You live here?''

''I've knocked about the world a bit, but this is where I'm based. I own the local dive shop.''

She might have known he was a diver. Not quite as tall as his friend, he shared Rogan's broad-shouldered physique, and had the look of someone who spent a lot of time near the sea. She'd have guessed a surfer if it hadn't been for his connection with the Brodericks.

''Are you related to Rogan and Granger?'' She supposed he could be a cousin or something.

He shook his head. ''Nope, but Rogue and I have been hanging out together off and on since primary school. He'll look after Camille, don't worry about that.''

Her gaze flew back to him. How had he known she was concerned for her friend, who had fallen in love with a man Sienna couldn't help thinking was all wrong for her? A man Camille herself had admitted was the very antithesis of what she'd thought was her ideal.

He said, ''There's no news about the stolen shipwreck items?''

She supposed if they were such old friends it was natural for him to be in Rogan's confidence. She'd been asked to keep very quiet about the antique coins, jewelry and watches she'd been entrusted with. She'd explained when Camille enlisted her expertise that she'd have to take the head of the archaeology department partially into her confidence so she could use the university facilities, but she'd told no one else. ''The police don't seem to have any ideas.''

She felt unreasonably guilty about the theft, although Camille and Rogan had been very understanding. It wasn't her fault that the laboratory where she'd been painstakingly removing a century and a half of verdigris and various accretions from the artifacts recovered from a wreck site somewhere out in the Pacific had been burgled while she was in hospital. Fortunately not before she'd taken full sets of photographs.

Other things had been stolen. Sienna's students had been excavating a recently discovered pa site. The palisaded Maori village from which tattooed warriors had once defended their families against attack had long gone, leaving only a grassy terraced hillside. The dig had yielded priceless jade and bone ornaments and weapons to be studied before finding suitable homes with tribal descendants of the original owners or in museums. But these precious artifacts had now disappeared.

"Nothing's been recovered," she told Brodie.

"Well, I guess there's more treasure under the sea, where Rogue found that lot," Brodie said. "And Pacific Treasure Salvors will be back there as soon as the divers and equipment are ready, hopefully before anyone else gets to it."

Although the Brodericks had done their best to keep quiet about their discovery and refused to talk to the media, it was an open secret that the *Sea-Rogue* had found a treasure ship, and rumor was rife about the new company's plans. Even the name they'd given it was a dead giveaway. She supposed they'd seen no point in trying to disguise its purpose, since the secret was out anyway.

Sienna bit at her thumbnail, a frown creasing her forehead. Despite Camille's assurance that the salvage would be carried out with due regard to the wreck's historical importance, she wasn't at all sure her friend hadn't been dazzled by her dashing new husband into a false sense of security. Apparently the Broderick brothers' father had been obsessed with finding a treasure ship, and Rogan looked to be following in the old man's footsteps.

"What's the matter?" Brodie asked curiously.

She dropped her hand. "I'm not sure about this company—disturbing a historic wreck."

Brodie folded his arms, his eyes assessing her. "You want the ship to remain on the bottom of the ocean, untouched, until it rots away?"

"I'd just like to know that nothing of archaeological significance is lost because of ignorance or greed."

Brodie's eyebrows lifted. He said in a deceptively mild tone, "Don't you trust Camille to make sure that doesn't happen? She's the official researcher and a qualified historian."

"She's in love!" Sienna shot back at him. "It tends to skew people's thinking." As Brodie cast her an inquiring look, she said hastily, "I'm sure she'll do her best, but archaeology isn't her specialty, and..."

"And you're afraid that Rogan will influence her." Brodie appeared slightly amused. "Don't you realize the guy is crazy about her? He'd do anything for Camille. She only has to lift her little finger."

"That may not last." A shadow touched her heart, but she tried to keep it from reaching her face.

His expression was quizzical. "Cynic," he accused. "A bit young for that, aren't you? Twenty-five?"

"Twenty-seven." She was well aware that he was fishing. He'd be about Rogan's age, presumably—thirtyish. "Age has nothing to do with it. I'm being realistic."

"Have you ever been in love?"

Something inside her quivered. "Of course. Haven't you?"

Brodie looked past her, and his eyes glazed. He said slowly, "Not...like that."

Involuntarily she turned to see what had taken his attention. Camille and Rogan were framed in the open doorway, holding each other's hands and for the moment alone. And it wasn't the sun that lent that almost blinding glow to Camille's face, or kindled the fierce light in her new husband's eyes.

The picture held Sienna spellbound for a second, and an unaccountable lump rose in her throat. Rogan said something to his bride, and she gave him a smile that positively dazzled. He lowered his head and touched his lips to hers. It looked like an act of homage, and Sienna recalled the words from the traditional marriage service he'd spoken in the chapel earlier, "With my body I thee worship...."

She experienced a return of the poignant sense of desolation that had unexpectedly pierced her when a radiant Camille and blazingly proud Rogan had turned from the altar to begin their married life.

Brodie said softly, "You don't think that will last?"

Wrenching her gaze away, Sienna lifted a shoulder. "Who knows? All I'm saying is I wouldn't count on it." For Camille's sake she fervently hoped it would, but experience made her cautious of such predictions.

Brodie's blue gaze was suddenly penetrating. "Want to bet on it?"

Shaking her head, she said, "I don't gamble."

"That figures."

It sounded like a derogatory comment, but she didn't reply, instead shifting her attention again to the moored boats. "Is one of those the *Sea-Rogue?*" Camille and Rogan planned a short honeymoon on the boat they owned, before its refitting was completed and they put it to work as a dive tender for Pacific Treasure Salvors.

"She's farther round the bay," Brodie told her. "At the old fishing wharves."

Sienna nodded. She looked away from the boats and started to get up. This time Brodie didn't stop her.

"Well, nice talking to you," she said distantly as he too rose to his feet.

He cocked his head, his questioning eyes openly doubting her sincerity, but he didn't follow when she made her way to the now empty doorway.

Sienna found Camille who said, "I might go up and change soon. Are you all right? You look a bit flushed."

"I'm fine," Sienna insisted. "I've been sitting out in the sun." Although Brodie had made sure she was under the shade of the umbrella.

"Oh, yes. Granger was hunting for you but he said Brodie seemed to be looking after you."

"I don't need looking after!"

Camille smiled at her vehemence. "You do look a bit fragile, and I suppose it brings out the protective instinct in the male of the species."

"They can keep their instincts to themselves as far as I'm concerned." A long time ago Sienna had learned there was no sanctuary in a man's arms. That the only person she could rely on to look after her was herself.

Regarding her thoughtfully, Camille evidently decided not to comment. "It's only about two weeks since you came out of hospital. You would have said, wouldn't you, if you weren't up to being my bridesmaid?"

"I told you," Sienna replied, "it's a pleasure. I didn't want to miss it." In truth, the pleasure was mixed with concern on her friend's behalf. Impressed despite herself by Camille's steadfast certainty, she hadn't dared voice her own reservations.

A little later they went upstairs and Camille shed her wedding gown in favor of more practical cotton pants and a shirt. Most of the wedding party then decamped along the foreshore to see the newlyweds aboard the *Sea-Rogue* for their short honeymoon cruise, and as the boat slipped out of its berth some of the onlookers threw streamers across the widening gap and Camille tossed her bouquet to the wharf.

Sienna stepped back, her hands resolutely at her sides, but Granger deftly caught it, and when he presented it to her with one of his grave smiles and a faintly lifted eyebrow, she could hardly refuse to take the flowers.

Back at the hotel Granger told Sienna, "I've booked us a table for dinner here at seven-thirty. Camille's mother and some other people will be joining us."

Supposing that entertaining Mona Hartley was part of her bridal-attendant duties, Sienna said, "I'll get changed and meet you in the dining room later."

In her bathroom she freed her hair from its knot of curls and brushed it out, hoping it wouldn't spring back into its usual wild corkscrews too quickly. The floor creaked as she crossed the old kauri boards to her suitcase and pulled out a plain sand-colored skirt and a sleeveless cream top embroidered with amber beads. The mirror in which she checked her appearance before going downstairs had a heavy carved wooden frame on which stylized Maori patterns were mixed with depictions of roses and lilies.

At the foot of the stairs she saw Brodie, one hand thrust into a pocket of his dark trousers, his collar open and his jacket slung across one shoulder. He watched her descend, his gaze swiftly encompassing her from head to toe and returning to her face with a gleam of masculine appreciation lurking in the vivid depths, and she wished she'd thought to take the old elevator instead, but for only one floor it hadn't seemed worth it.

"Ready for your dinner?" he asked her.

"I'm having it with Granger," she said coolly, fighting a ridiculous sense of pleasure at the way his hair gleamed in the light from a chandelier overhead, the blond streaks turning to gold.

"I know. Me too," he replied, walking at her side as she made for the dining room. "I offered to wait for you."

She wasn't late, but when they entered, two women already sat with Granger at the round table—Camille's mother and another middle-aged woman.

Mona looked pinched and put upon—not unusual in Sienna's experience. The other woman, whom Granger smoothly introduced as Mollie Edwards, a good friend of his and Rogan's late father, was cozily rounded with brass-colored curls framing her rather overpainted face, and a wide smile.

Sienna took to her immediately, but to help Granger out—and also to avoid having to talk too much to Brodie, whose presence she was all too conscious of at her side—she devoted a good deal of her attention during the meal to Mona. The woman had just seen her only child marry a man Sienna had a strong hunch she didn't approve of. Though it seemed that

Mollie's presence had more to do with Mona's offended air than did the loss of her daughter.

Granger occasionally caught Sienna's eye with a hint of grateful appreciation in the turquoise depths of his, and attempted to keep the conversation general around the table.

Brodie had discarded his suit and wore casual gray pants and a T-shirt. When his bare arm brushed against hers as he reached for salt, Sienna felt as though the tiny hairs on her skin had been charged with a current of electricity. It must be the dry seaside air, she thought, confused. The same phenomenon that caused her clothes to crackle sometimes when she shed them.

Mollie was excited that Rogan and his brother, along with Camille who had inherited half of the *Sea-Rogue*, were planning to raise the treasure their late father had discovered. "Barney always knew he'd find it someday." She wiped a small tear from her eye with her table napkin.

Mona gave a scornful little laugh. "I have my doubts about this whole thing." She speared a piece of fish on her plate. "Camille won't even tell me what all the excitement is about. After all," she complained, "my husband was Barney's partner, I think I'm entitled."

Granger studied her for a moment, then said quietly, "I'm sure you can keep a secret, Mona. Rogan's already recovered coins and a few pieces of jewelry from the wreck Barney found. The cargo, if we can recover it, could be worth a great deal."

Brodie swallowed a mouthful of his rare steak. "Even passengers' effects might bring in quite a lot of money, coming from a historic wreck."

Mona sniffed. "What difference can that make?"

Granger explained, "Sunken treasure accrues value from its history. A romantic shipwreck story and a certificate of authenticity make for a better price at auction."

Sienna commented, "It's an artificial inflation. Part of this whole business of commercial treasure hunting."

Brodie turned to her. "Can you give an expert opinion,"

he asked her, "on the possible worth of the pieces Rogan had?"

She had to meet his eyes, finding them blindingly blue and disconcertingly close. She could see her own face reflected in them, giving her an odd feeling of unwanted intimacy. For a moment she couldn't recall what the conversation was about. Pulling herself together, she said, "The brief I was given was to try to find out where and when they were made, to help identify the wreck. I'm sure Rogan and Granger will get the highest prices possible."

Mollie's look at Sienna was disappointed. "You sound as though you disapprove."

Brodie said, sounding amused, "Sienna's suspicious of treasure hunters." His eyes teased her, still holding her gaze until she wrenched it away as Mollie spoke to her.

"Why?" Mollie asked. "*You're* too young to be bitter and twisted about it." She directed a meaningful look at Mona, who almost choked on another morsel of fish.

Granger's gaze went to Sienna. "I'm sure you have good reasons. Would you like to tell us what they are?"

Sienna suspected he knew very well, or could at least make an educated guess. But the men obviously hoped, by throwing Sienna into the arena, to avoid open female warfare.

Ignoring the over-respectful look that Brodie turned on her, she said, "Old shipwrecks contain a lot of information about life in former times. Ships might remain preserved in mud or sand for centuries, until someone disturbs that protection and leaves them open to decay."

Beside her Brodie moved slightly, and she heard him take in a breath as though about to say something, but without giving him the chance, she continued defiantly, "Nothing should be removed from a wreck before an archaeological survey is conducted and the site properly mapped."

Mollie looked dubious. Brodie tipped his chair and hooked one arm over the back of it to lazily study Sienna. He said, "It costs a hell of a lot to salvage a wreck properly. Even archaeologists aren't keen on going ahead without hard evidence that it's going to be worthwhile. And most of them don't have the money or expertise to do it.''

Mona gave a genteel snort, perhaps of corroboration.

"It seems to be a constant dilemma,'' Granger agreed, confirming Sienna's suspicion that he hadn't needed to be informed of the problem. "It's only by bringing in investors that anyone can exploit a remote, difficult wreck—and investors expect a profit."

Sienna acknowledged that reluctantly, glad to concentrate on him instead of Brodie. "Only, irresponsible divers can ruin a heritage that belongs to us all. Priceless objects have been melted down for their metal. It's criminal!''

Brodie was still regarding her, his gaze turning curious. "Not all treasure hunters are looters and vandals," he told her. "And your colleagues can be so pigheaded that in the end no one benefits."

"Pigheaded?" She flashed him a hostile look.

"What's the point of barring salvors from exploring wrecks that are breaking up and being scattered all over the seabed? Or due to go under earthworks in harbors and be buried for all time?"

"I hope that wouldn't happen."

"It *has* happened. And *that's* criminal, surely? Salvage is damned hard work.'' Brodie let his chair drop back to the floor and leaned toward her, one strong forearm on the table. "Dangerous too, with far more disappointments than successes. Most of what divers recover goes to museums or private collections, where they're cared for and available for people like you to study.''

"But treasure hunters' primary concern is money,'' Sienna objected. She gave him a challenging stare, her passion for the subject making her bold. The prickling sensations running up her arms must signal antipathy for his argument, she thought.

He looked at her almost pityingly. "It's not a sin to be paid for what you do. And guys who dive for treasure aren't in it just for the money. There's a thrill in finding something precious that's been under the sea for a hundred or even a thousand years. You'd know that.''

''Of course!'' She knew how it felt to unearth a Victorian china cup or a pre-European carved Maori implement, and speculate who had owned it, who had crafted it, how they had lived so long ago, how and when they had died.

Granger regarded her thoughtfully across the table. ''I know you have a secure position at the university, Sienna,'' he said, ''but I wonder if you would consider joining Pacific Treasure Salvors as our official archaeologist?''

Chapter 2

Sienna stared back at Granger. "Me?"

He didn't smile. "Camille mentioned before you got ill that she'd like to have you on board. I was going to broach this to you tomorrow, but as the subject's come up..."

Brodie glanced Granger's way, and some kind of wordless exchange briefly passed between them. Sienna wondered if there was a reason Camille hadn't done the asking earlier. Maybe the men had wanted to check her out.

Mollie's eyes sparkled. "It sounds exciting. If I were you, dear, I'd jump at the chance. I've got a little investment in the company myself. For Barney's sake."

Mona looked as though she was about to roll her eyes.

Sienna was bemused. Of course she didn't want to be any part of a treasure hunt. Did she? "I don't think—"

Brodie interrupted. "You'd get to make sure things are done the way you think they should be."

Granger added, "Camille said you're experienced at scuba work."

"I've done some," Sienna admitted. She'd learned to dive

as a teenager, so in her student days when an ancient Maori canoe was discovered buried in the silt of a tidal estuary, she'd been seconded by the professor in charge of the underwater excavation and had taken advanced courses to improve her skills. "But most of my wreck diving has been recreational."

Granger said, "I hope you'll give our offer some thought. I'll be happy to supply details anytime."

Even as she shook her head, starting to say thanks but no thanks, Brodie argued, sitting back in his chair again to fix her with a direct look. "If you're really worried about the site being ruined this is your chance to make sure that doesn't happen."

Sienna hesitated, and Granger flicked Brodie a slightly amused glance. "He's right. But your university job isn't something to be treated lightly. Nor, I understand, is possibly risking your reputation among your peers. I know a lot of archaeologists regard working with treasure salvors as incompatible with their profession."

Granger's understanding and Brodie's challenge made her seem stuffy and overcautious—and more interested in preserving her position and salary than in her avowed mission of saving precious remnants of the past. She directed a suspicious look at Granger, but his expression was perfectly serious, his eyes blandly meeting hers.

"There's no immediate hurry to make a decision," he told her. "The *Sea-Rogue* won't be sailing again until the hurricane season's over, and we have a top-notch salvage team and the necessary equipment in place. Camille intends to finish the semester. Maybe if you decide not to take the job you could recommend someone."

Then he turned to Mona, offering to refill her wineglass, and the subject was dropped.

After she'd gone to bed, Sienna lay listening to the breakers gently washing the sand, the occasional sound of a car passing by, voices carrying on the clear night air.

She shouldn't even be thinking about Granger's surprising proposition, but her mind wouldn't let it go.

What he was offering could be an escape from a niggling worry that she'd put to the back of her mind.

She'd scarcely thought about Aidan Rutherford, her head of department, since coming to Mokohina.

Aidan had visited almost daily when she was in hospital, bringing flowers, books and exotic foodstuffs that he hoped would tempt her appetite. He'd even volunteered to keep an eye on her home and water her plants and feed the little cat that had adopted her.

One afternoon, he'd caught her hand in his and leaned toward her, saying her name in an urgent undertone. But when her startled gaze flew to his earnest brown eyes he'd suddenly dropped her hand, sat back and pinched the skin on the bridge of his long nose, his expression hidden as he muttered, "I hope you'll be better soon. I…we miss you in the staff room."

On her first day back at work his rather melancholy face lit up with relief when she walked into his office. He'd come round his desk and taken both her hands, then brushed a light kiss across her cheek, and after stepping back there was color in his normally sallow cheeks. He'd passed a hand over his thinning hair before retreating behind his desk and assuming a businesslike manner, to her considerable relief.

If Aidan ever showed signs of more than friendly interest they were both in trouble. He was married.

Not only married, but with a delightful brown-eyed daughter of six years.

Apart from an aversion to messy extramarital affairs between colleagues that led to gossip and tensions and sometimes wrecked careers and lives, and Sienna's own moral and very personal objections to breaking up a marriage, no way could she be responsible for hurting a child.

He was the kind of man she'd hoped one day to meet, but he was definitely off limits.

Maybe she was mistaking concern at her illness for something else. But even though she tried to believe that, she couldn't shake the uneasy knowledge that lately Aidan had been looking at her in a way she found disquieting, hurriedly shifting his gaze when he saw she'd noticed.

There were soft footsteps in the passageway, and someone quietly opened and closed a door. A light flickered against the window for a few minutes, then went out, leaving the room seemingly darker than before.

Resolutely Sienna closed her eyes. Images of the day imprinted themselves on her lids like a moving slide show. Camille's radiant face, the sunlight that had flashed briefly on the gold band Rogan placed firmly on his bride's finger, Granger reaching to catch the bouquet that now sat in a vase on the low table by the window. She had no idea what she was going to do with it. Probably leave it for the hotel staff to take care of.

The last clear picture she saw before drifting off was of Brodie Stanner looking at her with studied concentration when she threw back at him his question about ever having been in love. And she heard again the strange intensity in his voice as he lifted his gaze to watch Rogan and Camille and said, "Not like that."

Rogan had arranged for Granger to drive Sienna to Auckland where he had his home and legal practice, and she was booked on a flight to take her from there farther south to Palmerston North, where she'd pick up her own car and drive to her house near the Rusden campus.

On the way he told her what terms the company could offer an archaeologist, and at the airport insisted on carrying her bag to the counter. He bought a newspaper, and while she checked in, he glanced over a couple of pages.

As Sienna turned back to him with her boarding pass in her hand he gave a soft exclamation and frowned down at something he was reading.

"What is it?" she asked.

Granger looked up, his mouth hardening. "James Drummond's broken his bail conditions. Apparently he hasn't been seen for two months.''

It was a moment before she connected. Then a cold shiver attacked her spine. James Drummond had been indirectly responsible for the death of Granger and Rogan's father.

''Damn.'' Granger's voice held unusual force. ''And damn the judge who let him stay out of jail until the trial. Now there may not be one.''

''He threatened to kill Camille and Rogan!'' He'd been prepared to stop at nothing to get at the *Maiden's Prayer* and her treasure before the Brodericks. Even murder.

''Yes,'' Granger agreed grimly. ''Though I don't suppose they're in any danger now that there's nothing he can get from them. He's probably only concerned with saving his own skin. He'll be lying low somewhere. Maybe out of the country.''

In a way Sienna hoped so. ''Didn't he have to hand over his passport?''

''As the police said when they opposed bail, he has contacts in the shipping industry from illegally exporting prohibited heritage items out of New Zealand. Let's hope Rogue and Camille don't find out about this until their honeymoon's over. It could put a damper on it.''

He refolded the paper and handed her a card, saying, ''Call me if you need any more information about the job, and I do hope you're going to join us. Camille would be pleased.''

A few days after Sienna's return to the dig with her students, the team unearthed a cache of carved Maori weapons that might date back as far as pre-European times, and she invited Aidan to visit and give his advice.

After agreeing with her assessment and helping secure the site, Aidan offered to treat the team to a drink in celebration, and at the conclusion of a couple of hours in a pub she found that her car wouldn't start. ''My own fault,'' she admitted ruefully to the young men who fruitlessly opened up the engine and peered at the interior, jiggling wires. ''It's been iffy lately but I was just too busy to get it checked.''

Rain began to fall, it was dark and she didn't fancy sitting around waiting for help. "I'll get a taxi," she said, "and call the AA in the morning."

"I'll run you home," Aidan offered, having already piled several students into his car. One of them got out and insisted on her having the front seat.

Aidan dropped off the students first at their hostel, and then in silence drove her to the small house she rented in the center of the city.

Drawing up outside, he sat frowning through the windscreen as she unfastened her seat belt. "I'm sorry," he said, "if I've not been good company tonight."

"You're always good company, Aidan," she assured him, pausing as she fumbled for the door handle.

He gave a strained laugh. "Tell that to my wife," he muttered. "She thinks I'm a bore—I don't know what kind of life she expected with an archaeology lecturer, but it's not lively enough for her. And my salary won't stretch to the sort of lifestyle she'd like."

Sharon Rutherford always gave an impression of being restless and bored at any university function she attended, and it was fairly obvious she didn't want to be there.

"I'm sorry," Sienna murmured uncomfortably. Her fingers closed about the handle.

"Don't go yet." He turned to her with a pleading expression.

"Won't your wife be wondering where you are?"

"I phoned her, said good night to Pixie and promised to give her a kiss if she's still awake when I get home." His daughter's name was Priscilla, but he called her Pixie.

"Give Pixie a hug for me," Sienna said, beginning to open the door.

"That's very sweet of you." As she turned away he said her name in a desperate undertone. "Sienna, I—" He grabbed at her free hand, holding tightly, then pulled the other one into an equally fierce grip and lunged toward her.

Sienna sharply turned her head to the side. Dragging herself away, she said firmly, "Good night, Aidan. Thanks for the lift."

As she hurried to her front door, he restarted the engine and roared away with an uncharacteristic screech of tires.

Her heart was pounding, and she felt a shivery dismay.

Aidan was close to the ideal man she had quite consciously set up in her mind, a man she could respect and admire. Who seemed to respect and like her. But although they worked closely together, at times she'd almost forgotten that he was male.

It crossed her mind that Brodie Stanner would never have allowed her to forget that important fact. When she was with him she hadn't been able to put it out of her mind for a minute. He'd simply exuded masculinity and hadn't bothered to hide his interest in her. Not that she supposed it was exclusive. There'd been that blonde at the wedding reception, and no doubt if nothing had come of that he'd found another woman to take his fancy by now. Perhaps more than one…

Impatiently she dragged herself back to the immediate problem.

She couldn't—*wouldn't*—allow Aidan to endanger his marriage and embroil her in the resultant mess. The thought of following in her father's footsteps made her feel sick.

She'd been fifteen when her parents' marriage had been torn apart by his affair with a woman he'd worked with. Two families had been shattered by the inability of two people to stand by their vows.

No way was she going to be the cause of another man making the same mistake. Why couldn't he have maintained the comfortable working partnership of the past two years?

She went to bed torn between pity for Aidan and a muted anger that he'd clumsily tipped the neutral balance of their relationship. Once that balance had shifted, they could never regain their previous equilibrium. And the tension would spill into her work.

Next morning she phoned Granger Broderick and said, "I'm interested in that job with your company."

* * *

Sienna allowed the university authorities to believe that her health was the main reason for her requesting indefinite leave of absence from the end of the semester. Her normal appetite hadn't returned and she was aware that her colleagues worried about her. The professor emeritus who had filled in while she was hospitalized was happy to return for the next semester. But when she confessed to Aidan that she was going to work on a marine archaeology project he was taken aback, even shocked. Sitting opposite her at his desk, he dropped the pencil he'd been idly playing with and stared as though he didn't believe what he was hearing. "This is connected to those artifacts your friend from the history department brought to you that were stolen?" Surprising her with his vehemence, he said, "Sienna, I'd advise you to have nothing more to do with that!"

"I know some archaeologists feel that working with treasure hunters compromises their integrity, but—"

"You don't realize what you're getting into!" He leaned across the desk, his expression full of tension, his pale skin seeming even more so. "The field is full of thugs and thieves. Haven't you had enough trouble already?"

"What do you mean?"

"The burglary, and…well, isn't that enough? Suppose you'd been here when they broke in? Heaven knows what they might have done to you."

He could have a point. Needing to keep her private assignment separate and secret, she had worked on the pieces in her own time, at all kinds of odd hours, so she might well have been in the lab alone when the burglars made their move. "It's kind of you to be so concerned," she said, touched despite herself, "but you said yourself that the break-in probably had no connection to those particular pieces, and more likely someone heard the students talking about the Maori jade ornaments and carvings we'd recovered from the dig. They were just lucky that the treasure hoard was here too."

"I'm sure that's true," Aidan conceded. "Unscrupulous collectors will pay handsomely for ancient Pacific art, and of course the export restrictions only make it more desirable and raise the prices. But I still don't like this idea of yours. Won't you reconsider? I hate to lose you, Sienna.'' He looked bothered, his brown eyes pleading.

Hardening her heart and sternly reminding herself why she'd decided to leave, Sienna shook her head. ''I'm sorry, I've made up my mind.''

By the time she arrived in the north and drove along the winding coast road to the little port at Mokohina, then checked in at the Imperial, dusk was sneaking down from the hillside that half circled the town and lights were going on in the venerable villas and newer homes that populated its slopes.

She freshened up and ate early, while the dining room was less than half filled. Through the windows she could see the lights of anchored yachts and powerboats reflecting jaggedly in the water. After eating she was drawn across the road to admire the starry night and the moving gleam and glitter of the sea, and enjoy the cool, salty night air.

She began to stroll along the waterfront, in a surprisingly short time drawing near the old wharves.

Camille had joined her husband on the *Sea-Rogue* several days previously, and there had been a note at the hotel inviting Sienna to call when she arrived if she wasn't too tired.

She had no trouble identifying the old wooden ketch with its distinctive cabin structure, featuring a door instead of a lift-up hatch, even before checking the lettering freshly painted on the bow.

A light glowed in the main cabin, and the deck was an easy step across. She noticed a sticker on the bulkhead advising that the boat was burglar-alarmed, but although a sturdy padlock hung on the catch, the narrow door was open and her tentative call brought Camille up the short, steep companionway to greet her with a hug.

''Come on down,'' Camille said. ''We're just finishing dinner. Have you eaten?''

"Yes, and I don't want to interrupt your meal," Sienna protested.

But Camille urged her down the companionway. "You can have some dessert with us. I bet you didn't have one at the hotel." And when they reached the saloon, "You remember Brodie?"

He was seated at the built-in table, his alert blue gaze giving Sienna a minor jolt when he turned to give her a nod of recognition, taking in the brand-new scoop-necked, fitted scarlet top and hip-hugging jeans she wore.

Camille said, "Move over, Brodie, and make room for Sienna."

"I didn't know you had a guest," Sienna said when Rogan waved her onto the seat next to Brodie. "I'm sorry—"

"Stop apologizing," Camille scolded, and Rogan added lazily, "Brodie's not a guest anyway. He's a worker."

Camille said, "And if it wasn't for him I guess I'd be the one having to climb the masts with a paintbrush or screwdriver and get down into the bilge to fix cables."

Rogan grinned at her. "Of course," he said. "What do you think I married you for?"

Camille laughed. "I'm dishing up apricot mousse, Sienna. Do you want cream or ice cream with it?"

Even as Sienna said, "Just the mousse," Brodie cut in with, "Give her both."

Camille planted a scoop of ice cream and a dollop of whipped cream into the dish before handing it to Sienna with a slight, apologetic smile. "You don't have to eat it all if it's too much."

Evidently marriage had turned Camille into the kind of woman who automatically obeyed male commands. Sienna dug her spoon into the mousse.

The dessert was melt-in-the-mouth delicious, and the short walk must have woken her appetite, because she finished the mousse and even ate some ice cream before pushing aside her dish.

She declined more, but Brodie enthusiastically accepted another helping before Rogan suggested coffee on deck.

They sat on cushioned seats in the cockpit at the stern, Rogan with his arm about Camille's shoulders and Brodie and Sienna side by side opposite their hosts.

Brodie lounged back in the seat they shared, a foot away with his arm resting along the coaming behind her, and although he didn't touch her, she found his proximity unsettling, her nerves sending tiny electrical pulsations up both her arms.

Camille asked, "Did you find someone to look after your cat?"

"One of my students is house-sitting. She'll spoil him." Sienna paused. "Granger mentioned you thought you could find somewhere for me to store my car?"

"Brodie's offered half of his garage to you while we're at sea."

Sienna turned to Brodie. "Thank you. I'll pay you a rental—"

"You won't. No problem." His look dared her to argue.

"Well, thank you," she repeated.

Camille said, "How's your brother, Sienna? You stayed with him on the way up?"

"He's fine. But my car was broken into in the night while it was parked outside his place, and my luggage got stolen. Including my scuba gear."

Camille looked shocked, and both men stiffened, scowling. Brodie's eyes searched Sienna's face, his mouth going hard.

Rogan asked, "You reported it to the police?"

"Yes, but I had the impression they have more important things to worry about. They said if it was any consolation the thief was good at his job—he picked the lock without damaging the car. I filled in an insurance claim though I doubt they'll pay out the full amount of the stuff that was taken."

Brodie said, "I'll fix you up with scuba gear, on credit if you like. Come and see me at the dive shop."

"What a horrible thing to happen," Camille sympathized. "Are you okay for clothes and stuff?"

"I bought some in Hamilton. Basics, and I won't need much more on the boat. Fortunately I'd taken my laptop out of the car. I left it with my brother, since you said I can use the on-board computers."

Rogan asked, "It doesn't have information on it about our artifacts?"

"No, I've never kept that on the hard disk. I carry a password-protected disk in my bag that's always with me." Laptop computers were a prime target for theft, and Camille had impressed upon her how important it was to keep her notes confidential.

Even Aidan had no idea what was in them. When asking his permission to use the laboratory facilities, she'd told him she couldn't talk about the work and had kept the artifacts in her own padlocked steel locker, only taking them out when she was alone after hours. But the burglar had made short work of the lock.

"I think," she said, "after breaking into my car the thief tried to get into the house, but my brother heard something and scared him off. We didn't realize the car had been tampered with until the morning."

She'd been upset, of course, but thankful nothing irreplaceable had been taken. "I've sent Granger copies of my notes. I presume he's keeping them in a safe place?"

Rogan said, "My big brother's office is in an old bank building and he's got a strong room with a steel door a foot thick where he stores sensitive records." Perhaps to make some kind of amends for even vaguely querying her discretion, he asked, "You have an older brother too?"

"Younger. It's thanks to him I learned to scuba dive. We were on holiday in the Bay of Islands when he was twelve and I was fifteen, and he was mad keen to learn, but my parents would only let him if I agreed to keep an eye on him." Their last holiday with both parents—perhaps that was why she remembered it so vividly, every moment seemingly clear in her mind.

"You didn't want to dive?" Brodie queried, disconcertingly closer to her than she'd expected as she turned to him.

"I wasn't against the idea, just not crazy for it the way he was." She'd been more interested in collecting shells and occasional bits of flotsam, wondering if some of the pieces of wood she picked up that had obviously been shaped by tools had come from shipwrecks or drifted from the shores of other lands. And how long they'd been floating on the wide Pacific.

There had been no hint that dreamy, untroubled summer of the cataclysm that was about to descend on their lives. Yet only a few weeks after their return, her father had announced that he was leaving to live with another woman who was expecting his child. Her mother too had seemed stunned, apparently having had no more clue than Sienna or her brother about their father's secret life.

"If you're planning to dive on this expedition," Brodie said, "you'll need a certificate of fitness."

A little nettled—as if that were any of his business—she said, "I sent Granger a letter from my own GP, but he told me Rogan wants me to see a dive doctor here. I'll do it tomorrow," she assured the other man. It seemed Rogan preferred all the crew members to go to a doctor he knew and trusted. "I won't need to buy an air tank, will I? Granger said they'd be supplied."

"Yep—on the salvage barge there'll be air and gases for scuba, as well as a surface-supply system for the helmet divers on the bottom and a decompression chamber."

It sounded like a well-equipped expedition. Obviously some thought had gone into preparations to ensure efficiency and safety.

Not much later Sienna got up to leave, pleading tiredness. Brodie said, "I'll walk you back to the hotel."

"I'm sure it's perfectly safe."

He said flatly, "Rogue's dad got jumped not far from here."

Surely that was different—she'd gathered that Barney Broderick had been carrying some clue to the treasure ship he'd found, so it had been no random mugging. But obviously Brodie wasn't going to be put off by her protest, and Rogan and even Camille were looking approving. It seemed politic to give in rather than start a pointless argument.

Brodie leaped onto the wharf, now slightly above the deck level, and extended a hand that she couldn't refuse without an obvious snub.

His fingers were warm and hard, closing firmly about hers before he hauled her effortlessly onto the old, cracked boards, steadying her with a hand on her arm.

"Thank you," she said politely.

"It's a pleasure."

Sienna thought she detected ironic amusement in his voice, but it was dark now and she couldn't see his expression. She began to walk and Brodie fell in beside her, hands thrust into the pockets of his jeans, his ambling stride tempered to her pace. Yet he seemed oddly alert, peering down a darkened alleyway as they passed and occasionally glancing behind them.

"Are you looking for someone?" she asked.

His gaze returned to her. "No."

Moments later he said, "You don't think it's a bit odd that your lab was burgled and then your car?"

Jolted, she stared at him. "Theft isn't that uncommon, especially from unattended cars left on the road, according to the police. And it was miles away from the burglary."

"Hmm." They walked around a curve and into an area that was better lit, where cafés were still open, a few hardy souls sitting outside although it was autumn. Brodie appeared to relax a bit. "Why did you take the job after all?" he asked.

"Well, because I…" She floundered, not about to tell him the real reason. "Because it sounds interesting. And as you said," she added, "if I want to be sure the site is properly surveyed and not damaged, the best way is to be on the spot myself."

"Rogan won't go roaring in like a bull in a china shop.

And with you and Camille both on board I'm sure you'll make your views clear."

Sienna muttered, "Camille seems to have sold out."

"How do you mean? She's the one who insisted on asking you to join the team."

"I'm not insulting her," Sienna assured him. "I just mean that…well, marriage has changed her."

"It's made her happier," Brodie said bluntly. "Is that a crime?"

"Of course not. I'm happy *for* her. I suppose it's inevitable."

"What is?"

Sienna struggled to explain. "Her first loyalty now is to her husband. Before…well, it was different." Both she and Camille had nursed their own reasons for being wary of the male worldview. Now Camille was happy and loved, and Sienna felt an irrational desolation. She hadn't lost her friend, but things would never be quite the same.

"You think she's gone over to the enemy?" Brodie asked.

"I'm not anti-man." She knew all men weren't like her father. Her own fatal weakness prevented her from establishing a relationship with one of them.

"You relieve my mind," Brodie said. "Rogue's changed too. I guess marriage does that to people. Alters their perception of life or something." Thoughtfully he added, "I never thought he was the marrying kind of guy."

"What kind of guy would that be?" she asked, and he laughed, not bothering to reply.

Not Brodie's kind, she presumed. Camille had mentioned that Brodie owned his own house in Mokohina as well as the local dive shop and dive school. She'd gathered that Rogan's friend had settled down, but he didn't look at all the settled-down type to her. "Have you ever been married?" she asked. There had been no sign of a wife at the wedding.

He laughed again. "Do I look like it? No."

"That's what I thought."

"What—that no woman would have me?"

"I'm sure plenty of women would have you," she replied, "and probably regret it later." As her mother must now. Her father too had been a man who naturally attracted female interest. Even as a teenager she'd known that other women envied her mother. Quite possibly the woman he lived with now hadn't been the first to deflect his attention away from his wife. Perhaps the others had the good luck—or forethought—not to get pregnant.

Brodie grinned down at her, not noticeably insulted. "You could be right. I'm probably not great husband material. Have *you* ever been married?"

"No." How had they gotten into this conversation? It was becoming too personal. Reaching the grass verge opposite the hotel, Sienna said hastily, "Thank you for seeing me back."

She swung away, stepping onto the road as headlights suddenly swept over her, an engine roared and the car she hadn't seen or heard leaped out of the darkness.

Chapter 3

A hard hand grabbed her arm, hauling her back onto the grass and clamping her against an equally hard male body, and Brodie let fly an explosive word that seared her ears.

The car, which had almost scraped her jeans, accelerated away. Still held against Brodie's unyielding chest, her face pressed to his cambric shirt, her nose inhaling his warm male scent and the palm of one hand splayed against his hammering heart, Sienna trembled with reaction, her knees watery.

"What the hell did you think you were doing?" he demanded roughly.

Sienna straightened shakily away from him. "I just didn't see the car coming. It was stupid."

He released her, his gaze critical as she stepped carefully back, making sure she was still on the grass. "If you can't be more sensible than that, maybe a dive expedition is no place for you after all!"

Her chin jerking up, she said, "I think Rogan is the proper judge of that. I made a mistake—it's not a habit."

"I hope not."

"If it's any business of yours—"

"It is." The assertion was uncompromising and surely inappropriate.

She protested, her voice rising. "Even if I were a complete idiot—which I'm *not*, thank you, he was going way too fast anyway—does it have anything at all to do with you?"

"Of course it bloody does!" He was obviously angry too. "As dive master on this voyage—"

"As—*what*?" Her voice lifted another octave.

"As dive master," he repeated with exaggerated clarity. "You didn't know?"

Slowly Sienna shook her head, stunned. "Nobody told me," she said. And then, "Don't you have a business to run here in town?"

"I have well-paid, competent staff," he said shortly. "I'm a partner in PTS—you didn't know that either?" He peered at the shocked expression on her face.

Dumbly she shook her head again.

"And dive master," he reiterated. "I'm the one who approves the dive team and I'm the one who has the say about who goes down, if and when, once we're on the site."

"I'm sorry." She'd thought he was being overbearing and meddlesome and annoyingly male, but apparently he'd been at least partially justified. "I didn't realize you were involved."

"Up to my neck," he said. After a small pause he conceded, "You gave me a fright. I guess you're tired after your long drive, and that driver *was* gunning the engine."

An apology of sorts for snarling at her, she supposed.

He took her arm again in a firm grip and checked for traffic on the road before guiding her across to the hotel. Clamping her lips together, Sienna reminded herself that the meek would inherit the earth.

She didn't feel meek. She felt unsettled, dismayed and vaguely angry, as though she'd been deceived in some way, though of course that wasn't so. Everyone had probably taken it for granted that someone else had told her of Brodie's role in the new company. And it didn't really matter. Only, she wished the dive master were someone less irrefutably...male, in a way that disturbed her more than she wanted to admit.

At the foot of the broad steps to the door he asked her, "Will you be all right now?"

"Of course. I don't need a nanny."

He grinned, his good humor apparently restored. Thrusting his thumbs into the belt of his jeans, his eyelids lowering, he said, "Good, 'cause I'm not one."

No, she thought, looking up into his gleaming eyes. There was nothing nannyish about his earthy sexual magnetism.

She said hastily, "Good night, then. Thank you again for seeing me home."

"See you tomorrow," he promised as she climbed the steps.

When she reached her room she had an immediate sense of something alien in the air, a faint, indefinable feeling of intrusion. Looking around, she saw her replacement collapsible suitcase sitting open on the luggage rack with the so-far unworn clothes still neatly folded inside, just as she'd left them. Nothing seemed to have changed, except that the bed was turned down.

A staff member had entered in her absence, that was all. Relieved, she went to draw down the old-fashioned Holland blind, pausing as she noticed Brodie's broad-shouldered figure mooching along the foreshore.

Something stirred inside her, a warm spiral of purely physical reaction. Uneasily, she recognized it for what it was—a sexual response.

Brodie Stanner, with his lopsided grin and frank appraisal of her face and figure, was going to be one of the team she'd be living in close proximity with—for perhaps months. And that bothered her. He spelled danger, large as life and twice as threatening.

He'd made no secret of the fact that he found her attractive. But by all the signs he found any personable woman attractive, and was one of those men who generously spread his favors around without discrimination. And without any particular thought. A here today and gone tomorrow sort of guy.

Mindless, meaningless sex wasn't something that had ever interested Sienna. Sex for her had never been meaningless, although it had not brought her the security she'd once hoped for, when she was too young to understand her own need and looking for love in all the wrong places. She'd long ago given up on that futile search.

And she had little doubt that if Brodie Stanner had anything in mind, it was no more than a short, wild fling. That was not for her—and neither was he.

Sienna's GP had already assured her she was fully recovered from her earlier sickness, although a bit underweight, but she was relieved to emerge from the dive doctor's surgery with the necessary certificate in her hand.

The little town was quite busy, and when she reached the wharf the *Sea-Rogue* was abuzz.

Alongside a couple of other men Brodie was loading boxes and bags from a pile on the wharf into a forward hatch, his shirt discarded and his fit, lithe body bending and straightening in a rhythm of physical exertion that had a sort of primitive beauty. Rogan stood by with a clipboard, checking things off and occasionally examining a label.

Brodie stopped work for a second and lifted a hand in greeting. Rogan glanced up as she stepped aboard, and smiled at her. "Camille's in the saloon. She's expecting you."

"Thanks." Sienna jumped lightly into the cockpit, and descended to the saloon where she found Camille studying a computer screen incorporated into a bank of instruments.

The two women spent a couple of hours going over the documentation on the *Maiden's Prayer* that Camille had collected from various sources and the information Sienna had garnered on the stolen samples.

Sienna said, "Can we transfer my notes from the CD to your computer?"

"Yes, that would be a good idea. We've been careful about

it because the boat's been burgled before, but we sail in a couple of days and the burglar alarm seems very efficient. You probably heard it last night, when we woke half the port.''

''Last night? I dreamed about a fire engine…'' She'd forgotten about it, but now she recalled a vivid dream involving sirens and fire, a feeling of impending doom as flames licked behind her while Brodie Stanner climbed a ladder to her window and held out his hand. She'd hung back, afraid to take it, until he'd said commandingly, ''Come with me, I'll save you.''

Some chance, she thought now. From the fire to the frying pan…

Camille was saying, ''It seems to have been a false alarm. Rogan shot out of bed and raced up on deck, but no one was there. The thing might have been set off by a line flapping in the wind, although it's not supposed to work that way. It did show that if someone tries to break in now, judging by last night's performance, it'll bring people running from all the boats nearby.''

After transferring the information Camille handed the disk back, saying, ''It's a good idea to keep a spare, just in case.''

''I wasn't able to find much really.''

''Still, you never know when something that seems unimportant or unrelated will match up with another fact and tell us something useful. You know how it is with research.'' Camille hesitated. ''I'm sure it's all right to tell you, now you're a member of the team. We have the ship's bell, but we're keeping that under wraps, so don't mention it to anyone else. You're the only one who knows apart from Granger and Brodie, Rogan and me.''

They lunched on deck with Rogan and Brodie. After delivering the stores, the other men had driven off.

''Did you get your doctor's certificate?'' Brodie asked.

She fished it from her capacious bag and handed it to him, along with her dive certification.

A man strolling along the wharf stopped at the *Sea-Rogue*. "Rogan Broderick?" he inquired.

"That's me." Rogan stood up.

The man was fiftyish, his brown hair thinning, eyes hidden behind trendy wraparound sunglasses. His casual shirt and slacks looked as though they probably sported designer labels. Uninvited, he leaped aboard and held out his hand to Rogan. "Fraser Conran," he said. "And this is your brother?" He turned to Brodie.

"No." Brodie denied it, not offering his name.

For a moment the stranger didn't react, then he smiled thinly, and Camille said, "Do I know you?"

He shifted his attention to her. Then she said, "We met at James Drummond's house," her expression changing from uncertainty to hostility.

Jolted, Sienna recalled that Camille had spent time with Drummond before she discovered he was a crook and a killer.

Conran didn't seem to notice the sudden chill in the air. "A bad business, that." The smile fading, he shook his head. "I didn't really know him well, but his antique stores seemed aboveboard—he was well known, respectable. Hard to believe…though, of course, he hasn't been found guilty yet."

"He's guilty," Rogan said curtly. "What did you want?"

Fraser Conran turned back to him. "I hope I'm not going to be tarred with the same brush because I knew the man. We were business acquaintances, that's all." He paused, but no one reassured him on that point. "I heard you were looking for investors for a…venture. I have some cash to spare. Perhaps we could talk?"

"You heard wrong," Rogan said. "Our investors have all been by invitation. We don't need any more."

"Really? Treasure hunting is very expensive, I'm told— my understanding was you can hardly have too much capital."

"Thanks for the offer, but I'm sure you can find other ventures to spend your money on. Probably less dicey ones."

"But not so interesting."

There was a silence, then Conran shrugged. "If you change your mind, here's my card."

Rogan reluctantly took the card the man handed over before climbing back onto the wharf. They watched him depart, strolling without hurry.

Brodie asked Rogan, "What do you make of that?"

Rogan shook his head and turned to Camille. "Do you know anything about him?"

"Not really. I didn't recognize him right away, but he was with some other people who sailed up from Auckland for the weekend. I think James hoped to sell something to him."

"Did you get the impression he tried to give us just now that he hardly knew Drummond?"

Camille chewed briefly on her lower lip. "It's hard to say. James told me the people were business contacts."

Brodie said, "He's not the first one to come fishing, is he, since word of the new company got out?"

"No," Rogan agreed. "And not the first who seemed a bit dodgy, either. Just as well we had Granger to rustle up investors he could vouch for." He looked at the card.

Brodie asked, "What does he do?"

"Shipping agent, it says."

"I guess Drummond knew plenty of those."

"Some of them might have been legitimate," Rogan allowed. "But I wouldn't trust anyone who had anything to do with Drummond."

Sienna and Camille helped to get supplies stowed neatly in every available storage space on the boat in preparation for their departure, and it was late afternoon when Sienna found herself being walked back to the hotel by Brodie again.

Along the way he said, "Camille told you we're sure now the wreck is the *Maiden's Prayer.*"

"She said you'd found the ship's bell, but not to say anything."

"Had you found any confirmation in the stuff Rogan brought up from the bottom?"

"There was nothing to refute it, but I didn't want to jump to conclusions."

"Are you always so cautious?"

"Preconceived ideas are not good science."

"Y'know," he said thoughtfully, "I have the feeling you might have some preconceived ideas about me."

"I don't know why you should think that. And if I did, I wouldn't let them interfere with doing my job."

"You realize we're all going to be living pretty close together for a few months?"

"I've never had a problem getting on with people." Trying to sound serene and confident, she couldn't help feeling that instead her voice was decidedly cool and a little snippy. Well, perhaps it wasn't a bad thing. She'd hate him to guess the effect he had on her—the way his smile warmed her very bones and his blue gaze gave her pleasurable little shivers up her spine.

He seemed ready to drop the subject. "Does your brother still dive?"

"Sometimes. But he tends to master a skill and then go in for some new challenge. At university he joined the mountain-climbing club, and he's still a member of a search and rescue team. When he moved to Hamilton to take a job as a mechanic he learned to fly. Now he's working for an aeronautical engineering firm there and doing night classes to improve his skills. He seems to be showing signs of settling down."

"You approve of that? Settling down?"

"Isn't it what you did? Have you got bored with being a shopkeeper?"

He gave her a keen look. "I've never given up diving. I combine my shop and dive school with occasional commercial assignments. The shore work gives me a steady income and means I don't have to scramble for jobs—I can pick and choose where I go and who I work with."

"And you chose Pacific Treasure Salvors?"

He grinned. "Not too many people can resist the lure of long-lost treasure. Even you."

Sienna didn't bother to deny that. She knew most of the work would be tedious and painstaking, and much of the wreck's cargo—maybe the bulk of it—might already be lost forever in the depths of the sea, buried under layers of coral, destroyed or scattered irrecoverably by time and tropical storms. Nevertheless she was excited at the prospect of being involved.

She essayed a wry smile of acknowledgment, and Brodie broke into an answering one that lifted her spirits in a way no other man ever had. Plenty of women would have fallen for him instantly. No wonder he seemed a shade piqued that she'd shown no inclination to do so. She mustn't allow him to discover how fragile her brittle defences really were.

She sighed, assailed by a wistful longing that lately had recurred too often, and Brodie said, "What's the matter?"

"Nothing. I'm still a bit tired."

He frowned. "Are you sure you're up to this trip?"

"You saw the doctor's certificate. There was a lot of work to do before I left, but I'll have time to recover before we reach the wreck." The exact location was confidential but she gathered it was at least a week's sailing from Mokohina, and she knew from Camille that Rogan was concerned that, while he assembled his crew and equipment, looters might get to the site before they did. But also determined that the expedition was properly equipped and staffed.

Brodie cast another covert glance upon her but didn't argue anymore.

Next day Sienna started out to find the dive shop, not in any particular hurry. On the way she dawdled over a display of local art for sale, mostly depicting seascapes or rural scenes, and at a shop-window mannequin wearing a rather nice jade-green stretch top.

A teenage boy in baggy shorts and T-shirt, with a knitted beanie hat pulled low over his eyebrows, was reflected in the glass, apparently looking too, but when she turned he ducked his head and mooched off to stare into the window of a nearby computer shop while she walked on.

She was turning a corner when something tugged hard at the bag she held, and she instinctively tightened her grip, swinging round as the beanie-wearing youth she'd seen earlier tried to wrench the bag from her hold, his brown eyes stark and wide below the hat.

Sienna kicked him hard in the knee, jerking the bag away from his loosened hold as he doubled up with a cry of pain, and a man and woman rounded the corner.

"Bitch!" the boy gasped, and then he saw the two people approaching, backed off and began to run, almost being mown down by a car as he dodged across the road.

The couple stopped, bewildered, and the man asked, "Are you all right?"

Sienna was breathing fast, her heart pounding. "Yes. He tried to snatch my bag. I'm okay."

The woman exclaimed in disgust, "That sort of thing never used to happen in Mokohina. You ought to tell the police."

"Yes," Sienna said. But the boy had disappeared and by the time she reported the incident they'd have no hope of catching him. "Thanks." If these people hadn't come along she might still be tussling with the bag snatcher or been knocked to the ground while he made off with his booty.

After the couple walked on, she waited a few minutes to calm down and resume her normal breathing pattern, then continued to her destination.

When she entered the shop Brodie was helping two giggling young women choose gear for their first dive lesson. One of them looked up at him, pushing back a mane of shining dark hair, and cooed, "Will you be the teacher?"

Brodie's glance at her held amused appreciation. "Sorry," he looked regretful, "I'm not going to be available for a while. But we have several very well qualified staff members."

The girl looked disappointed. "It's your picture on the brochure we picked up at the motel."

That, Sienna thought, would bring young women in droves to the dive school.

Brodie was saying, "I own the business. Don't worry, Hemi will see you right."

"Is he as good-looking as you?" the girl asked, casting him a sidelong look.

Brodie laughed. "Better. And he's younger than me. You'll like him."

A female assistant, tall and fit-looking, her skin the light golden-brown of manuka honey, was suppressing a grin of her own as she left off arranging a display of snorkels and face masks and approached Sienna. "Can I help you?"

"I'm waiting for Brodie," Sienna told her.

The assistant let the grin surface, her gaze sliding to her boss. "You might be waiting for a while."

Apparently she'd been mistaken for one of his fan club. Sienna said crisply, "I'm the archaeologist for Pacific Treasure Salvors."

At the sound of her voice Brodie had looked up. He motioned the assistant to him and said, "Take over here please, Jen." Then, excusing himself from the girls whose wistful looks followed him across the shop floor, he invited Sienna. "Come with me."

He led her into a roomy storeroom-cum-office, where he picked up a bulky jacket-type buoyancy compensator hung with all the necessary accoutrements. "I picked this out for you, a new model that's tested well. It excludes sand, a plus when you're picking up stuff from the seafloor. Try it."

Standing behind her, he helped her into it, and then came round in front and adjusted the waist strap.

She could see the faint gleam of incipient whiskers on his chin as he completed the task. He pointed out the various instruments integrated into the system. "In the water it'll give you greater freedom of movement than older systems and fewer hoses to manage." He stepped closer again. "There are just two nice big buttons to press for gaining neutral buoyancy."

Neutral buoyancy prevented a diver from sinking fast to the bottom or bobbing about on the surface; once achieved, it allowed full control of movement in the water.

Brodie looked up from checking the fit and met her eyes. For a moment she was lost in the blue depths of his, only aware of how intense the color was, and then of the sudden flare that lit them before he gave her a slow grin, his eyebrows lifting slightly in teasing, hopeful inquiry.

Hastily Sienna looked away, a pulse beating unevenly at her throat. Neutral buoyancy was what she needed, she thought—a way of controlling her feelings so that she neither sank once again into the dangerous depths of misdirected love nor floated aimlessly into a shallow affair.

She touched the buttons he'd pointed out, experimenting, and Brodie stood by with his hands thrust into his pockets and a studiedly casual expression, watching her familiarize herself with the system.

"What do you think?" he said.

"I think it's probably expensive." She peered at a swing tag hanging from the front, confirming her assumption.

"I'll give you a twenty-five percent discount. I can provide you with something cheaper, but believe me, this will be worth having once we're out there in the deep ocean."

"You're the expert." Twenty-five percent must be near cost price. "PTS is going to pay me very well for going on this trip and I'll have some insurance money coming for the gear that was stolen from my car, so yes." Although temporarily at least it would make a hole in her bank account. "And thanks for the discount."

Taking the jacket from her, he smiled. "You won't regret it."

"Is that a promise?" she asked lightly. Lightly, she'd decided, was the only way to deal with this man.

"I'll bet on it."

"You're the gambling man." She recalled him offering to bet her that Camille and Rogan's shining love would last. "I don't do bets."

"Ah, yes. The cautious type," he teased, his eyes laughing at her. "Well, that's good—taking risks underwater can be fatal. Why are you looking at me like that?"

"Like what?" Sienna wasn't aware she'd been looking at him in any special way, except that the light in his eyes had a mesmerizing effect and she'd been caught by it, not thinking at all but unable to look away.

"As if you don't believe me."

What had they been talking about? Mentally she shook herself. Taking risks underwater, of course. Diving was always risky. Her instructors had made sure everyone knew the strict rules that governed the occupation, regularly hammering home the safety aspects. "You don't strike me as the cautious type," she told him. How did a gambling man cope with the necessary precautions?

He said grimly, "I am, underwater. Guys who do stupid things in this business don't live long."

Sienna went a little cold. "Have you ever done anything stupid?"

"Coupla times," he grudgingly admitted. "When I was young and thought I was superhuman. But not anymore. I figured my luck was about to run out."

"Is that when you decided to buy a shore business?"

Brodie laughed. "No, that came later. The thing is," he said, sobering, "the second time I damn near took Rogue with me. He put himself at risk to save my sorry butt. Kicked it later for me, and I don't blame him. I swore I'd never put someone else in danger again just because I felt invincible. No one is. Remember that when you're at the bottom of the sea."

"I'm not likely to forget." Sienna had some sympathy for him. In a way she'd experienced a similar situation, not physically but emotionally, finding herself disastrously out of her depth before she fully realized what had happened. But it wasn't, she reminded herself, a matter of life and death. Just as Brodie had survived his moment of truth, she'd survived the gaping wound in her heart.

It hadn't been easy, and it wasn't her first such mistake, but she was determined it would be her last. She'd never again been quite so vulnerable. Nowadays she was in charge of her emotions, not allowing them to escape her control. Life was much more comfortable that way.

"Something the matter?" Brodie asked, startling her.

Her expression must have betrayed her. She thrust the unwelcome memory back into her subconscious where it belonged. "Nothing," she said brightly. "I need all the other gear too. Wet suit, flippers, mask, dive computer…"

He helped her choose the rest of her equipment, and when they were both satisfied, she said, "How do you want me to pay for this? Is a credit card okay?"

"Sure, or leave it until we get back. I'll deliver it all to the boat for you. Are you moving to the *Sea-Rogue?*"

"I think I'll stay on at the Imperial until we leave tomorrow." There wasn't much privacy on board, and Camille and Rogan might need as much of it as they could get before the boat sailed. Since their Easter wedding, they'd only snatched weekends together while Camille finished the semester and Rogan made preparations for PTS's project.

"Let me know when you want to park your car at my place," Brodie offered. "When I'm not here I'll be at the *Sea-Rogue* or my place."

"Where do you live?"

"Five minutes' walk. If you wait around until closing time—" he glanced at his watch "—which isn't far off, I'll show you. Why don't you have dinner with me there? We could get to know each other a bit before we start the trip."

Sienna knew it was important to get on with other members of the crew, but stalled, giving herself time to consider. "Can you cook?"

"Sure I can cook. Did you think I was offering so you'd cook dinner for me? You won't have to lift a finger—and *that's* a promise."

She didn't actually say yes, but somehow he took it for granted that she'd accepted, and half an hour later he was ushering her through a wicket gate and along a short path to a tiny cottage with a disproportionately large garage toward the rear.

A curve of corrugated iron hooded the veranda at the front of the cottage, giving it a sleepy look. Wide wooden steps creaked as Brodie led the way up them and opened a lead-light-paneled door flanked by long old-fashioned windows.

Inside, the board floors had been varnished to a soft sheen and dressed with rugs. The furniture was minimal but Brodie pointed her to a big, comfortable sofa—chosen, she assumed, to accommodate his large body when he wanted to sprawl on it and watch the small TV set that sat in a corner.

She guessed that someone had removed a wall, replacing it with a wide arch that defined areas of the roomy living space. Besides the sofa, there were two double-seaters, a low coffee table and the TV trolley, while bookshelves lined one wall. The kitchen was separated by a polished wooden counter doubling as a dining table, with two high-backed wicker chairs pushed under it on the sitting-room side.

"Drink?" Brodie offered, opening a cupboard. "Gin, beer, wine—white or red?"

Sienna settled for white wine and he poured two. After handing hers over, he plunked himself down in one of the two-seaters. Lounging back with his long legs spread in front of him, he inquired, "Do you like nasi goreng?"

"It's a rice dish, isn't it? I think so. I like rice."

"Good." He raised his glass. "To the *Maiden's Prayer* and a more successful voyage for us than *her* last one."

"I should hope so!" Sienna said, and tasted the wine—cool, fruity and with a pleasant zing to it.

He drank some of his wine and lowered the glass. "How long have you known Camille?"

"A couple of years, since I started at Rusden." Longer than her husband had known her. "I hope Rogan appreciates her."

"He does. Rogue's a lucky man. She's gorgeous."

"She is beautiful." Sienna didn't have Camille's spectacular looks, only she had never been short of men to take an interest. But she'd become wary of being too eager and open, of giving too much and receiving too little. She would never fall into that trap again.

"So are you," Brodie said.

"Please, I don't need any empty compliments."

"The compliment," he said, "was sincere. Clumsy," he acknowledged with a wry grin, "but sincere."

Sienna couldn't help a small laugh at his chagrined expression.

He picked up his glass and said, "I'll start the rice."

"Can I help?"

"Nope. I told you, all you have to do is appreciate while I work."

Not hard, she thought. Any female—and she was one—could hardly fail to appreciate a man as good-looking as Brodie, especially when he was cooking for her, with evident enjoyment and expertise. As a seduction technique it was probably almost fail-safe. Not that he seemed to have any such intention at the moment.

She moved to one of the wicker chairs and they talked about the planned voyage while he chopped and sautéed and added ingredients to the mixture simmering on the stove.

He refilled her glass and she began to feel pleasantly relaxed, resting her elbows on the counter in front of her while a tempting aroma filled the big room, and night began to darken the corners.

Brodie switched on lights in the kitchen, but behind her the room remained shadowed.

He handed her a fork and put two well-filled plates on the counter, then pulled out a stool from under it and sat down opposite her, offering red wine.

"I'll stick to white," she said, allowing him to refill her glass again. She'd be walking to the Imperial so wasn't too bothered about drinking, but would make this the last glass. She didn't want to go reeling back to the hotel. And besides, experience and the tug of reluctant attraction that Brodie engendered in her was a warning to take care not to let down her accustomed guard over her emotions.

The nasi goreng was fragrant, spicy and delicious, but she couldn't quite finish the pile he'd heaped on her plate, pushing the remains away regretfully.

"You don't like my cooking?" he growled.

"It's wonderful, but just a bit too much for me." She looked up and realized he'd been teasing.

"You didn't do too badly," he conceded.

He put crackers and a couple of cheeses on the counter, which she nibbled while he made coffee.

"Shall we sit over there?" he suggested when he'd poured it, indicating the darkened sitting room. "There's a light switch by the door if you want to turn it on."

Wondering if he'd noticed her slight hesitation, Sienna flicked the switch, then settled on one end of the big sofa.

Brodie took the other end. "We could watch some TV if you like," he offered.

"I don't mind, if you want to."

"Not specially. Most of it's pretty depressing."

Brodie probably didn't allow himself to be depressed often. He seemed like the kind of person who tackled life head-on and if something bothered him he'd do something about it, not sit around thinking how awful it was. The way Sienna tried to organize her own life. She didn't want to sink into the kind of despair that had engulfed her mother after her father's defection, which still dimmed her enjoyment of life and prevented her from moving forward. A long time ago Sienna and her brother had realized that they were little compensation for the loss of a husband.

"Want to tell me?" Brodie offered softly, bringing her gaze to his face.

"Tell you what?"

"Why you look as if you have some secret sorrow."

His perception was startling. Her voice brittle, she asked, "Doesn't everyone?"

Extraordinarily, for a second she'd been almost tempted to confide in him the story of her parents' divorce, her mother's subsequent ongoing misery and hopelessness, and her own struggle to overcome feelings of utter abandonment.

Fortunately her normal defenses quickly came rushing to the fore. Pouring out her heart to a virtual stranger wasn't in her nature. Maybe she'd had more wine than she realized.

Determinedly she shook away the shadow that had fallen over her and laughed, proving to herself and Brodie that she could. "You don't want to hear about my misfortunes." It was a banal story anyway. Divorces happened every day, and most people—even children—recovered from the trauma and went on with their lives. As she had, eventually.

Lifting her coffee, she finished it and put the cup down. "Time I went home. Thank you for dinner, it was great."

She reached for her bag and stood.

Brodie rose too. "I'll see you back to the hotel."

"It's not far, and there are streetlights."

Remembering the attempt to take her bag, she didn't argue, shamingly grateful to have his large, intimidating presence at her side.

She strode out purposefully and of course he easily kept up. The streetlights glowed on the blond streaks in his hair, and she averted her fascinated eyes to look at the harbor with its ghostly boats riding on their anchors.

Outside the hotel she said briskly, "Thanks again for a delicious meal. And for seeing me home."

"No problem." As she was about to go up the steps to the lighted doorway he seemed to come to a decision and caught her arm, turning her to face him again.

For a moment he just stared into her face, his gaze intent, and she said, "What?"

The skin about his eyes crinkled as though she'd said something funny, but his expression remained sober. Then he dipped his head, and even as her lips parted in astonished recognition that he was about to kiss her, his mouth met hers firmly, warm and confident, lingering for all of two seconds.

As soon as she began to pull away he lifted his mouth, and without letting go her arm he drawled mysteriously, "Yeah... well."

Chapter 4

Sienna blinked. She ought to have protested, should have pushed him away, but he'd taken her by surprise.

Brodie released her and stepped back. "Good night, Sienna," he said, and turned on his heel, leaving her staring as he swung off down the street, his hands in his pockets, his back straight, the street lamps gleaming on his hair.

"Yeah, well…?" she murmured, injecting indignation into the echo of his words. What did he mean by that—the kiss and the comment?

"Oh, what the heck," she thought crossly, mounting the steps to the hotel foyer. He probably always kissed women good-night when he'd escorted them home…if he wasn't invited in. And it had hardly been the kiss of the century. Just a sociable gesture.

But her lips tingled from the touch of his; she couldn't banish the feeling of the slight, experimental movement of his mouth over hers. And she could still see the disconcerting glitter in his eyes, hear the exact nuance of his voice as he'd stepped away from her and uttered that odd phrase.

* * *

Brodie glanced back just as Sienna disappeared through the open front door of the Imperial. The taste of her mouth—surprised, soft, parting slightly under his—lingered on his lips and in his mind. Tentative, unsure, but not closed against him.

His body stirred pleasurably. He'd wanted to kiss Sienna ever since he'd first seen her at Rogue's wedding, had wondered what it would be like. Now he knew that it was just as sexy and sweet and exciting as he'd imagined—even more so—and it wasn't enough.

She didn't give much away—a contradictory puzzle of a woman, determined to appear composed, cautious, competent. He was sure she was all of that—in her job. But that luscious, vulnerable mouth and the occasional haunted look in her eyes when she dropped her guard told a different tale, at odds with the cool personality she tried so hard to project.

"Yeah," he murmured again. The kiss had confirmed that suspicion to his satisfaction. "Well…" Where did they go from here? Sienna aroused in him unfamiliar sensations—burning curiosity about why she was so determined to fend him off despite the small signs that she wasn't as indifferent as she'd like, and something uncomfortably like compunction. He'd never been a pushy kind of guy—hadn't needed to be. If a woman indicated she was taken or—rarely—just not interested, he'd shrugged off the rebuff and moved on. This time he didn't want to move on. He wanted Sienna.

Whatever her problem, she wasn't cold. And he'd love to prove it someday.

He began a pleasant fantasy about just how he could do that, and was still lost in it when he turned a corner to the narrow street that wound uphill toward his house. The street lamps were yellow but dim, with pools of darkness between them.

Approaching his house, when he pushed open the gate he hardly registered the hint of movement under the shadow of the veranda. He was still thinking about Sienna and wondering if those sweetly rounded breasts were as soft as her lips, and he was almost at the veranda steps when he heard the creak of one of the old boards. The back of his neck prickled, his shoulder muscles tightening, ears alert for any sound, all his senses telling him to exercise caution.

Then a large black shape erupted toward him and another came around the side of the house.

He lunged at the nearer one, collided with a thud, grabbed the man and got a stranglehold on his throat, but the second man was on him and a hard blow to the side of his head set his ears ringing, another one forcing him to let go. He rounded on his assailant and threw a couple of punches that were returned in kind, then the first intruder lifted his foot and kicked out. The boot landed fair and square in Brodie's stomach, making him gasp hoarsely and double over.

Whoever they were, they seemed more intent on escaping than beating him up, and by the time he got his breath back, they were long gone.

Disgusted with himself, he stumbled up the steps and unlocked the door, slamming it shut behind him. Damn, he must be getting soft. Time was when he'd have had those two on the ground, no sweat.

A quick inspection showed no forced locks or broken windows. Maybe the intruders had expected him to stay away longer. Or perhaps they were just opportunists who'd noticed a darkened house and decided to try their luck. Whatever, they didn't seem to have actually gotten inside.

He phoned the police number and the system rerouted him to someone miles away in Whangarei who promised to pass on a message. Mokohina's sole representative of the law was probably already out on a call.

Brodie put down the receiver and rubbed at a swelling on his cheek. He could taste blood where a tooth had cut into the inside of his lip. His head hurt too, with a thumping ache.

It was years since he'd been in a scrap like that. Rogue would have something to say about him letting them walk all over him.

Rogue…Could this have anything to do with Pacific Treasure Salvors and the *Maiden's Prayer?* Wasn't it too much of a coincidence on top of the theft of the artifacts from Sienna's lab and the burglary of her car?

She'd been here tonight. Did someone imagine she might have left something with Brodie that was worth stealing?

A clutch of anxiety wrenched his innards. He picked up the phone again and dialed the number of the hotel, asking to be put through to Sienna's room.

She answered, sounding surprised, and he said without preamble, "Is there a chain or bolt on your door?"

There was a pause before she said, "Yes, but—"

"Make sure it's on."

"I will when—"

"Do it," he snapped. "Now!"

"Brodie—"

"*Now!* Don't argue."

He must have got through to her. The next instant the phone banged down on something hard and there was silence for two seconds. Then she picked up the receiver again. "All right, it's done. What's this all about?"

"And don't sleep with your window open," he said. "I just got jumped by a couple of heavies—"

"Where?" she asked quickly. "Are you all right?"

"Yeah, I'm okay." He shouldn't be pleased that she sounded shocked and worried. "In my own front yard," he continued, answering her questions in reverse order.

"Did you call the police?"

"Yeah, yeah. It's you I'm worried about."

"*Me?* I'm not the one who's been mugged!"

"You were here tonight, and you've had two burglaries so far."

There was silence, and he wondered if she was scared. He wanted her to be scared. Enough to take care, but heck, he didn't want to freak her out. "It's just a precaution," he said soothingly. "In case there's any connection."

Another two seconds ticked by. "Someone tried to snatch my bag today," she said.

"*What?* When?" He had to fight down something uncomfortably akin to panic. "Why didn't you tell me this before?"

"It didn't seem that important. He didn't get it—I kicked him and he ran off. He was just a kid, really. A teenager."

"You fought him off?" She didn't have red hair for nothing, apparently. Well, almost red.

"You needn't sound so surprised. I'm not helpless."

Obviously not. For a second he enjoyed the picture of her downing a mugger. *Where* had she kicked him? The place it hurt most, he hoped. "Did you tell the local cop?"

"No, I mean to though."

"This can't all be down to chance," he said.

"They do say things come in threes."

"James Drummond—he's holed up somewhere…"

"Not in Mokohina, surely!"

"No, he's too well known here, but he's probably still in contact with people who can do his dirty work for him. Maybe he's masterminding all this."

"Whoever burgled the lab has already got the artifacts that came from the wreck. What else could they want? And why attack you?"

"I don't know. But for God's sake don't open your door to anyone you don't know. We're sailing tomorrow. I'll come over and take you to the cop-shop first, then the *Sea-Rogue*. Don't move from the hotel until I get there."

She argued but next morning he was at her door first thing, accompanying her down to breakfast in the dining room before they reported the attempted bag-snatch.

When the constable had taken the details, Brodie said, "It's not the first time something like this has happened. Her car was burgled in Hamilton, and before that some stuff was taken from her place of work. Tell him, Sienna."

The constable looked thoughtful. "Some people do seem to have a rash of unrelated incidents, but…you're on the *Sea-Rogue* team?"

"I will be from today."

"Hmm." The policeman tapped a pen against his teeth.

"I'll pass this on to Whangarei, and what's this about an incident at your house, Brodie?"

Brodie said, "After Sienna visited." He described the "incident," then asked, "There's been no sign of Drummond since he skipped bail?"

Frowning, the constable shook his head. "Pity the judge didn't remand him in prison. Confiscating his passport and freezing his assets is all very well, but my guess is he's left the country anyway."

When the constable had finished writing his report, Brodie lingered and the policeman said, "Anything else?"

Brodie pushed back a stray lock of hair from his forehead. "What's the story about murder at sea?"

The constable sat back. "If you mean the deckhand James Drummond's man allegedly murdered—"

"No, this is something different. Nothing to do with Drummond, as far as I know."

"What are we talking about?"

"Well, we found this skeleton."

"Where exactly?"

"Um...out in the Pacific. International waters."

"That complicates things for a start." The man looked pained. "How old was it? And why do you think this...person was murdered?"

"Maybe the bullet that was still inside the skull?"

The constable's expression didn't change. "That would be a clue. Bullets can be identified. Is it still there?"

Brodie shoved his hands in his pockets and briefly looked at his feet. "I...um...removed it. And then I dropped it. I've no idea how old the bones are. I'm no expert."

"You dropped it? Where?"

"In the water, when we were surfacing. I was putting on my glove, meaning to tuck the bullet inside, but—" he shrugged "—my dive time was up, and I was trying to hang on to a line and put the glove back on at the same time. I lost my grip on the bullet—it was only small—and the damn thing went to the bottom. We couldn't stay down any longer and...well, it's gone.''

The constable rubbed a hand over his cheek, grimacing. ''Could you find it again?''

''The bullet? I doubt it. The bones, maybe. But they could have been swept away by now, or taken off by sharks—though there wasn't any flesh left to interest them.''

Sienna's own flesh crawled at the picture he'd drawn.

The policeman said, ''There's no evidence of a crime, in other words. Unless you can find the skeleton and bring it back for the forensics guys. It's probably ancient. Do you want to formally report this?''

Obviously he wasn't advising it.

Brodie shook his head. ''Forget it. I just kinda thought maybe we should mention it.'' He deduced the cop thought the department, notoriously short-staffed as it was, had enough work on hand without chasing after some vague story of a probably historical and unprovable crime way beyond their actual jurisdiction.

Outside, on their way back to the Imperial to collect Sienna's things, she said, ''It bothered you, finding a skeleton.''

''Nah, I've seen others. But since it wasn't an accidental death and we were there at the station...'' He shrugged. ''Well, the cops aren't interested. And Rogue wouldn't want them sniffing around where we're trying to work anyway.''

He took Sienna's bags and her new equipment on board the *Sea-Rogue,* then they drove to his house where he opened up the garage for her to park her car.

They walked down to the *Sea-Rogue* together and settled into their respective compact cabins before Brodie helped Rogan to cast off. After clearing the harbor entrance, the *Sea-Rogue* emerged into a choppy sea under a blue sky hung with billowing white clouds, and Rogan cut the engine.

Sienna dodged out of the way as the men attended to the sails. Soon the boat was on automatic pilot and skimming over the waves, heading north.

Camille made sandwiches and brought them up on deck.

She sat close to her husband under an awning that shaded the cockpit, and Brodie moved along the seat opposite, tacitly inviting Sienna to sit beside him. He rested his arm on the coaming behind her, not touching her. She found it unsettling, but tried not to show she was conscious of his every breath, every slight movement. That she wanted to lean back against him and feel his arm curve around her.

Afterward Sienna helped Camille clean up in the galley, getting accustomed to the roll and sway of the boat.

"You don't get seasick?" Camille inquired.

"I'm taking pills." They made her feel a bit spaced out, but she knew that in a day or two she wouldn't need them. "Are we supposed to do the meals because we're the only women on board?"

Camille said, "I'm supposed to do them because I volunteered. You don't need to."

"Sorry." Sienna gave her friend a sideways smile. "I don't mind helping."

"Thanks. I expect everyone will help if I need it. But when we're on site the men will be doing most of the physical work—I'm not qualified for helmet diving, and they are. So I said I'd cook. And maybe I can help you catalog artifacts or something if you tell me what to do."

In the days that followed, life on board soon settled into a rhythm in tune with the sea and the sailing of the boat. Whenever they sat in the cockpit together they took the same places, and each time Brodie stretched out his arm behind her, Sienna experienced the same renewed awareness, as if some kind of invisible charge spanned the small space from his arm to the sensitive skin at the back of her neck. All she could do was try to ignore it and hope devoutly that he wasn't picking up on her feelings. Sometimes she caught him looking at her as if trying to work something out that puzzled him. And occasionally she surprised a gleam in his eye that made her breath catch before he quickly looked away, leaving her wondering if she'd imagined it.

Everyone took turns to keep watch for other shipping and

hazards like floating logs or lost cargo containers, as the boat forged across water that changed from green to blue to inky. Schools of fish flashed by in silver streams, and pods of sleek dolphins leaped in graceful unison from the water, arching back into it and playing in the boat's white wake. Once, as Sienna was scanning the horizon just before sunset, a whale spouted in the distance.

Just over a week after they'd·left Mokohina, in the dark of the early hours, she pulled on jeans and a jersey to go on deck for her turn to stand watch.

Brodie was wedged into a corner, a black, bulky shape.

"Good morning." Sienna sat down, folding her arms against the chill. "You can go and get some sleep now."

"Not sleepy," he said. "And it's a great morning."

The sea was like black glass, a line of light just beginning to show on the horizon. Stars still shone overhead, but gradually they faded as the morning glow overtook them. Dimly she could see Brodie's face in the gloom.

He shifted his feet, crossed one ankle over the other and tipped his head back. "Sometimes I wonder why I ever decided to become a landlubber, even part-time."

"Don't you have the best of both worlds?"

He lowered his head to look at her. "Yeah. I can take off whenever I want and go sailing, diving, but the shop and the house are always there. One day..." His voice trailed off and he looked away, toward the horizon. The water hissed at the *Sea-Rogue's* hull, and the sails moved as if breathing in the ghostly morning light.

One day, she guessed, his restless spirit might lead him to abandon things that tied him to the shore and resume roving like Rogan, whose only home was the boat. "The sea isn't always as peaceful as this," she reminded him.

Brodie laughed. "Don't I know! It can be wild and unpredictable. That's one of the things I love about it. You never know what to expect. And underneath that calm surface it holds so many secrets, so much to discover and explore. It's beautiful and mysterious and once you penetrate its depths, it casts a spell that never lets you go.''

The light was growing stronger, throwing his face into relief, and even though his eyes were shadowed, she could feel the intensity of his gaze.

"That's why you became a professional diver?'' she asked him. "Because the sea cast a spell over you?''

He gave a soft laugh. "You could say that.''

"Rogan told me you both entered dive school when you were teenagers. Did you always want to be a diver?''

"I knew I wanted to do something on the sea—or in it. If I'd known how hard it could be…'' He laughed softly, shaking his head.

"But you don't regret it?''

"Never. Once I was far enough along to realize what I was getting into I was hooked on the life. Learning the trade's a tough, relentless testing ground, not for weaklings or waverers, and the survivors have proved they're the real thing—sea people. The ocean weeds out anyone who can't hack it, throws them back to shore where they belong. I like the dive shop, dealing with people who feel the same way I do about the sea, but sometimes I need to be out there again. Underwater—'' his voice changed to a deeper, slower note "—where there's a peace like nothing on earth that gets right inside you.''

Sienna too had experienced that, had been able to forget for a time all the emotional traps that had her constantly on guard, pretend the other world on dry land didn't exist.

A diver was weightless, floating, and there was a feeling of being suspended in a calm inner space, of time stilled. Although beneath the sea there were hidden currents, and noise too—fish made little popping noises, coral creaked and crackled, and there was always the reassuring sound of the regulator providing air for the alien human who dared enter that secret kingdom.

The crack of light on the edge of the ocean widened and blazed orange, heralding the return of the sun. Already she could see the faint stubble on Brodie's chin and cheeks, and the sunrise reflected in his eyes as he watched the light catch her hair. Deliberately she looked away, afraid of the insistent, relentless tug of attraction that signaled danger.

"Diving," Brodie said, "was something I took to from my first time. Making a living at it seemed like a job made in heaven." He paused, then asked, "What made you decide to be an archaeologist?"

Disconcerted at the question, although she supposed she should have expected it, Sienna didn't answer immediately. "I suppose," she said, "it sort of grew on me. When I was ten I read a book about the pyramids and was fascinated. At high school I had a history teacher who spent her holidays working on digs in New Zealand, and by the time I entered university I knew what I wanted to do. Resurrect the past and preserve it."

"Uh-huh," Brodie said, nodding.

Something in his tone made her ask, "You have a problem with that?"

"Nope. I was just...thinking."

"About what?" Sienna asked involuntarily.

"What makes a girl like you want to live in the past?"

"I don't *live* in it! I study it." Even as she defended herself, she wondered if in a way he was right. It was soon after her parents' marriage broke up that she'd decided to make archaeology her career. Maybe deep down the desire to go back in time had something to do with it.

Brodie sometimes had an uncomfortable way of making her question her own self-knowledge. "We can learn a lot from the past," she said.

"Does knowing how people lived their lives hundreds of years ago teach you anything about living yours?"

"Maybe not directly, but we don't know ourselves if we don't know our history. Does diving teach you about living your life?" she queried.

"Hell, yes," he said. "It's taught me how precious life is, and not to waste a moment of it. That I only have one, and taking risks is part of it, but always to be prepared for the hidden hazards. To be responsible for myself but watch out for my buddies, and trust them to do the same for me. To take opportunities when they come and make sure I have a backup in case things go wrong.''

''That's why you bought the shop,'' she surmised. If anything happened to his diving career he'd still have that.

''Right.''

The sun had paled and risen above the horizon. The breeze picked up and he brushed a windblown strand of hair from his forehead with his fingers. ''This is the first time you and I have been alone since we came on board,'' he said.

Sienna knew that. But she said, ''Oh?''

For a moment he was silent, then he told her, ''I thought maybe you were avoiding me.''

She tried to look surprised. ''It's difficult to avoid anyone on a small boat. I thought we'd seen quite a lot of each other.''

Brodie made a sound suspiciously like a grunt. ''Yeah, and people generally get to know each other pretty quickly.''

''I suppose.'' She'd learned a lot about Brodie from things that came up in his conversation with the others. Small things like the fact that he'd once won a school speech contest, that he'd fallen off his bike when he was ten and broken an arm, that he had brothers and sisters he seemed casually fond of.

She'd noticed that he liked to read techno-thrillers and true-life adventure books, and shared a stack of diving magazines with Rogan. And he was seldom ruffled, although he wasn't above using a few choice words when a sail didn't behave or a line came loose.

''Have you ever been to Parakaeo?'' he asked.

The remote island was where Rogan had arranged to meet up with more divers, and he'd had the salvage barge towed there from Rarotonga.

''No,'' she answered. ''Why aren't we picking up the barge and the extra divers at Rarotonga?''

''Less chance of word getting round about our plans,'' Brodie said, "or of anyone following us to the wreck. Parakaeo's a quiet little place with a population of less than three thousand, with a small tourist trade, mostly ecotourists and people in the know about what a great, unspoiled dive site it is, though lately they've had a few cruise ships calling. I'll show you around when we get to it."

The island was a volcanic cone covered closely in glossy tropical foliage and tall coconut palms, with limited flat land near the sea, some of it taken up by an airstrip.

The only real town had been built along the foreshore, and sprawled onto the lower slopes of the long-extinct volcano that aeons ago had risen, spitting fire and steam, from the depths of the sea. A shabby freighter was moored near huge storage sheds where workers were loading the ship, the sickly-sweet smell of copra permeating the air.

When the *Sea-Rogue* dropped anchor in the harbor a horde of brown-skinned children swam out to the boat and splashed around it, calling, "Hello, hello, Mr. Rogue, Mr. Brodie!" Ducking and diving, they surfaced with big grins before racing back to the white sand of the beach and running and leaping away to spread the news.

By the time Rogan and Brodie had launched the inflatable dinghy and rowed to shore with the two women, a small welcoming committee of adults had gathered on the wharf, the women in flowered dresses, the men wearing either shorts or brief brightly colored pareus mere lengths of cotton—about their hips.

The women draped leis of fragrant frangipani flowers around the visitors' necks, and there were smiles and handshakes all around.

Excited congratulations greeted Rogan's introduction of his wife. Camille was heaped with leis up to her chin, and someone placed a garland of scarlet flowers and green ferns on her head.

One of the women turned to Brodie, standing aside with

Sienna, and asked, "Brodie—you brought your wife too?"
She beamed at Sienna.

Brodie shook his head, his mouth sloping into a grin as he
sent a glance at Sienna. "Sienna's Camille's friend."

The woman shrugged philosophically. "One day, eh?"

Brodie's gaze went again to Sienna and lengthened. For a
moment he said nothing, his eyes glazing as if he'd been
struck by some slight shock—perhaps the mention of a wife
had been unwelcome—before he agreed equably, "Sure.
Maybe."

Under a palm-thatched roof near the wharf an open-air market did desultory business in taro, yams, fruit and rainbow-
dyed pareus, while across a dusty road a row of shops with
drooping awnings snoozed in the humid heat.

The whole party walked slowly uphill to a large, airy house
with wide-open doors and windows letting through a cooling
breeze laden with the heavy, sweet scent of frangipani. Coconut cakes and orange juice were served, and Camille and
Sienna were introduced to Tu, a chunky, deep-chested islander who ran a local diving school and had been keeping
an eye on the salvage barge for Rogan.

Rogan asked him, "Have our divers turned up yet?"

"Tilisi's here, of course. Joe's at the hotel, waiting for you
guys to arrive. The other two are flying in tomorrow from
Raro. And the barge is ready to go, I think, but you'll want
to inspect it before it's towed to the site."

"Have there been any strangers around lately?" Rogan inquired. "Anyone asking questions?"

Tu shrugged. "Divers, yachties, a guy came in on a motor
cruiser, had some questions. Said he was a writer researching
a book on the hidden Pacific."

Brodie and Rogan exchanged glances. Rogan asked, "Did
he see our barge?"

Tu grinned. "It's not easy to hide something that big on
an island this size. I told him it was for pearl diving. Dunno
if he believed me."

It was some time before Rogan extricated his team from

the welcome party, and they climbed to the two-story pink-and-white building that was the island's only hotel.

They found the two divers in the hotel bar. Joe was a red-headed, weathered Australian who was an experienced salvor, Tilisi a former graduate of Tu's diving school who had several years of commercial diving experience. They greeted Brodie and Rogan with insults and back-slapping before being introduced to the women.

Tilisi shook Sienna's hand and gave her an admiring smile. "I never knew archaeologists were so pretty!"

Sienna laughed. He seemed so disingenuous, with his dark eyes and smooth brown cheeks.

Brodie said, "Watch him, Sienna. He's not nearly as innocent as he looks."

Tilisi's expression was wounded. "Brodie—I thought you were my friend!"

"Yeah, and I know you too well." To Sienna he said, "I've seen him take in too many women with that 'I'm just a poor native boy' act."

"I'm not easily taken in," she retorted.

He gave her a considering look. "Uh-huh."

Tilisi's eyes sparkled and he lightly punched Brodie's arm. "I could tell a few tales about you, my *friend!*"

Brodie laconically acknowledged, "I guess."

If she were a gambling woman Sienna would have taken a bet on it. For some reason the thought irritated her.

Later they all inspected the barge, moored at a wharf near a small boat-building business, and Sienna declared herself satisfied with the facilities provided for her, including big plastic tubs where artifacts in danger of deteriorating once removed from the sea would be immersed in salt water.

Rogan had a few last-minute modifications he wanted done, but everything should be completed within a day or two.

"I promised to show Sienna around," Brodie told him. There were still several hours of daylight left. "Do you need me?"

"Go ahead. We'll see you later."

"Camille might like to come," Sienna suggested.

"Sure," Brodie agreed. "Camille?"

Rogan looked inquiringly at his wife, who shook her head. "Rogan's promised to give me a tour tomorrow."

He grinned. "She can't bear to be away from me." He hooked an arm about her waist, pulling her close.

It didn't take long for Brodie and Sienna to traverse the main street and poke about the market, where they bought mangoes that they took to the beach to eat, leaning over to let the juice drip to the sand.

Brodie laughed as Sienna wiped the last of the juice from her chin, and she couldn't help laughing too. "Delicious," she pronounced, "but messy."

They rinsed their hands and faces in the shallow wavelets creeping up the beach, and Brodie said, "Would you like a drink of coconut milk, fresh from the tree?"

Dubiously she looked up at the tall palms that edged the sand. "Are you offering to get it for me?"

"Think I can't?" His eyes glinted at her.

"I'm not making any bets."

"Chicken," he chided. "Take a chance for once. Though you'd lose anyway."

"Show-off," she retaliated. Just being with him, enjoying sparring with him, smiling back at the challenge in his eyes, was danger enough for her.

Brodie laughed.

She'd seen the Cook Islanders on Rarotonga, including children, shinny barefoot up the coconut palms to cut down the big yellow globes. Now she watched as Brodie slipped off his boat shoes and belt, tied the belt about his ankles and started up the smooth pale bole using the same technique as the islanders did with a piece of twine or plaited palm leaf. He reached the top and took out a sturdy diving knife from its sheath. "Stand back," he called to her.

A coconut thudded down, followed by another. Within seconds he was back on the ground, grinning in triumph. Sienna, pretending awe, applauded.

He used the knife to open up the yellow outer casing and then the hard, fibrous nuts. The juice was cool and sweet, and when it was gone he broke the nuts into pieces so they could enjoy the crisp, moist white flesh. "That was sublime," Sienna said when she'd had enough.

Seated on the sand beside her, he threw a grin at her, then gathered up the remains and buried them in the sand. "Wait for me," he said. "I won't be long."

Sienna sat on the beach, her knees in light cotton pants drawn up, her chin resting on her hands, eyes shaded by the brim of a linen hat. The water rippled, the sun turning it into a dazzling mass of stars. She felt happy and drowsy and yet very much alive.

Brodie was back within ten minutes, astride a motor scooter.

"Where did you get that?" she asked him.

"Borrowed it. Hop on."

She hesitated only a moment. Then, feeling unusually adventurous, she climbed onto the pillion seat.

"Better put your arms round me," he advised. "Once we're out of town the roads are a bit rough."

He wasn't kidding. As they wound up the mountainside between banana and pineapple plantations, and forests of breadfruit trees and giant yellow-flowered hibiscus interspersed with the ubiquitous coconut palms, the road became narrower, rutted and pocked. Brodie slowed the scooter to a crawl, and Sienna clung to him, her breasts against his broad back, her hands linked at his waist.

His stomach was taut, and through the material of his T-shirt she could feel his body heat. She tried to block it from her mind, concentrating on the occasional glimpses of the sea, the children they passed, riding bareback, two or three to a horse, the workers in the banana plantations who looked up and waved, three women gossiping on a porch as they prepared the evening meal. But she was still acutely conscious of Brodie's body so close to her own, the steady rhythm of his breathing against her arms, her breasts.

Eventually the road became little more than a grassy track, and the scooter snarled to a stop before a carved gateway that straddled the path.

"From here we walk," Brodie said.

The path was too steep for anything else, winding under the trees that closed overhead, making a dim green tunnel.

After five minutes they emerged into a dazzle of sunlight on a small granite plateau.

Far below, beyond the thick green trees, they could see the town and its little harbor. Beyond that the ocean spread out in a vast splendor of shimmering blues and greens.

Shifting her gaze, Sienna realized that from here they could see almost the entire island. Clusters of houses sat among the banana groves and pineapple fields, and white strips of sand bordered tiny coves. Canoes and dinghies were drawn up on most of the wider beaches.

A larger craft lay at anchor on the opposite side of the island from the main harbor. A fishing trawler of indeterminate color, its steel hull streaked with rust, its deck littered with ropes and nets and stacks of plastic bins.

Brodie commented, "She isn't local."

"How do you know?"

"No one on this island can afford a boat that size."

They stayed a few more minutes, then Brodie said they'd better go, to make sure they were back before dark. They had arranged to have dinner with the others at the hotel.

They found Camille and Rogan and the divers enjoying drinks on a terrace overlooking the harbor. Brodie hooked out a chair for Sienna, and they ordered drinks.

"Had a good day?" Rogan inquired.

Brodie looked at Sienna, waiting for her to reply. "Lovely," she said honestly. It was a long time since she'd enjoyed herself so thoroughly. "Brodie's a good tour guide."

He raised his glass at her in acknowledgment of the praise. His eyes held warmth and his grin made her heart miss a couple of beats. *Careful,* a nagging inner voice warned, but she ignored it, recklessly downing her gin, lime and tonic, and allowing Brodie to order her another.

She was among friends, there was safety in numbers, and she'd had a truly nice time today with Brodie, learning about the island he was obviously fond of and knew well. The day wasn't yet over, and the relaxed and friendly atmosphere of Parakaeo was seeping into her soul. She didn't want to be uptight, cautious, afraid of her own susceptibility. And surely by now she had enough experience and self-knowledge to keep her emotions under control while allowing herself some innocent pleasure?

Later they all had dinner together, enjoying fresh fish, pineapple and taro. The hotel put on a floor show of traditional island dance, beginning with a graceful women's dance, their hips swaying in long pareus tied below their waists, and their arms and hands making fluttering movements like birds on wing.

Men joined in, circling the women, slapping their bare brown chests and clapping their thighs together. The dances gradually became less languid, the clacking wooden drums beating faster and faster, the women's hips rotating rhythmically. After a particularly frenetic number and enthusiastic applause, the performers invited the audience to join them.

Rogan dragged Camille, laughing, to her feet, and it was obvious he was no novice, while she quickly picked up the rhythm. Tilisi approached Sienna, and she yielded to his coaxing and followed him onto the floor, trying to imitate the island girls who had been dancing since they could walk.

"You're good!" Tilisi encouraged her. "You've done this before."

She had, taught by a Rarotongan girl who had befriended her on a visit to the Cook Islands a few years before, and whose twelve-year-old brother was the last man she'd danced with.

Tilisi grinned at her and she smiled back, beginning to feel quite uninhibited.

Brodie appeared at Tilisi's side, dropped a word in his ear, and the young man laughed, whacked his friend on the shoulder and went off to find one of the island girls to dance with. Even as Sienna faltered, Brodie smoothly took over where Tilisi had left off, snapping his fingers to encourage her.

Spreading his arms wide, he curved them about her without ever quite touching her, and maintaining eye contact, a gleaming challenge in his. Evidently this wasn't his first time either.

She'd had two glasses of wine at dinner, not enough to make her drunk, but perhaps, after the gin she'd imbibed earlier, it had the effect of making her uncharacteristically reckless. Under Brodie's intent blue stare she deliberately exaggerated the movements of her hips, refused to let her glance modestly drop as some of the girl dancers did, and instead let her gaze lock with his in a silent, erotic war.

Chapter 5

The drumbeat seemed to be in sync with Sienna's racing heart, and when the drummers abruptly stopped and the dancers stilled, her heart continued to race. She was breathing fast, and there was a faint sheen on Brodie's forehead. For a moment they stood facing each other, their eyes still engaged in a silent duel of desire.

Not a genuine emotion, she told herself, shaken by the strength of it. They'd both got caught up in the sexual energy generated by the drums and the eroticism of the island's traditional entertainment.

The other dancers were leaving the floor, returning to their everyday selves, laughing and talking. Camille and Rogan quietly disappeared through a side door.

Sienna dragged her gaze from Brodie and he followed her to their table. She gulped a couple of breaths to calm herself and return to normality.

The rest of the dive crew were about to repair again to the bar. ''The last chance we'll get for a decent drink for a while,'' Joe said.

"Do you want a drink?" Brodie asked Sienna.

Hot now, and feeling exhilarated and yet nervy, she eyed the moonlit seascape outside. It would be nice to stroll along the waterfront after that delicious meal and the strenuous exercise, and let herself come down from the high engendered by the dance. "You go and join your friends. I think I'll go for a walk."

"Not on your own. I'll come with you."

Alarm tingled through her. "Surely this is the safest place on earth?" The island seemed very peaceful and everyone had been markedly friendly.

"I'm not letting you out there in the dark alone."

She could see she'd have no luck dissuading him. Changing her mind would make it obvious she was avoiding his company, which she had enjoyed all day, and besides, she discovered with a hint of defiance, she really didn't want to dispense with it.

They took the narrow winding road with no footpath down to the foreshore, wandering along until they came to the end of the town, where the road petered out and only a dirt path continued at the edge of the trees.

Sienna halted, but Brodie decisively took her hand in his and forged on.

She needed his guidance because, although the moonlight was brilliant and white, the trees shadowed the rough path, and once or twice she stumbled.

They emerged at a small cove, a curve of pale sand with a high headland at the other side crowned by a huge, flat-topped rock. These blocks of granite cropped up all over the island, remnants of the long-ago explosions when it had been born out of fire and brimstone.

Brodie led her across the sand to another, steeper path, and at the top climbed onto the big rock, using footholds he obviously knew well, and turned to haul Sienna up after him.

Moonlight shimmered across the water. She could see the harbor where the *Sea-Rogue* lay gently rocking at her anchors, a couple of fishing boats nearby, and half a dozen canoes lying on the beach, some sporting outboard motors.

The lighted windows of the town and a couple of yellow streetlights gleamed not far away. Nearer, in the darkness a fish leaped, momentarily a twisting sliver of silver caught in the moonlight before it splashed back into the water. She took a step to peek over at the foot of the headland, where thunderous waves licked whitely at the rocky face. Attacked by an unexpected moment of vertigo, she hastily moved back, and cannoned against Brodie.

His arms came about her waist. "Watch it."

"Sorry," she gasped. She hadn't known he was so close behind her.

He was still holding her securely. "You okay?"

"Yes. I didn't realize it was so far down."

"You're scared of heights?"

"Not more than most people, I think. It was just steeper than I expected. You can let me go now."

"Suppose," he drawled, "I don't want to?"

Sienna held her breath. She couldn't answer, though common sense told her she ought to say something to break the moment, indicate that the hard body warming hers, the arms wrapped gently about her, were unwelcome. Only they weren't.

He turned her to face him, and looked down at her. The high brassy moon sailing in a star-crowded sky gave a faint patina to his hair but his face was shadowed, his eyes dark.

She tried to persuade herself that her heart was pounding because of the small fright she'd had when she looked down, that she didn't push away from him because of their precarious position on the rock, although it was big enough for several people.

But she knew that if she'd said no he wouldn't have kissed her, wouldn't have lowered his mouth to hers and covered her lips, parting them under an insistent, persuasive pressure and commencing an intimate, lingering exploration that made her knees weaken, her body flood with heat.

The salty tang of the sea and the heavy, sweet perfume of frangipani blossoms rose about them, and she inhaled them along with the subtle male scent of Brodie's skin. Her own skin was so sensitized she could feel the cool moonlight on her closed eyelids, and when Brodie raised his head at last, and lifted one hand to briefly touch her cheek, she felt an invisible shiver of pleasure all the way to her toes.

Brodie drew in a heavy breath and let it out. Sienna was as dizzy as when she'd looked over the edge of the cliff. She'd never been kissed quite that expertly and thoroughly in her life. Never felt so alive and aware, and yet as if she were floating on a dark, satin sea. The feeling was wonderful, hypnotic, yet she was conscious of the dangerous depths below. If she let herself be carried by the persuasive current of sexual hunger, she could drown in those depths, be pulled down once again into the darkness and cold of utter despair.

Long-cherished caution warred with temptation. Biting her lip, finally making an effort to pull away from him, she said thinly, "I…think we should go back now."

It sounded inane.

"Sure," Brodie said after a moment. He released her and moved, jumping down before turning to help her. When she reached the ground he held her with two hands at her waist, and pressed another lightning kiss on her lips, leaving them tingling and warm. Then he led the way back, and didn't comment after they gained the roadway again and she pulled her hand from his to jam it into the pocket of her trousers.

Back at the boat he saw her to her cabin and gave her a crooked grin when she slipped inside with a quick, firm "Good night."

Had she thought he expected to be invited in? Brodie wondered as he crossed to his own cabin, the grin fading into a frown. A man could hope but…

Usually after ten days' sailing people knew each other's hot buttons, who snored and who didn't—he didn't think Sienna did—and something about their background. For long periods the boat was under autopilot and all that was needed was an occasional change of sail and a watchful eye on the weather and the water. That inevitably led to talk, and to some personal information being exchanged.

Sienna was noticeably reticent in that regard.

He'd told her one night, when they were alone in the cockpit, about his four brothers and sisters, scattered about the world in various jobs, and about his mother, a schoolteacher still working at a little country school—and his father, who had been a fisherman and died at sea.

"It didn't put you off a life at sea?" she'd asked, looking at him curiously.

"Nope. I guess I inherited his genes. It was a hard life and there's not much money in it these days."

"Doesn't your mother worry about you?"

"She's never stopped any of us doing what we want to do. Do you have a mother worrying about you now?"

"I'm an adult, she knows I can take care of myself."

"And your dad?"

"I don't see much of him." She sounded indifferent. "They're divorced."

"Do you mind," he asked, "not seeing him?"

She was silent for a while, watching the horizon where the stars met the night-black sea. "I suppose it's my own fault," she said. "I couldn't forgive him, and when my brother and I visited him I was unhappy and sulky."

"He was the one who walked? Was there another woman?"

"Yes," she said reluctantly. "He has a new family anyway."

"How old were you then?"

"Fifteen. I'm fine. I got over it ages ago."

"And forgave him?"

"I'm glad he's happy."

She wasn't happy; he could hear it in the husky note in her voice, see it in the way she'd turned away from him.

Before he could ask any more questions she'd stood up and

said she was going to help Camille in the galley. End of discussion. He could sense her pulling down a mental blind to close him out, putting up shutters. Gathering that cool and impenetrable manner about her like a protective cloak. Probably regretting that she'd opened up to him even that far.

It was the only time she'd done so. And he'd been careful not to crowd her, telling himself not to force anything, be patient.

Then tonight she'd backed into him and her sweet body was soft and warm against him, and pure physical reaction had him instantly heated up. She hadn't resisted when he turned her to him, her face lifting to his in the moonlight, her eyes huge and dark, and her mouth a naked temptation. He'd hardly dared breathe as he found it with his, kissed her with a feeling that something important was happening here, that he mustn't mess up or he'd regret it for the rest of his life.

Not exactly kissing him back, she hadn't objected either, pliant in his arms, her mouth passively accepting his careful seduction. But when they'd drawn apart she had simply suggested they go back, with no hint that it had affected her in any way at all.

Closing his cabin door behind him, he fumbled for the light switch, still thinking about the kiss and Sienna's reaction.

He saw his own reflection in the cool glass of the porthole, ghostly against the night, looking frustrated and baffled.

A picture came into his mind of the first time he'd seen Sienna. He closed his eyes and saw the little seaside chapel again, Sienna following the bride and groom with her bewitching mouth curving into a strangely poignant smile, and the sunlight playing on her glorious hair.

Today someone had asked him if Sienna was his bride.

Abruptly opening his eyes, he shook his head to clear it, stared at his reflection, gave it an astonished grin. He was getting wa-ay ahead of himself here.

If Sienna had any idea of what he was thinking—well, half thinking, maybe—she'd run a mile.

And so would he if anyone else had suggested it.

He thrust a hand through his hair and turned away from the porthole.

Rogue's wedding had unsettled him, made him think about things that had rarely even crossed his mind before.

Sienna would look great in a shimmering long white dress with a veil—and even better without them, in his arms, his bed...

Another grin, slightly shamefaced, curved his mouth as he hauled off his T-shirt. He shouldn't be thinking about her like this.

But he couldn't help it. The more he saw of Sienna, the more he wanted her.

There was no damn privacy aboard the boat, and now things could only get worse, with the rest of the team joining them, although they'd be sleeping on the dive barge.

He'd just have to be patient. Maybe that was a good thing. He and Sienna would be working side by side. They'd surely get to know each other better, and without sex getting in the way.

Blinking at that thought, he paused in the act of unzipping his pants. Since when had sex *got in the way?* He'd always thought it was a pretty good means of getting to know a woman he liked. A damn fine one, in fact. Quick and easy and decidedly pleasant.

Easy, yeah. His conscience twinged.

Somehow he knew quick and easy wasn't going to cut it with Sienna.

The following day Rogan and Brodie went off to finish fitting out the barge. Camille and Sienna spent the morning housekeeping on the *Sea-Rogue*, then made a picnic lunch that they took to share with the men.

Sienna avoided Brodie as much as possible, glad that the others were there to prevent any private conversation. She couldn't banish last night's torrid kiss from her mind. When she did catch Brodie's alert, considering gaze, his mouth curved in a knowing smile before she hastily averted her eyes.

After lunch the two women went shopping, and along with more practical things like foodstuffs, they bought some tie-dyed pareus, mere lengths of light, cool cotton to wear in the tropical heat.

Sienna was still wearing one later during dinner at the hotel. Brodie's gaze lingered on her bare shoulders for a few moments, and she tried to quell a thrill of pride at the admiration in his eyes.

While everyone else lingered over drinks afterward, she slipped away outside, went down to the beach and strolled along the sand. Brodie wouldn't approve, but she needed time alone, time to think, to remind herself she couldn't face another emotional upheaval in her life, that she'd already been down that road with men too much like him. Too much like her father. A dead-end road she never intended to travel again.

The pale sand curved into a little cove where the trees were thick and dark, a sliver of moon giving the calm water of the lagoon a faint sheen, the foaming breakers on the reef a ghostly white.

The sand was still warm, and even wearing only the thin cotton pareu over minimal panties, she felt sweat dewing her skin, trickling on her forehead and between her breasts, dampening her underarms.

She took off her sandals and walked to the edge of the water. Looking about, she saw no one in sight; she might have been alone on the island. The only sounds were the palm leaves clicking against each other, the distant boom of the breakers, the nearer swishing and rippling of the wavelets cooling her toes.

Possessed of a reckless impulse, she tossed her shoes onto the sand and undid the knot holding the pareu and threw it after them, where it drifted for a moment in the air before settling in an uneven blur of muted color. Then she walked into the water until it was deep enough for swimming.

It felt glorious—liquid satin, cool and sensuous against her bare skin. She swam with a slow breaststroke, then floated for a while on her back, looking up at the splendid extravagance of the stars crowding the night sky.

When she waded back to the beach she felt refreshed, stimulated, alive. She was conscious of her body in a new way, as if she'd never been at home in it before, as if the water had washed away all inhibition. As if like Venus she were newly emerged from a seashell. Her breasts peaked and tingled, and her skin seemed to feel every tiny salt droplet that ran over it.

She found the pareu and was straightening with it in her hand when a faint movement among the trees caught her eye, a paler shape amid the dense, dark foliage. Instinctively she clutched the material with both hands over her breasts, calling sharply, "Who's there?"

The shape emerged upon the sand—male, large, wearing jeans and a light T-shirt. "It's only me." Brodie's voice. "It's okay, Sienna. Sorry, I didn't intend for you to know."

It wasn't okay. Her heart pounded. "Have you been spying on me?"

He strolled closer, not replying at once. "Watching you," he admitted. "I followed you from the hotel—I told you last night you shouldn't wander about alone. Obviously you didn't want company so I kept out of sight. I had no idea you meant to go skinny-dipping."

"It was an impulse. You…sh-shouldn't have watched."

"I know." His voice lowered. "I couldn't help it. You were so beautiful. Like something out of dreams and legends—a mermaid. Magical, mysterious."

Treacherously, she was conscious of a jolt of shocking pleasure, of sizzling excitement. She took a deep breath and the pareu slipped, baring one breast.

She ought to pull it back into place. Instead she simply stood there, while Brodie's dark gaze, shadowed in the moonlight, remained fixed on her face. Then he reached out slowly and did it for her, but his hand lingered, his knuckles pressing gently against the tender skin just below her armpit, then moving the edge of the material farther round as if to wrap it about her. "You should put this on," he said softly, "if you want to be safe."

Afterward she told herself it was the atmosphere of the island—the moonlit beach so far from home, the swaying palms, the silver-tinted lagoon, a setting straight out of a TV ad for Pacific holidays. And the rich, exotic scent of frangipani mixed with the heady tang of the sea. But in truth it was the man—Brodie, with his own unique male scent, his gentle hands, his seductive, deep-ocean voice, his confession that he'd followed to watch out for her—and kept watching because he couldn't resist temptation—that gave her the courage to push aside her customary caution and seize the moment with all its hidden hazards, its disregard for future complications.

"Maybe I don't want to be safe," she said, "tonight." Even now a tiny part of her mind, not totally lost to common sense, supplied the caveat.

For long seconds Brodie simply stared down at her, not moving. She wondered if he was going to reject her after all. She should have been relieved, but dread made her close her eyes.

Then she felt his warm breath on her face, his lips featherlight against her eyelids, first one, then the other. "Open your eyes, Sienna," he said, his voice deeper than ever and not quite steady.

She did so reluctantly, staring up at him, his face still only inches from hers.

He said, "I want to make love to you. Is that what you want too?"

He wasn't going to let her get away with any pretence of being swept off her feet, not knowing what she was doing. She could back out now and he'd let her.

"Yes," she said, scarcely above a whisper.

She slid her arms about his neck, and he took up the invitation, pulling her close, one hand flattening against her back, the other closing about the top of her thigh, sliding over the curve above, then settling at her waist as his mouth covered hers, finding it eager and open for him.

He was gentle, but she found she didn't want gentleness. Taking his cue from her, he gathered her closer and kissed her thoroughly, his tongue plunging into her mouth, his hand finding again the rounded, naked flesh of her behind, then moving to her breast before he wrenched the cloth from between them and spread it on the sand, bearing her down on it even as he snapped open his jeans.

She helped him get rid of them, haul off the T-shirt, remove her damp bikini panties.

Never had she been so wanton, so lost in turbulent sensation, so impatient to explore a man's body with her hands, lips, her own skin pressed against his, so excited when she felt him respond with a deep shudder, realized that already he was fully aroused. Wanting her as she wanted him.

He was trying to take his time, his hands everywhere on her body, stroking, exploring, teasing. The moonlight revealed in the tautness of his face the fierce control he was exercising and the glitter in his eyes, now seeming black as the night about them.

She was torn between wanting to prolong the dizzying lovemaking and the driving desire to reach the pinnacle that was coming nearer with each kiss, each touch of his fingers, each time her own fingertips traced his wonderfully muscular shoulders, his strong back, or plowed into his hair as he lowered his mouth to her breasts, her navel, the tip of his tongue arousing her to unbearable heights of desire.

Finally she told him with her body that she needed him *now*—inviting him in to the ultimate focus of pleasure, meeting his deep, strong thrusts with gasps of delight, moving to encourage him, finally giving herself up to ecstasy such as she'd never known before; she knew that he was with her, they were cresting the wave together, then slowly coming down on the other side into the shallows of spent passion.

She closed her eyes, exhausted, her head cradled on his shoulder, and slowly, slowly, came back to earth.

Brodie kissed her hair, her cheek, then—lingeringly—her mouth. He eased away from her and only then she realized he'd been prepared for this. Stupid to feel a slight chill at that. It was sensible of him, especially after last night when they'd shared that sexy kiss in the moonlight. He must have anticipated something like this. Even while she was pretending to herself that it would never happen, that she still had control over her increasing desire for him.

In the aftermath she felt empty, oddly emotionless. Not even regret penetrated the vacuum that seemed to surround her.

Brodie moved away, and she sat up, knelt on the sand and wrapped the pareu around her, knotting it tightly under her still-tingling breasts, trying to blot out the intimate attention he'd given them—given every part of her.

He watched her for a minute, then hauled on his clothes, the rasp of the zip as he did up his jeans, sounding loud in the silence.

She pulled her panties back on, now sandy as well as damp.

"You okay?" he asked her.

"Yes." But when he reached out to touch her she shied away. "I need a shower." She began walking back toward the boat.

He thrust his hands into his pockets and walked beside her, head bent. "I must say you surprised me." He sounded as though something bothered him. "I didn't expect…"

"Let's not start analyzing." She had surprised—shocked— herself. It was as if some other woman had taken over her body, her mind. A woman she didn't know, couldn't trust. Who might lead her into unknown depths that frightened her. She could lose herself in those depths, let herself be taken by the powerful currents of mindless, needy sentiment, and drown in a fatal emotional maelstrom. "It happened," she said, desperate to regain the safe shore of reason, of prudence. "It was nice, it's over."

"Over," he repeated. "Yeah?"

"Yeah." Deliberately she echoed the word, and increased

her pace. She'd been a little mad, for a short while. Now she had to return to sanity, to reality. Protect herself. Brodie was silent for the rest of the walk to the boat, and there she went straight into the shower and afterward to bed. Tomorrow they'd leave the island and there'd be little opportunity for any private encounter. Perhaps she'd recapture a sense of proportion, of judgment. But she wished Brodie wasn't going to be on board.

Next day the *Sea-Rogue* set sail again, with the island's one tugboat, having escorted the cargo ship out of the harbor, now towing the salvage barge where the other members of the dive crew would eat, sleep and work.

On arrival at the site almost twenty-four hours later the barge was secured near where Rogan said the wreck was located, just far enough off to ensure its anchors couldn't damage anything on it. The *Sea-Rogue* was tied up alongside, and with barely contained excitement the divers, and an engineer from Parakaeo who was to man the winch, transferred their gear to the barge and readied themselves for work.

One of the new divers, a large, square-jawed American known as Hunk, had medical training, and the other, a Norwegian called Olin, owned a range of camera equipment that put Sienna's waterproof snapshot camera to shame. He told her he had photographed underwater all over the world and supplemented his diving income by selling his pictures to magazines. He was also a computer wizard and could, Brodie said, make any electronic machine "sit up and sing."

Brodie and Rogan had both spent time studying the use of sidescan sonar and magnometers, equipment designed to locate anomalies on the seafloor.

"At sea," Brodie said, "it's always handy to be able to turn your hand to more than one thing. Cheaper too. And the fewer people who know about this the less chance there is of word leaking out about where we are exactly."

He and Sienna made a preliminary dive so she could physically survey the site before it was disturbed any further.

They went down on scuba, although later the divers would be using surface-supplied air, which would allow them to stay longer on the bottom.

Sienna followed Brodie into the blue depths, trying not to be distracted by the reef with its rainbow-hued corals, waving seaweed, and the fish darting about among them in flashes of silver, yellow, blue and orange.

When Brodie pointed, she experienced a shivery thrill at the sight of the long curve of the downed ship's hull, almost hidden under its covering of sand and marine growth.

They swam toward it, and Sienna saw a dark, uneven shadow that when they came closer revealed itself as a large, jagged hole in the sea-worn timbers.

Brodie planted a buoy line to mark the location of the wreck, then he caught the edge of the hole and peered down into the blackness. Lifting away from it, he motioned Sienna to follow, and they swam in increasing circles from the buoy line, systematically traversing the area. There were lumps of coral, some of which might be hiding artifacts, but little on the surface that looked like goods scattered from the wreck.

When they surfaced and climbed on board the barge where Rogan and the others waited, Brodie pulled off his mask, looking grim. "Someone's blown a hole in her," he said with disgust.

Rogan swore, Camille gave a shocked "Oh no!" and the other divers looked glum. Sienna, her own mask in her hand, said, "That hole wasn't there before?"

"No," Brodie said. "Not where there's one now."

Sienna's heart sank. Heaven knew what sort of damage the explosion might have caused.

Rogan asked, "Did you go inside?"

"Nope. They've made a mess of it. There's a lot of smashed timber in there, including some pretty heavy beams, and God knows what else."

Rogan suited up himself, and went down with Camille and Joe.

After surfacing, Rogan said, "Accessing the ship through

that hole carries too much risk of getting trapped, or snagged on something.''

''I wonder if the guys who did it tried?'' Hunk the American said. Everyone was wondering how much of the treasure might have been taken.

''They'd have to be crazy,'' Brodie told them. ''It's a death trap.''

Rogan decided, ''We'll keep uncovering the ship and see how much there is before we try clearing the hole.''

Next morning at dawn a ship was clearly seen, anchored not far away. A rusty-hulled fishing trawler.

''Damn, they can't stay there,'' Rogan said. ''If they put nets down they could snag our machinery, or even the divers. It's far too dangerous.''

Brodie lifted binoculars to his eyes. ''The *Scorpio.* I'm pretty sure she was anchored at Parakaeo. There was something on the radar screen last night, probably her.''

Rogan said, ''At Parakaeo? I didn't see her in port.''

''She was anchored at the other side of the island.''

''I'll see if we can raise her on the radio.''

The *Scorpio's* captain, Rogan reported minutes later, was polite and immovable. ''He says we're on his fishing ground, that they've fished here regularly.''

''That close to the reef?'' Brodie queried. ''Has he brought up any bits of wreckage or cargo?''

''Probably,'' Rogan muttered. ''Maybe they're responsible for the hole in the wreck's hull.''

Joe, the redheaded Australian, said, ''Some fishing boats use dynamite to stun their catch and bring the fish to the surface.''

''That's illegal, isn't it?'' Sienna asked.

''Yeah,'' Joe confirmed, and grinned. ''But on the high seas, who's to know?''

Rogan said, ''Anyway, I've told him we have certain legal rights on the site, and asked him nicely to move on. We can't force him.''

Brodie offered, "We could make fishing uncomfortable, with our airlifts. The bubbles might scare the fish away."

Sienna gave him a dubious look. "He has just as much right to be here as we do, doesn't he?"

His gaze rested on her for a moment, and she felt as if he'd touched her with a warm finger, sending a tiny shiver down to her toes.

"The Pacific's a big ocean," he pointed out. "There are plenty more fishing spots but only one *Maiden's Prayer*." Turning to Rogan, he said, "Can we offer him compensation to move on?"

"I'm not keen to do that in case it's exactly why he's here. He's turned up just when we're ready to start, and I somehow doubt it's pure coincidence."

"He wouldn't be stupid enough to lower his nets near our anchors," Brodie suggested. "We can make a start, anyway, if we stick close to the barge."

Rogan agreed. "The first thing is to airlift some of the overburden of sand off the wreck. We don't know if the complete hull is here or bits of it have scattered for miles. And Sienna, you can see how well our new computer program works for you in practice."

The program he'd briefly introduced her to while they sailed toward their destination would show her a virtual grid superimposed on the video picture the divers would send back to the barge from their helmet-mounted cameras, improving on laboriously setting out physical grid lines underwater.

Sienna said, "There could be breakable items down there. Crockery's valuable in an archaeological sense, even if not in market terms."

"We'll take it gently," Rogan promised.

"Yeah," Brodie agreed. "We don't want to accidentally smash anything."

She thought his gaze this time was meant to be reassuring, but the warmth in his eyes almost undid her. Without even trying he could remind her of a tropical night that she desperately wanted to forget.

Once the first two helmet divers were down, connected to the barge by their yellow air hoses, and the airlift was creating a five-foot-wide circle of bubbles on the surface, Sienna and Brodie sat side by side in the control center set up on the barge, watching the underwater operation on computer screens.

She tried not to notice when his bare arm brushed hers. Tried to concentrate on the picture before her and not on the way a sun-kissed lock of hair fell over Brodie's forehead when he leaned forward to study something that had caught his eyes on the screen, nor on how surprisingly long his eyelashes were, and so much darker than his hair, or how strong and brown his blunt-fingered hand looked when it moved the computer mouse to zoom in on whatever had interested him.

The man was just too sexy for her peace of mind. She wrenched her attention back to the computer.

Chapter 6

Sand churned in opaque clouds, making it difficult at first to clearly see the divers systematically moving the ends of the airlifts, like giant vacuum-cleaner hoses, over the buried ship.

Sienna knew exactly where they were, the numbers on the screen indicating which square of the grid they were in. On deck Rogan and Camille were watching the filters for anything brought up with the sand.

The first thrill of anticipation ebbed away as the work progressed and nothing of interest was recovered. Lumps of coral retrieved from the filters were just what they appeared to be. Several fragments of wood were put aside in a tub of water for examination later. A round object retrieved by one of the divers, causing brief excitement, turned out to be a modern fishing float.

Brodie shifted uneasily and muttered, ''Someone's cleaned out the surface stuff, at least.''

''Are you sure Rogan didn't collect more than he's letting on?''

Brodie turned to give her a hard stare. "Rogue's not a cheat. Or a liar."

"But he's big on secrets," she pointed out. "Joe told me he and the other divers didn't have a clue where we were going."

"Rogue didn't want it leaking out. Anyway, the first time he dived the site, Camille was with him. And the second time, I was."

"What about when he was in Rarotonga to organize the dive barge? After all, who else would have known where to look?"

"A navy ship picked up him and Camille the first time. The captain was sworn to secrecy, of course, but the crew could have put two and two together, specially when the papers got wind of the story and the reporters started making up theories because Rogue wouldn't talk to them. And James Drummond's on the loose somewhere. He knows where it is. And his skipper."

"Who's in prison," Sienna reminded him. The man had confessed to everything he'd been charged with, and swore that Drummond had been the mastermind behind it.

"Yeah, but he could have talked to his mates in there— and they don't stay locked up forever."

When the first divers came up and entered the decompression chamber to purge their systems of nitrogen, two more replaced them and the work continued. More of the hull became visible, much of its timber remarkably almost intact. Then came the first real find of the day—one of the divers pushed aside the mouth of the airlift and stooped, then held up something that, though heavily encrusted, was obviously a candlestick.

Sienna leaned forward, zoomed the computer in on the picture, and clicked for a still shot that the computer would automatically store. Brodie, in telephone communication with the divers through a headset, said, "Put it in the basket, Joe."

Joe gave a thumbs-up signal and carefully placed the candlestick in the wire basket that had been lowered nearby, before returning to his painstaking work.

Sienna noted the exact location of the find and said, "Did you and Rogan think of using those new machines that pick things up underwater?"

"They're designed for areas too deep for divers," Brodie answered, his eyes on the screen in front of him, "and they're very expensive."

A little later Joe's partner found some shards of china. Then a complete coral-coated wine bottle, more china shards and an apparently undamaged china plate joined the other artifacts. But the main task at the moment, Brodie said, was to determine which end of the ship was which, and how much of it was there. Sometimes a portion of a shipwreck might be found, with the rest perhaps being miles off in deeper water, carried by the current when the ship broke up.

At the end of the day the basket was hauled up and its contents collected by Sienna and carried to the cabin on the barge set aside for her work.

The fishing boat had moved off for a time, trawling in a desultory fashion back and forth, always within sight. But it returned to the same anchorage before darkness fell. Rogan spent some minutes with his hand shading his eyes, staring across the water.

After a hearty dinner that she helped Camille cook, Sienna left the table early and returned to her lab.

Brodie strolled in while she was carefully chipping coral from the wine bottle with a rubber mallet.

"How's it going?" he asked, looking over her shoulder. "You're not afraid of breaking the glass?"

"Not if I'm careful," she said. "It takes patience."

Brodie looked at her bent head. She seemed almost oblivious to him. On the island he'd felt she was nearly ready to allow him to get beneath the surface of her firmly maintained outer shell, when she'd spent most of the day with him, danced with him, let him kiss her as they stood on the headland. And finally made love to him so generously, so unreservedly. Only to clam up immediately afterward, shutting him out of her mind, her heart.

He said, "Sienna...on the island we were as close as two people can get, at least physically." Her hand rested on the table in front of her, still clutching the mallet. Clutching it quite hard, he noticed.

"It was a beautiful night," she said. "We were both affected by all that tropical romance."

Excuses, he thought irritably.

Sienna lifted her hand again and gently tapped at the coral. A small piece fell off, revealing a bit more of the bottle. "It was nice," she said.

Nice? It had been more than that. Special. Something to be treasured—and repeated. He looked down broodingly at the painstaking way she was removing the hard coating that hid the delicate artifact.

Sienna hid her real self behind a protective layer of indifference and even cynicism. But she wasn't as tough as she made out. Underneath she was as fragile and brittle as the glass she handled with such care. Brodie knew it.

Restlessly, he shifted position to lean against the table where he could see her face. She had her hair tied back out of the way, but her eyes were hidden by her lashes as she turned the bottle to access another portion of it.

He couldn't believe the episode on Mokohina had meant so little to her, when he'd found it a mind-blowing experience. What was she trying to hide? Or hide from? "I thought," he said carefully, "that we had something going there."

She lifted a shoulder. "We had a good time."

"I hoped there might be better ones to come."

Fleetingly her eyes met his. When she looked down again she said steadily, "If you mean you hoped to sleep with me again, I'm sorry—it's not going to happen."

Tempted to ask, Wanna bet? Brodie refrained. Almost thinking aloud, trying to fathom this baffling turnaround, he said thoughtfully, "You don't hate me."

That got her attention. "Of course I don't hate you!" Her cheeks went a deep pink.

He watched with interest. "Who *do* you hate?"

"No one!"

Not even her father—she'd said she was glad he was happy. Taking a gamble, he said, "What about the guy—or guys— who hurt you in the past?"

The color in her cheeks faded and she looked away from him. "No one goes through life without being hurt."

"So badly you've shut yourself away from enjoying life?"

She glanced up then, her expression hostile. "I have a very good life. I love my job, I have plenty of friends and a brother I'm close to, and my mother. Do I seem so miserable to you?"

"You just seem…enclosed," he said. "As if you're afraid to let yourself go. What are you scared of?"

"I'm not afraid!" She flashed him a fierce look that made him grin. She sure wasn't intimidated by him, although he could have picked her up with one hand if he were so inclined.

"Prove it," he said.

Her eyes turned suspicious, then scornful. "You'll have to do better than that," she said with deliberate sarcasm. "I'm not going to bed with you again just to show you don't frighten me." ·

Brodie laughed outright. "There was no bed that first time, as I recall. Just you and me and the moonlight on the beach. And it was enough, wasn't it?"

"Yes." She sat back, her gaze on the work in front of her. "It was enough, and I don't need to repeat it." She turned the bottle, stubbornly refusing to meet his eyes. "I have to get on with this. You're distracting me."

That might be a good sign, Brodie hoped as he straightened and strolled toward the door. "See you later," he said, and turned briefly, catching a wistful expression on her face as she stared after him. But she quickly dropped her head, fixing her eyes on what she'd been doing.

Maybe he'd imagined that look after all.

* * *

Sienna tightened her hold on the mallet and stared at the wine bottle, not seeing it. A strange sensation fluttered in her stomach, and she firmly quenched it.

She should have treated Brodie as she did Tilisi, who flirted with her, his brown eyes teasing, obviously not at all serious, making her laugh with his exaggerated dejection when she failed to respond. But he always bounced back even more outrageously. It was a game, a natural reaction of a certain type of male to any attractive female who happened to be around and apparently available. And she was the only one handy at the moment.

Tilisi was easy to handle, but with Brodie she'd been unable to keep it light, to laugh.

She'd succumbed once so he thought he might get lucky again. And perhaps he was a bit piqued that since leaving the island she'd tried to be pleasant and aloof and make it clear that a mistaken incident in the tropical moonlight wasn't going to lead anywhere. A new experience for him, very likely.

Well, it wouldn't do him any harm.

A few days later the trawler disappeared over the horizon and off the radar. Apparently the skipper had decided there was no point in hanging about any longer.

The divers cleared away more sand, revealing that much of the wreck's hull was remarkably intact. The winch lifted the larger pieces of timber out of the jagged hole in the side.

Soon Sienna was busy cleaning and cataloging other finds. Half a dozen rusted muskets found lying together in a heap were carefully lifted to the barge. Sienna was able to date Joe's candlestick as circa 1840 and a pocket watch that Tilisi found as manufactured in 1850. With only six helmet divers working on air supplied from the surface, Brodie was one of the team as well as supervisor. When Rogan took his place in the computer room Sienna couldn't help noticing a drop in her inner tension, a curious flatness in her mood.

After surfacing from a dive, Brodie handed her a gleaming fob chain as Rogan left to go back on deck.

"It's beautiful," she exclaimed. "And as good as new."

Gold didn't tarnish or pick up much in the way of accretions underwater. It survived for centuries.

Brodie stood by as she fingered the chain, each finely wrought link a work of art. "Gold lasts forever," he said. "I guess that's why it's traditionally used for wedding rings."

Sienna glanced at him, then put down the chain. "A gold ring will certainly outlast any marriage. Especially now."

"Now?"

"Divorce is an easier option than it was in earlier times. People can just walk out when they want to."

"Like your father?"

She glanced up again swiftly, then looked away, pretending to study the chain again. "I was generalizing." She wished she hadn't told him about her father.

Brodie said, "My parents are still together after forty years."

"Nice for you."

"Hey!" he objected softly.

Sienna looked up at him, feeling guilty. "I don't mean to sound sarcastic."

"It *is* nice," Brodie told her. "And something to aspire to, if I ever get married."

"Well, good luck."

He was looking at her thoughtfully. "You sound as if you think I'll need it."

"It's not personal."

It was a moment before he spoke again. "Did you ever think about getting married?"

The blunt question surprised her. "All little girls dream of a white dress and veil to go with the handsome prince who's going to carry them off to a castle where they'll live happily ever after." She laughed but it came out a little strained. "Unfortunately princes are thin on the ground."

"You're waiting for one to come along?" Brodie queried. When she looked at him again he was giving her a quizzical grin.

Obviously he wasn't taking this conversation seriously.

"Heavens no! I was snapped out of that—" She stopped abruptly there. "I'm not waiting for anyone. I have more important things to do. Like cataloging this chain." She picked it up again and moved to the computer that held her records.

Ignoring the hint, Brodie watched her for a few minutes, then turned to pick up a shiny sovereign from several on the table.

"Why would a ship heading for America be carrying British coins?" he wondered idly.

Glad of the change of subject, she told him, "British money was standard in Australia by the 1850s. Before, gold or silver coins from almost any country were used—in the eighteenth century Spanish dollars were the closest to a universal currency. The miners could have exchanged the sovereigns for dollars once they got home, but they probably carried most of their gold as dust or nuggets, or bars."

Brodie nodded and spun the sovereign on its edge, then caught it and carefully set it down.

"Apart from a few coins," Sienna said, "there's no sign of any gold hoard so far."

"The *Maiden's Prayer* had a bullion safe. We haven't found that yet."

"Suppose there's nothing in the safe after all? Camille could only guess from the records and the rumours at the time the *Maiden's Prayer* had sailed as to how much gold was on board."

"The signs are good. We won't quit until we know for sure, one way or the other. Rogan doesn't give up easily."

Sienna turned from her computer notes. "Do you?"

His head tipped to one side, he regarded her as if she were a chess board and he was planning some kind of tactic. Then he smiled slowly. "No," he said. "I've never been a quitter, Sienna."

The way he said her name sent a flutter of something like apprehension into her midriff. To her relief, he turned and left her without another word.

* * *

After another week what looked like the broken bow of the ship was exposed, its shattered, worm-eaten timbers stark testimony to the fatal collision with the coral that had violently torn it open. Sienna urged Rogan to call a temporary halt to operations while she went down to inspect the newly revealed section in person.

"Twenty minutes is all the time you'll have," Rogan warned.

Brodie said, "You take over as dive master, Rogue. I'll go down with Sienna."

They finned down quickly to the dead ship, Sienna wearing only a brief two-piece swimsuit with her fins and dive gear, Brodie a big, sleek presence at her side in dive pants but with no top under his buoyancy jacket. They wouldn't be down long enough to get too cold.

Broken timbers told their mute tale of long-ago tragedy. Several fish shimmered away through the clear water that deepened to murky green in the distance.

Sienna peered into the cavity, not yet entirely clear of sand, noting every detail and taking photographs. Timber that had fallen inward mixed with the remains of what had probably been the seamen's quarters, and a jumble of objects that might have been almost anything, crusted with a century and a half of sea-growth.

A bulkhead blocked them from going farther. Brodie's hand circled Sienna's wrist, pulling her after him. They left the bow to inspect the hole blown in the middle of the ship. They didn't touch anything, but Sienna took more photographs, and on deck again she compared them with the pictures on the computer and typed in notes.

Brodie leaned on the back of her chair, making occasional comments, adding his impressions to hers while Rogan, standing next to him, asked a few questions. Camille sat next to Sienna in Brodie's chair.

Brodie said, "It looks as though the ship struck the reef, then sank and slid down the slope, either immediately or over time. Between the wreck and the reef she could have spilled a lot of stuff on the way.''

"The magnometer might pick up any large amounts of metal in the ship now we've got rid of some of the sand,'' Rogan suggested. "Even handheld metal detectors might find something.''

Sienna drew in another grid line on the computer and numbered it, concentrating on her task, while aware of Brodie only inches away. "Metal detectors miss a lot. China, wood, other materials. And I don't want anything moved until I've mapped exactly what we've got down there.''

"Ah…Sienna,'' Rogan said, "divers' wages don't come cheap.''

Brodie asked, "When can we put them back in the water?''

"I'm almost done. Tell them, pick up everything that isn't part of the sea flora or fauna, and whatever it is, not to move from that spot until I've logged it. And anything small or fragile needs to be brought up by hand.''

"I think they know that.''

Sienna twisted to look at him. "Sometimes people get excited and forget.''

"I'll remind them again,'' he promised.

The divers sent up basketfuls of nails and ship fittings, table utensils, an inkwell and more china. Tilisi found a silver thimble, dented and dulled with verdigris, but after an electrochemical bath followed by thorough washing and a final polish with a baking soda paste it regained its sheen. Sienna began fitting together some of the broken china pieces, with help from Camille.

After two weeks they could see the outline of the ship, the bow smashed where she'd struck the reef, and other timbers stoved in or rotting away but many in quite good condition.

"She must have settled into the sand pretty quickly,'' Brodie said as he and Sienna watched Tilisi and Olin below clearing more sand away. "If she sank in a storm she could have been buried almost immediately.''

Sienna nodded. When they were both intent on the job they were doing, she could almost forget how his very presence disturbed her. She'd worked hard at ignoring the prickling awareness that she felt every time he came near, and Brodie seemed to be treating her with much the same casual friendliness he extended to the rest of the crew. She ought to be relieved. Instead she felt a kind of hollow chagrin.

On the seafloor, Tilisi stooped and poked at something, then quickly backed off. His voice came through the receiver at Brodie's ear. "Bones, boss. Human."

"Don't touch them unless they're in the way," Brodie ordered. "See if you can find a hatch."

"Sure thing." Relief in his voice, the diver waved an acknowledgment and moved along the hull.

Rogan came in and watched as the airlifts were shifted to where the divers might find a hatchway. Joe followed him, saying, "Can I come in?"

Rogan shrugged without taking his eyes from the screen. Sienna was conscious of a muted excitement mounting in the small space.

The sand churned as the airlifts sucked it away, and the screen became cloudy. Then dimly she saw a dark corner of a square and Brodie gave a grunt of satisfaction.

"It's open," Tilisi reported. "But there's a lot of sand."

Brodie said, "The poor bastards probably used the hatch cover for a raft when the ship was going down."

"Or," Rogan surmised, "the impact blew it off."

Sienna could imagine the panic when the sailors and passengers realized the ship was sinking. "It must have been terrifying," she murmured.

Brodie cast her a glance. "Pretty grim," he agreed.

Camille slipped into the cabin and Rogan hooked an arm about her waist.

The hole became larger, almost all of the hatchway now exposed, and Olin asked, "Can we go in?"

"No!" Brodie said sharply. "Your time's almost up."

"Aw, boss—"

"I want you on deck in fifteen minutes. We'll send some-one down on scuba to have a look."

When the divers had surfaced and entered the decompression chamber Brodie began suiting up.

Sienna said, "You're going down?"

"There could be all kinds of hazards in there. The umbilicals might get tangled or cut. I won't ask my divers to go in until I've checked it out for myself."

"You need a buddy diver. I want to go."

Bending to pull on his wet suit, Brodie looked up.

"I want to check it out before we start removing things, to get some idea of the layout."

"Too risky." He shook his head. "I'll take one of the guys."

Sienna raised her eyebrows. "It's my job. That's what I'm here for, remember? And you know I'm qualified for this."

Brodie, hauling the suit to his waist, paused. "Okay," he said grudgingly. "Get your wet suit—you'll need some protection from snags and hazards inside the ship. But stick by me and do as you're told. Remember who's dive master."

As if she could forget.

Brodie shone a beam of light into the darkness, then slipped through the hatchway, followed closely by Sienna.

He looked back to check on her, and she gave him the signal for okay. Dimly she made out jumbled shapes piled together: the rusted hoops of broken barrels, smashed boxes, and a litter of smaller objects that had spilled from them—bottles, tools, coins, even shoes and boots that were still recognizable.

This must be a cargo hold. Sienna snapped pictures and tried to memorize where everything was as they swam above the chaos, until stopped by a heap of shattered timbers where light filtered through from the hole blown in the side of the ship.

Brodie signaled they should return and she started to follow him back, then paused when a strange dizzy sensation passed over her. She felt lightheaded, lethargic. An orange-and-blue striped fish darted by and she half-turned to watch its progress, fascinated by its colors and wondering where it was going. Another fish followed, gleaming and jewel-like, so pretty she reached out to touch it, unable to resist. She felt as if she were dreaming. Maybe she was…

Her sluggish brain warned her, *This isn't right—wake up!* She must get herself to the surface but, disoriented, she was no longer sure which way to go.

Then a hand closed about her wrist and she was tugged around to face Brodie, scowling behind his mask and holding his dive computer in front of her.

Sienna slowly raised her hand in the okay signal. *Concentrate,* she told herself. Her mind felt foggy. *You have to get out of here.*

Brodie pulled her with him out of the hold and into clear water.

At the first decompression stop on the way to the surface, her head began to clear, the peculiar feelings completely gone by the time Brodie hauled her after him onto the deck of the barge.

As they removed their masks he turned to her, demanding, "What were you doing down there?"

"I got distracted," she said. "Sorry."

He looked at her closely. "Are you all right?"

"Yes, perfectly." She was now. Whatever happened had been temporary.

Joe asked, "Anything interesting down there?"

"There's a lot of stuff to sort through," Brodie said. "It's hard to tell yet."

Rogan looked from Brodie to Sienna. "What happened?"

"Nothing," Sienna told him.

"Dunno." Brodie was still watching her even as he stripped off his suit.

The others dispersed, but he and Sienna were both still in the brief swimsuits they'd worn underneath their wet suits when Brodie said, "I want to talk to you." He took her arm and walked her to her workroom, where he firmly closed the door.

"Now," he said, "what really went on down there? Nitrogen narcosis?"

"Rapture of the deep? We weren't down far enough for that, were we? Nowhere near a hundred and fifty feet. It can't have been—"

But it had been alarmingly like the symptoms of the dangerous drunken sensation caused by nitrogen bubbles in the blood at depth.

Brodie looked grim. "Then something *did* happen to you. It can hit at less than a hundred feet."

"I told you, I just got a bit distracted—there was a fish…"

"And you were going to follow it."

"I wouldn't have been that stupid." Reluctantly she admitted, "I had a touch of dizziness but it only lasted for a minute."

"Because I got you out of there and into shallow water. Guys with narcosis have swum off into the deep ocean following some illusion and are never seen again—or they've been known to offer their mouthpiece to a passing fish," Brodie said. Then abruptly, "I don't want you diving anymore."

"You can't stop me diving!" Her head came up and her eyes flashed.

Brodie didn't remind her again that he was the dive master. His implacable expression said it for him.

"PTS is paying me good money to be their archaeologist," Sienna said. "You surely don't want it wasted."

"Better than wasting lives. You can supervise on the screen. It's worked pretty well so far."

"It'll be much harder now we're inside the hull. You saw what it was like down there."

"Yeah, I did. Dangerous."

"I need to do my job!"

"You need to be kept safe. That's my job."

Sienna stiffened. "I was perfectly safe—"

"With me," Brodie argued flatly. "And I intend you to stay that way."

"If I go to Rogan—"

"He'll back me up."

Sienna had no doubt he would. The two of them had been friends forever. "This is because I'm a woman, isn't it?" she accused. "Can't you forget that for once?"

"Forget it?" Brodie's glance encompassed her thin one-piece swimsuit and went all the way to her toes and back. A slow grin curled his mouth. "Uh-uh."

Chapter 7

Suddenly conscious of her near nakedness—and Brodie's—Sienna felt her cheeks heat again. Despite herself, her body reacted to his lazy scrutiny, a melting sensation spiraling through her.

Brodie's gaze dropped to her breasts, the peaking centers clearly visible through the flimsy Lycra.

Her teeth closed on her lower lip, and he looked up again, paused at her mouth. "Don't do that," he said softly. "You'll hurt yourself."

Then he stared straight into her eyes, holding them with his, a lambent blue flame hypnotizing her. She released her abused lip and his hand came up, the thumb gently smoothing the aching flesh. He made a little sound, his mouth briefly pursing. He stepped close to her, his body heat warming her, and bent his head.

He took her lip between his with tender care, his hand cradling her head. She shivered, but not with cold, and his other arm came about her, bringing her close against him. He stroked his tongue across her throbbing lip, coaxed her mouth open and kissed her more deeply, surely—erotically.

Somewhere her mind was feebly trying to make a protest heard but her body wasn't listening. It was absorbed in the new exciting sensations Brodie aroused with his lips, his tongue, and the hand on her bare back that held her against him.

His other hand moved from her nape and pushed down the thin strap over her shoulder, baring the upper slope of her breast. But when he took his mouth at last from hers and dipped his head, finding the burgeoning flesh, she somehow mustered a shred of sanity and the strength to say, "No!"

Brodie's head came up, glittering blue eyes met hers and a crooked grin crossed his face. She shoved at him, her hands on his bare chest, resisting the urge to caress, instead putting some space between them as she panted, "Let me go!"

Reluctantly he did, letting her move away. He raked a hand through his hair and squeezed his eyes shut, then opened them again. "Okay." Something like curiosity mingled with triumph in his expression.

Sienna could still taste him on her lips—a seductive maleness that was all his own. She scrubbed at her mouth with the back of her hand, and saw his eyes narrow, brilliant with something other than the naked desire she'd seen when she freed herself from him. He was angry.

Dropping her hand, she said, "If you think you can persuade me to give in to your high-handed decrees by kissing me, you're way off beam!"

Brodie stepped back, leaned on the closed door and folded his arms. "I might accuse you of trying to change my mind in the same way. It takes two."

"I wouldn't do that!"

"Neither would I." His face was hard. "I want you," he said bluntly, almost arrogantly. "And judging by what happened just now—and back on Parakaeo—it's mutual. You have a problem with that?"

"Yes, I have a problem! I don't want to get involved. If I thought you did, I'd never have...it wouldn't have happened."

"We won't have much chance while we're working on the wreck," he reminded her. "There's not a lot of opportunity."

"Just as well," Sienna decided. Temptation was one thing, opportunity something else.

As if in confirmation, there was a rap on the door and, even as Brodie moved away from it, Rogan came in.

"Everything all right?" he inquired, glancing from Sienna's still heated cheeks to his friend.

"Yes," she said. "I have to get changed."

She brushed past them both and hurried across the deck to the *Sea-Rogue,* going down to her cabin and pulling on long cotton pants and a roomy T-shirt.

Rogan turned inquiringly to Brodie. "What gives?"

"Seems she had a touch of nitrogen narcosis."

"At that depth?" Rogan looked skeptical.

"Yeah, which means she might be extra-susceptible. I told her I don't want her diving again."

"Uh-huh." Rogan's eyes didn't waver. "How did she take it?"

"Reckoned she'd complain to you—I said you'd back me up."

Rogan nodded. "So, you had a fight?"

Brodie gave a faint grin. "You could call it that."

"Sure you're not being overprotective?" Rogan looked at his friend curiously.

"She had that illness before she came on board. Maybe she's not over it."

"The doc gave her a clean bill."

"Still, she's not putting on any weight. I don't want to take any chances."

Rogan shrugged. "It's up to you. But I don't suppose she'll like it."

"She doesn't." She'd made that clear, but moments afterward she'd been melting in his arms, letting him taste her soft, sexy mouth, even briefly allowing him to press his lips to her breast. His blood ran hot at the memory.

Rogan's eyes lowered. His mouth twitched into a grin, and he said mildly, "I wouldn't go on deck yet if I were you, not until you…er…settle down."

Brodie rubbed a hand over his forehead. "Yeah." He grinned back, trying not to look embarrassed. "I'll get me a cold shower."

The divers recovered cooking utensils from what must have been the galley of the wreck, and some table knives, spoons and dishes from the main cabin. An intact box was hoisted up by the crane and opened on deck while everyone gathered around expectantly. The box contained spoiled, disintegrating clothing and shoes, and a rusty pistol.

Sienna carefully removed everything and added them to her growing list.

She was conscious of Brodie watching her as she tapped in the information. He watched her a lot, a constant reminder of her own weakness.

Despising her reaction to that devastating kiss after he'd decreed she wasn't to dive again, she recalled that she hadn't even tried to resist despite her anger.

Because anger had fatally mixed with another much more complicated emotion, once she'd seen that he was worried for her. All her determination to stand on her own feet and never, ever lean on a man again almost crumbled under the onslaught of that single thought—that he cared about her safety, her well-being.

The moment he'd let her go she'd flown at him with an accusation, glad when she'd seen his passion replaced by anger, a much safer emotion to deal with.

She clung to her own anger, letting the unfairness of his ban on her diving simmer under the surface of her civilized but deliberately aloof manner. If he thought she was sulking, fine. Better than him thinking he could seduce her again with his sexy grin, his knowing eyes, his breathtaking, too-experienced kisses.

* * *

A complete skeleton was discovered in a broken doorway of the wreck, still wearing a leather belt. Two small bags lay under the belt, as if they had once been attached to it.

There was sand inside the ship, half burying the skeletal remains. One bony hand rested on a small heap.

As Sienna and Brodie watched, one of the divers lifted the fleshless fingers away, revealing a corner of dark wood, and excavated a small chest bound with discolored brass bands.

The bags were carefully eased into plastic jars and brought to the surface along with the chest. Sienna took them into the workroom, where Brodie and Rogan flanked her as she examined the chest, finding it firmly locked.

She studied the lock. "I don't want to break into it unless I have to. We should look for the key in the vicinity of the skeleton. He probably kept it on him."

Brodie said, "Poor sod took the time to save his precious fortune when the boat was going down, and got himself trapped."

Sienna couldn't help a slight shiver. "The gold would have weighed him down anyway if he'd jumped overboard with it."

She picked up the first jar, noting its weight, and gently tipped it, letting the bag slide into her hand before she laid it down on a sheet of plastic she'd spread on the table. Using tweezers, she tugged gingerly at a plaited leather thong that held the neck of the bag, working patiently until it parted. Dully gleaming yellow grains and tiny shining flakes spilled onto the plastic sheet.

Rogan let out a slow whistle, and Brodie slapped his friend's shoulder and breathed, "Yeah!"

It was unmistakably gold dust.

A wave of optimism swept the crew, and they worked with renewed vigor and cheerfulness. A metal detector uncovered a key within a few feet of the unlucky miner's bones, and after cleaning it and scraping sand and rust out of the lock Sienna was able to open the chest.

Camille, Brodie and Rogan watched.

The chest held gold nuggets—irregular, shining lumps, from thimble size to as big as hens' eggs.

For a moment no one moved, then Rogan put an arm about his wife and kissed her, and Brodie exclaimed, "Eureka!" His hands cupped Sienna's shoulders, and he turned her to him, dropping a kiss on her mouth. It was so quick she had no time to protest, but a bolt of lightning seemed to shoot through her. Then he raised his head, his eyes aglow with a strange blue light, and stepped back, lifting his hands away.

Next day the divers brought up a gold chain with a diamond pendant, a pair of earrings to match it, a diamond-and-ruby ring, a brooch set with several kinds of precious stones and one of ivory intricately carved with tiny figures, buildings and trees set in a gold frame.

Found in a small heap, they had probably been stored in a bag or box that had rotted away with time.

"Some wealthy female passenger?" Brodie speculated, watching with Rogan and Camille as Sienna spread out the items on her table.

"Or," Camille suggested, "gifts from a homecoming miner for his wife or sweetheart."

Rogan said, "Possibly a saloon girl returning home with her due rewards from a grateful clientele."

Camille gave him a reproving look. "I like my story much better."

Brodie asked, "What's your theory, Sienna?"

"Any of those." She picked up the brooch with the ruined painting. "Or the saloon girl married a miner who had made his fortune on the goldfields and decked her out in diamonds and rubies."

"Happy ever after," Brodie murmured.

"Not exactly," Sienna reminded him. "But maybe she died, before disillusion had a chance to set in."

Brodie gave her a long, thoughtful look.

"All this stuff," Rogan said, "looks like passengers' personal effects. We haven't got into the cargo yet."

Within a few days, more bags of gold dust turned up. In the week following, scattered gold and silver coins were gathered, and a number of fob watches, some with chains attached.

"My guess," Sienna ventured, "is that the ship sank during the night. The men would have removed their watches before going to bed." They must have woken to the grinding crash of the ship hitting the reef—perhaps the terrifying sound of water rushing into the gaping hole in the bow—and fumbled in the darkness to find their way up on deck, where the only alternative to going down with the ship was to jump into an inky black, probably storm-lashed sea.

"What's the matter?" Brodie asked.

"I was thinking about the shipwreck. All these things belonged to people who drowned that night. It does make me feel a bit ghoulish."

"Yeah," he said. "But they're no use to them now."

Later in the day Brodie, Tilisi and Joe went spearfishing near the reef, promising to bring something for dinner. Tilisi got a large, very ugly grouper that would make a good feed of fish steaks, Brodie speared a smaller fish and Joe grabbed a big lobster hiding in a rock cleft.

They were about to return to the barge with their haul when Brodie thought he recognized their location. Signaling that he wanted to explore farther, he began to look for the skeleton he'd found when diving with Rogan.

It was still there. He checked his computer, left Tilisi holding his catch and finned down, drawn by renewed curiosity. Joe followed him.

Nothing seemed changed. He looked about futilely for a sign of the bullet he'd dropped, but it had probably been taken by the current as it sank, and could by now be deep in the sand almost anywhere along the reef. A metal detector might find it if it was still near the surface, but that was a slim chance.

About to leave, he took one last look at the skeleton. The sand over the arms had thinned, revealing more of the whitened bones. He hovered over it, fanned some more sand aside, revealing the long, whitened bones of a hand—and a gleam caught his eye. Gold.

Joe touched his arm, pointing upward.

Brodie ignored him for seconds, staring down at the circlet of gold around the skeleton's middle finger.

Joe was tapping his dive computer, signaling they'd soon be out of air.

Brodie acknowledged that, agreed they should leave, but something compelled him to reach down and carefully draw the ring off.

He felt like a grave robber.

Back on the barge they handed over their fish and Rogan took the catch down to Camille in the galley.

Pulling off his gear, Joe said rather grumpily, "You cut that a bit fine, didn't you, Brodie? Something special about that ring?"

Brodie lowered his air tank to the deck. "Nah, it's gold, though. Must be worth something."

Tilisi shook his head. "Bad luck." Most Parakaeoans had an aversion to touching the dead, even those whose bones had been under the sea for centuries.

"Can I have a look?" Joe asked.

Brodie handed the ring over, and the other man held it between thumb and forefinger, turning to examine it in the fading light. Somehow it flipped from his fingers, bouncing and rolling toward the edge of the deck, and he and Brodie both air-dived to reach it before it could fall into the water.

Brodie's shoulder collided heavily with Joe's, and his fist closed over the ring.

Joe swore, and Brodie said, "Sorry, are you hurt?"

"I'm okay." Joe scrambled up. "Did you get it?"

"Yup. I'll take it to Sienna."

Followed by Joe, he sought out Sienna in her workroom and laid the ring down in front of her.

There were no precious stones, but it had a half-inch black-enameled square that featured an exquisitely detailed gold urn and was framed by a gold snake, each scale carefully delineated.

"Is this old?" Brodie asked as Sienna glanced at him and picked up the ring.

"It's a mourning ring—probably Victorian, maybe even Georgian. They usually have a date inscribed on the inside." She peered at the inner surface, tilting the ring to the light, then lowered it again, and with a fingernail levered at the front. "Ah—it's one that opens."

He leaned closer to look; his breath stirred a curling tendril at her temple, distracting him for a moment. He wanted to finger the little curl away and put his lips to the pulse he could see beating under her fine skin. He forced his eyes back to the ring.

The tiny cavity inside the minutely hinged case was empty, but Sienna said, "There might have been a lock of hair in it at one time. Here we are." She read aloud from the back of the lid. "'Thomas Goudge died 16 May 1831 aged 45.'"

"Eighteen thirty-one?" Brodie felt a surge of relief.

"It's beautifully preserved. Which part of the ship did this come from?"

"It's not from our ship. At least, not from the immediate area. I'll try to give you a fix on its position, but it could be from an earlier wreck." Still feeling unreasonably guilty about removing it from its owner, he didn't mention the skeleton.

Sienna ran a finger over the gold design. "I'll make a note of this and put it in the safe on board the *Sea-Rogue* with the other jewelry."

"Would it have been worn by old Tom's widow?" Brodie asked, straightening. Somehow he'd assumed the skeleton was male, but he was no expert. "In memory of her dead love?"

"Not necessarily. Mourning rings were often distributed around family and friends at the time of the funeral. It might have been worn by a man."

The divers began to haul boxes out of the hold that were hoisted to the surface. Many of them were damaged or rotting, their contents so badly decomposed it was impossible to tell what the boxes had originally held, but the rescued goods included copper and brass ware and some Chinese porcelain dishes.

Camille went down on scuba to help salvage items that had been exposed when their containers broke or rotted away, and Sienna stored some sodden diaries and journals in the freezer for expert attention back on shore. They would be priceless treasures to historians.

One box yielded dozens of exquisite jade ornaments packed among rotted silk. Sienna and Camille carefully unpacked them. "Someone must have picked them up in China," Camille said, "or bought them from one of the ships that had sailed that way."

"Someone who knew a good investment when he saw it," Sienna commented.

She almost forgot being angry with Brodie while they watched the salvage operations, swapping guesses about what might turn up next, sometimes almost reading each other's minds.

The stern section was finally broached and Rogan was down with Joe on the last dive of the day when he reported, his voice coming strongly through the phone, "Looks like we've found the safe."

Brodie's arm came around Sienna's shoulder and his hand squeezed her upper arm as Rogan gave a thumbs-up. Catching the men's excitement, she turned to smile at Brodie, finding him grinning triumphantly at her.

He pushed his mike aside and closed the small distance between him and Sienna, his mouth descending on her parted lips, a lingering, firm pressure that set her heart galloping and made her tingle all over.

Then Rogan's voice crackled in, saying something Sienna was too hot and bothered to catch, and Brodie drew away.

"Yeah," he said softly, his eyes capturing hers before he withdrew his arm and sat back in his seat, readjusting his headset. "Hey, Rogue!"

The safe was big, and though crusted and corroded, still solid enough to resist their efforts to move or open it. The two men cleared away debris and sand, then reluctantly left it and surfaced.

"It'll be a hell of a job to get it out from where it is," Rogan remarked as he stripped off his diving gear. "We'll have to remove some of the hull timbers first."

Next day the winch wouldn't work, and the engineer spent all day trying to fix it, without success, his hands and arms black with grease, the air around him blue with curses. The divers confined themselves to retrieving small articles and shifting easily moved sand and debris.

Frustration was rife. Finally the engineer gloomily reported a cracked part.

"We could radio Tu," Brodie suggested, "and get him to send the tug out to us with a replacement part."

"Supposing he can find one on the island," Rogan said.

Brodie grinned. "If there's one within a hundred miles he'll find it and get it to us."

After midnight, hot and restless and unable to sleep in the stuffy little cabin below, Brodie sat in the bow of the *Sea-Rogue,* contemplating the stars and thinking about Sienna.

For weeks he'd tried like hell to maintain a neutral manner, to allow her some slack and not act on his frequent wild impulse to grab her and hold her, kiss her until she admitted that the growing need gnawing inside him wasn't all one-sided.

Sometimes he was sure he was right about that, when she snatched her hand away at an accidental touch, a faint flush staining her cheeks, her eyelashes fluttering down as she ducked her head to hide her expression. Or at the rare unguarded moments when her eyes met his and he saw them darken and go wider, her lips parting slightly, the fine skin at her throat subtly moving as she swallowed before she dragged her gaze from his and turned away.

But those glimpses of susceptibility were so brief and so quickly replaced by her usual cool containment, he wondered if he was fooling himself.

Sorely tempted to take advantage of the slightest chink in her formidable armor, he knew if he forced the issue she'd retreat into herself completely, like a sea creature hiding in its shell.

But yesterday he'd instinctively wanted to share the moment of elation when Rogan found the safe.

At the first taste of her lips he'd almost forgotten what was happening at the bottom of the sea, totally absorbed in the feel of her mouth under his, the intoxicating scent of her skin, the overwhelming desire to haul her into his arms and kiss her properly, drown in the depths of her.

Short-lived though it had been, the kiss simply confirmed what his body knew perfectly well. Something about Sienna made his blood roar, his heart pound, scorched his senses with an overwhelming need to penetrate the shell that hid her innermost self, to know her in every sense of the word, and certainly in the most intimate way of all. Once wasn't enough. And sex wasn't enough…

A cloud spread from the horizon, hid the lemon-slice of moon and covered half the stars. A cool breeze made Brodie pull his windcheater closer about his body as he wedged himself farther into the corner.

A dull *thwump* from below startled him, and a shudder seemed to pass over the *Sea-Rogue,* waves slapping at her sides, setting her rocking, the buffers protecting her hull bumping against the barge to which she was tethered.

Brodie's senses went on high alert, and he stood up, steadying himself against the movement of the boat, looking out at the blackness where the only sign of the ocean was an occasional tiny gleam.

Rogan, dressed only in shorts, appeared on deck, a flashlight in his hand. "What the hell was that?"

The shock would have been more obvious down below.

"Dunno," Brodie replied. "A whale?" A marine giant scratching the barnacles from its back on a handy keel, perhaps. Or maybe somewhere way under the ocean a small earthquake had occurred, a shifting of the seabed sending ripples of disturbance for miles.

Rogan shone the flashlight on the water that still heaved about the boat. He swore graphically and Brodie looked down into the light dancing on the bubbling swells.

As they watched, a dozen or so pale, dead fish rose like small ghosts from the depths, and floated, still and bleeding, on top of the water.

"They wouldn't!" Brodie said. "Right under our noses?"

"They have," Rogan answered grimly. "No whale. And nothing that was in the wreck would cause this. What's the betting someone's tried to blow the safe?"

Chapter 8

"What sort of idiot...?" Brodie burst out.

"A greedy one," Rogan said. "I'd say the explosion was a bit bigger than he expected. He might have killed himself if he didn't have the sense to get out of the water before the charge went off."

He moved the light over the water nearby, but they could see nothing but waves and blackness and the silver gleam of more fish floating belly-up.

"Could have damaged the *Sea-Rogue* too."

Camille emerged from the companionway, pulling on a jersey over slacks, and asking, "What happened?"

Rogan said, "We're going to find out."

No one on the barge seemed to have noticed the explosion. Its sturdy build and its size would have cushioned the effect, and after their underwater exertions the divers probably slept like the dead.

Sienna appeared looking tousled and apprehensive. They hauled on their gear. Brodie grabbed a second flashlight and the two men went overboard, scanning the *Sea-Rogue's* hull.

There didn't seem to be any damage, and they surfaced to reassure the women before finning down to the wreck, among dead fish and floating sand and debris that darkened the water still further. Visibility was almost nil.

They reached the wreck and made for the stern where the safe was, looking about them for signs of life—or no life.

Penetrating the swirling dimness as they approached their target, Rogan's light picked up a fresh, gaping hole.

The light hit the gashed timbers, and a second later a long, bulky black shape shot out of the middle of them—a diver illuminated in the beam.

Brodie kicked forward, with Rogan right at his heels.

The other diver swam rapidly away from them but Brodie surged after him, catching at the intruder's fin.

The man was quick and strong. He kicked out and the flashlight was knocked from Brodie's hand, still looped to his wrist but dangling, the light swinging crazily through the murky water as Rogan too made a grab for the poacher.

Like an eel, the man eluded their hands, then twisted round. Brodie saw a flash of steel and realized the guy had drawn his diving knife, the curved, serrated blade in his fist arcing through the water, slashing wildly at his would-be captors.

Raising an arm instinctively to ward off the attack, Brodie felt nothing, but saw a thin trail of red curling in the madly bobbing light, then Rogan was hauling him backward and the other man arrowed away into darkness.

Seconds later a glimmer of light briefly flickered some distance off and Brodie made to go after it, but Rogan's strong grip on his wrist stopped him, and only when he felt the throb of pain Brodie discovered he was bleeding, his wet suit slashed to halfway up his forearm and a long cut welling red into the water.

A huge pale shape glided past among the dozens of fish still floating about them, and then another followed the first, making Brodie sweat inside his suit.

Sharks attracted by the dead fish. With luck they'd be too busy feeding on them to bother the divers.

Rogan signaled in pantomime a fast ascent. He clamped a hand about Brodie's wound and started upward.

Very aware that he was bleeding, Brodie concentrated on letting air out of his buoyancy compensator and breathing steadily and slowly outward to avoid bursting his lungs on a nonstop ascent.

When an undulating gray body curved itself about and began circling, he closed his eyes and prayed as he never had in his life.

The two men burst through the surface and headed straight up the ladder to the boat.

On the *Sea-Rogue's* deck the lights were on, and Camille and Sienna leaned over the rail. Rogan pushed Brodie ahead of him and then hauled himself on board.

Brodie spat out his mouthpiece and burst into a furious stream of words, most of them unsuited to polite company, at the same time trying to stem the blood flowing down his arm and over his hand and dripping onto the deck. He heard Sienna's sharp intake of breath as Rogan urged him across the deck to the barge, saying, "We've got about two minutes to get ourselves into the decompression chamber. Camille—rouse out Hunk and get him in there with his medical kit while I help Brodie inside."

"I don't need help," Brodie growled. As if to contradict that, his brain seemed to begin a slow revolution inside his head and he swayed against Rogan.

Sienna was suddenly at Brodie's side, pulling off the T-shirt she wore, revealing scanty bikini panties and no other covering as she stuffed the T-shirt into a wad and slapped it over the long cut on his arm. "I'll hold it," she told Rogan, "while we get him onto the barge."

"It's nothing," Brodie said.

They both ignored him, and he stumbled between them over the rail onto the barge.

He should be reacting to the sight of Sienna's pretty, bare breasts. Unfortunately when she pressed against him as they steadied themselves on the deck of the barge, his wet suit prevented him from feeling anything.

The cut was stinging now, and throbbing. No wonder, he thought, with Sienna's surprisingly strong grip still pressing the makeshift pad onto it.

Things got a bit hazy then because he was concentrating on not throwing up. The consequence of a fast ascent, he supposed, although Rogue didn't seem to be feeling any ill effect. Thank heaven they had recompression facilities. Otherwise it would have been a choice between the sharks or the bends—and either could kill just as surely and nastily as the other.

At some stage Rogan took over from Sienna and she whisked back to the boat, presumably to get some clothes on.

Camille must have roused the medic in double-quick time—he entered the chamber with his hair standing on end and wearing a startling pair of black satin boxers patterned with red devils wielding pitchforks. The metal door clanged shut behind him and Brodie closed his eyes. "Hell," he muttered.

Four hours later Camille and Sienna were having coffee on board the *Sea-Rogue* when the men returned and changed into jeans. Brodie's arm was bandaged where Hunk had stitched him up. He felt much better, but thought Sienna was paler than usual. Had she sat up waiting for them?

She was wearing a pareu about her waist, with a fresh T-shirt, and he wondered if she had put on a bra, suddenly remembering her virtually naked body as she tried to staunch the blood from his arm. At the time it had all been something of a blur, but now he recalled the deck light falling on the pert tilt of her breasts, the inward curve of her waist, the cute little unadorned belly button that he had once explored with his tongue, the exact curve of her hips that, unforgettably, he'd been allowed to follow with his hands.

The picture was so clear he could almost feel what he

hadn't been able to through his wet suit, her arms wound about him, the softness of her breast pressing against his body.

Which reacted predictably. Hastily he sat down at the table, sliding along the banquette Camille had just vacated to go to the galley and lift the kettle.

"How did you do that?" she asked, handing him a cup of coffee and looking with concern at his arm.

Rogan said, helping himself to a cup, "He was knifed."

Sienna exclaimed, *"Knifed?"* Her cup clattered down.

Rogan briefly explained, and Sienna was definitely unnaturally pale now. But then, Camille looked sick too. "We have to report it," she told Rogan. "This is serious."

"By the time anyone gets to us," Brodie said, "the guy could be long gone. We've got no idea who it was."

Camille said, "Did you see a boat?"

"No," Brodie admitted. "It's pretty dark out there."

"Would you know him again?" Sienna asked.

Brodie grunted. "With a mask and snorkel and hood? Anyway I didn't get a good look at his face—I was watching the damn knife."

"How much did he get away with?" Camille asked.

Rogan answered, "Not much, if anything. He wasn't carrying any large amount of loot. Maybe he was just opening the safe so his pals could move in and grab everything."

"Doesn't make sense," Brodie objected. "They'd have to bring in machinery and there's no way they could keep that secret. I reckon he was working on his own."

"Yeah," Rogan said heavily. Turning to Camille, he asked, "Did you see anyone up and around when you went to fetch Hunk?"

"There were heads poking out everywhere when I went in screaming for him."

"You don't remember who was there—or not?"

Camille frowned. "It was dark—all I was thinking about was getting the medic on deck. Surely you don't think…?"

Rogan said, "If the guy down there was working alone and didn't have a boat he'd have to be one of our divers."

There was a silence around the table until Brodie said, "The team was handpicked. We know all of them."

Rogan nodded. "Well, they say every man has his price."

"We're paying them top wages," Brodie complained mildly. "Plus bonuses and a souvenir coin."

"Against a few gold bars, maybe it doesn't add up to so much."

Brodie looked down at his coffee. "Tilisi earns more in a week diving than his old man does in a year on the island...but maybe he could be tempted for the sake of his family." Tilisi was probably related to half the population of Parakaeo, and all of them had a claim on him. According to custom, the islander was expected to share everything he got with numerous uncles and cousins as well as his parents and sisters. Which left not so much for him.

Sienna sat up abruptly. "You think it's Tilisi?"

"No!" Brodie hunched over his cup. "If Rogue's right— and I hope to God he's not—it could be anyone."

Olin had complained the other day that what he got for his pictures hardly paid for his camera and equipment. Hunk wanted to make enough money to marry his girlfriend, buy a hotel in the islands and spend his life fishing and diving. Joe had dived on a dozen treasure wrecks for wages and seen investors who never got a foot wet walk away with millions. Maybe he'd got sick of it and thought he deserved more.

"The engineer?" he said aloud. "D'you think there really is something wrong with the winch, or..." Maybe the guy had been playing for time.

In the morning the trawler was back.

Rogan stared across the water at it sailing near the horizon, never out of sight.

"So maybe that's where our safecracker came from," Brodie said.

"It would take a damn good diver to find his way in the dark from the trawler to the wreck and back again without giving himself away."

"She could have come in much closer during the night. Without lights." They hadn't seen any, and in itself that was suspicious, surely. "Our lights were on. All he needed to do was head for them on the surface, then dive to the wreck and use a pocket light to find his way to the safe." Brodie remembered that brief glimmer as the poacher swam away. Shining his flashlight long enough to consult a compass perhaps, and make sure he was headed to the unlit trawler. But using a light too small to have attracted attention if anyone had happened to look over the side of the ketch or the barge while he was planting his explosive. An experienced man could have done it.

"He can't have gone back to the trawler while he waited for the explosion," Rogan argued.

"So he had a boat. Or if he surfaced at the other side of the barge and boarded it for a few minutes until it was safe to go back in the water, no one would have seen him."

"Yeah," Rogan conceded. He thumbed his bottom lip. "But if our diver came from the trawler, how did he know about the safe?"

Rogan was silent for seconds. "How do you think?"

Brodie's nape prickled, his stomach going hollow. His neck felt stiff as he turned to stare at his friend.

Keeping his voice low and hardly moving his lips he said, "You mean even if the diver wasn't one of ours, we've got a spy on board."

"I don't somehow think it's coincidence, the trawler turning up again now."

"Trust no one?" An acrid taste invaded Brodie's mouth.

"That's about it. And keep our eyes and ears open. And the control room locked. I don't want any radio messages going out that we don't know about."

"He could be using a satellite phone."

Rogan frowned. "Damn modern technology."

"I suppose," Brodie said after several seconds, "we could search the guys' bags."

"And start a mutiny? It's too late anyway. If our looter has pals on the trawler he's already contacted them. We'll keep watch tonight. Maybe bring out the guns.''

They were securely locked away, but it paid to keep a couple and know how to use them when at sea in some parts of the world. "You could be right," Brodie said. "We're a hell of a long way from the nearest police station.''

There was no concealing the fact that the safe had been blown, so no point in pretending that Brodie's wound had been some kind of accident. A rumble of anger and a nervous sense of urgency possessed the team. And frustration at the delay caused by the breakdown of the winch.

Tu radioed that he'd located a new part and the tug was on its way.

"With a cop on board," Rogan relayed to Brodie, Camille and Sienna. Camille had insisted he report the attempted theft and the attack on Brodie. The two-officer police station on the island had marshaled its forces to investigate.

"Meantime," Rogan told Brodie, "we bring up as much as we can by hand.''

To get at the safe the divers first had to clear debris left by the explosion—which explained, Brodie supposed, why the thief had been empty-handed when they discovered him. He hadn't had time to get to the safe itself.

Rogan and another diver were down when the safe was cleared. It was filled with wooden boxes in surprisingly good condition, most of them quite small but heavy. As the men on board hauled the first one up to the barge the divers accompanied it. Everyone crowded around to watch it being opened.

There was a stunned silence when the sun glinted on the box's contents. Then a concerted mixture of cheers, whistles and earthy exclamations erupted from the men.

The gold was in ingots. "Beautiful, beautiful ingots!" Hunk crooned as Brodie lifted one and passed it around for everyone to handle. Even Sienna experienced a moment of awe when she held the gold bar in her palm and turned it over to see the manufacturing marks on it. She handed it back to Brodie and he kissed it before replacing it in the box.

Since time immemorial gold had been admired and coveted for its undying beauty, becoming the universal symbol of wealth, never losing its seductive luster or its value. It had drawn men in every age to leave home, friends and family and cross the stormy oceans of the world aboard crowded, often unseaworthy ships in search of it, to work themselves to exhaustion in heat and cold, dust and mud, living in the most primitive of conditions while they wrested it from the ground, to risk danger and death for the sake of it—and sometimes to kill for it.

The underwater safe was crammed with gold—ingots molded in Adelaide from Australian gold, raw nuggets, more bags of gold dust, even sovereigns and a few American eagles. The barge hummed with excitement. The engineer went back to trying to repair the winch with a new determination, and soon announced he'd got it working again.

"Gold fever," Brodie said later as he and Sienna watched the divers below heaving more boxes into the basket for lifting to the surface. "The guys have got it bad."

"You're not immune."

"Didn't you get a thrill when we opened that box?"

"Yes, though I can't help thinking about what happened to the owners. So much blood, sweat and tears, and they never got home again to enjoy it."

"Yeah," Brodie said. "I hope they had a rip-roaring time of it while they could."

"They probably did. The goldfields offered plenty of entertainment, according to contemporary accounts. In fact the shopkeepers and entrepreneurs probably went home with more money than a lot of the miners."

"So maybe some of the passengers were sharks rather than honest, hardworking gold diggers grubbing the stuff out of the soil?"

"Shopkeepers aren't necessarily dishonest or lazy. You're one yourself."

"You got me there," Brodie acknowledged. "A low blow."

Sienna had to laugh, and he smiled at her, his eyes lit with humor and a disconcerting male gleam that despite her best intentions evoked an involuntary response, tightening her skin and warming her body.

"How's your arm?" she asked him, to distract herself from the way he made her feel and him from studying her with his too-penetrating blue eyes.

"Fine." He flexed it, and asked with a wicked slant to his grin, "Want a demonstration?"

"No." Hastily she shook her head and sat farther back in her chair. "I'll take your word for it."

Brodie laughed and returned his attention to the screen in front of him.

Late in the afternoon Rogan entered the control room. "The last of what's in the safe is coming up now. We'll transfer the gold on board the *Sea-Rogue,* lock it up, and as soon as the tug arrives we'll be out of here."

Sienna's head jerked up. "We can't leave yet! The archaeological survey isn't complete!"

"Sorry," Rogan said. "We've got millions of dollars' worth of salvaged cargo and we need to get it to a safe place as fast as possible."

"Money!" Sienna exclaimed in disgust. "Is that all you two care about?"

Brodie said, "Hey! That's not fair."

Rogan glanced at him. A thud on deck announced the arrival of the last box. "Explain to her, Brodie," he said, and left them.

"Explain what?" Sienna turned on Brodie. "That your precious profit is worth more than my research? That the only reason I'm here is to lend a false respectability to your treasure hunt? I should have known—Aidan was right."

"Who the hell's Aidan?"

"My department head at Rusden," she said. "He warned me not to trust treasure hunters. Thugs and thieves—"

"I object to that!" His chin was thrust out.

Sienna stood up. "And I object to being used."

"You weren't used!" As she made to leave he stood too and grabbed her wrist with his good hand, swinging her to face him.

She thumped a fist against his chest. "What would you call it then? Granger promised me Rogan would let me do the job properly! And now the minute he finds gold—suddenly, *poof!* That's it, we're done, let's go home and see how much we can get for our loot!"

"Listen—"

"I did listen, that was my mistake!" She tugged at his hold, trying to free herself.

"Whoa, there!" He clipped her arm behind her and brought her close, body to body, and before she could stop him his mouth came down on hers, hard and fierce.

It only lasted a moment, then he lifted his head, having effectively silenced her, and abruptly released her wrist, letting her step away from him. "*Now,* listen. You're way off beam. Rogue's worried. Have you forgotten how I got this?" He indicated his wounded arm.

Sienna looked at it, then up at him, resentful that even with one arm he could use his masculine strength against her, and obscurely angry too that he'd charged after the would-be thief and been hurt. When he'd arrived on deck bleeding she'd felt sick and had to steel herself to act sensibly and not scream or faint. "If you hadn't gone after him like some macho film hero," she raged, "he wouldn't have had the chance."

"So it was okay for him to pull a knife?" Brodie demanded.

"*No!* Of course it wasn't!" Remembering how much blood there had been and the sharks circling in the water, she inwardly shuddered. "But when you and Rogan disturbed him he ran—*swam*—away, didn't he? You chased him and he panicked. He probably didn't have any intention of killing you."

"He might be capable of it. We can't guess at what he might do next. I don't know how many guys are aboard that trawler, but they probably outnumber us. And as long as we stay here we're sitting ducks."

"The *trawler?* They're probably just waiting for us to vacate their fishing ground so they can go on with their business in peace."

"Or for us to lift the treasure so they can grab it for themselves."

"Aren't you being a bit melodramatic? You think *everyone's* out to steal the treasure!"

"Someone on board here could be in cahoots with the guys on the trawler. And we don't know who. Remember, James Drummond's a known killer. That trawler's been around too much, and behaving mighty strangely for a fishing boat. Rogue doesn't want anything like this—" he lifted his bandaged arm "—and maybe worse happening to Camille. Or you."

Sienna blinked at him. He sounded deadly serious and grimly determined. "Camille and I are grown women," she said, "and not wilting violets, in case you hadn't noticed."

He gave a faint grin. "I've noticed a lot about you." His gaze dropped momentarily, then he raised it to her face. Her breath stopped and her heart seemed to flip over.

The glint in his eyes had turned to a blinding glitter, like sunlight on the sea. Briefly he closed them, before focusing on her again.

Then he said, "For everyone's protection we ought to get out of here fast. We can't just abandon the guys on the barge—though if there is a spy he'll know the gold is aboard the *Sea-Rogue*. But once the tug gets here…"

"With the police," Sienna remembered.

"One cop isn't much of a deterrent. Still, safety in numbers and all that. If we stick together for the trip back to Parakaeo we're less likely to be attacked on the way."

"Attacked? Piracy?" It seemed fantastic, but then Rogan

and Camille had already been subjected to one such episode. If Rogan was paranoid she couldn't blame him.

"It's not as uncommon these days as people think," Brodie said seriously. "Word of a treasure hunt brings out the hyenas of the sea."

"All right," Sienna conceded. "Maybe Rogan does have good reasons." With Brodie's bandaged arm as a reminder of the lengths some people would go to, she reluctantly had to agree it might not be safe to linger at the wreck site. "But I want to make a last survey of anything that's left, and bring up what I can in the time we have."

"I don't think so, not after what happened last night."

"It's broad daylight now."

"No."

"Brodie!" She put her hands on her hips, eyes flashing.

"No. It's too risky."

Sienna stormed out and went on deck to find Rogan.

To her surprise, after listening to her arguments and giving her a long, brooding look, he said, "If you can persuade Brodie it's okay by me."

Camille insisted on a last dive too, and Brodie, following a low-voiced conversation with Rogan, reluctantly allowed it. Rogan went down with them, since Brodie wasn't supposed to get his stitched arm wet, and Sienna studied and photographed as much as she could in the limited time, sending up a last basket of fragments and unidentifiable coral-covered objects to the barge.

"The tug should be here by morning," Rogan told Brodie when the women had taken their haul to Sienna's workroom. "Tonight we show no lights and you and I keep watch."

"Okay." They were well out of shipping lanes and the reef was clearly marked on modern charts. It was unlikely that another craft would accidentally hit them in the dark.

Rogan repealed the strict no-alcohol regime he'd imposed on the team while they were diving, and at dinner he opened several bottles of champagne he'd kept aboard the *Sea-Rogue* for just this occasion.

Sienna was aware of undercurrents at the table. The gold was the main topic of conversation, and as for the blown safe, the consensus was that the trawler crew had guessed what the salvors were doing out in the middle of nowhere and had tried to muscle in on the treasure hunters' patch.

Brodie and Rogan didn't contradict the theory, both seemingly relaxed, leaning back with champagne flutes in their hands. But beneath apparently sleepy lids, Brodie's vivid blue eyes were watching the other team members intently, and a creak of the deck boards brought him instantly to his feet and out there to see what had caused it, with Rogan on his heels.

When they came back into the cabin all eyes turned to them, and Brodie shrugged. The atmosphere was thick with unvoiced questions and the party atmosphere dissipated. Joe put down his empty glass and stood up. "Think I'll turn in," he said.

There were murmurs and shuffles round the table, and the other men finished their drinks and went off to their bunks.

It was two o'clock in the morning. Brodie sat on the bow of the *Sea-Rogue,* his back against a bulkhead, peering through the darkness to where he'd last seen the trawler. A loaded rifle lay across his knees. Overhead, an awning cast a deep shadow.

A faint sound came to his ears, something that wasn't the shushing of the waves or the creak of boards contracting. Maybe a soft footfall.

He turned his head and saw a ripple against the blackness, a mere hint of movement on the barge.

Someone was moving over there, stealthily.

He lost sight of the darker shadow and wondered if he'd imagined it, then a light flashed for an instant. A second's wait, then another flash. Another second, another flash.

Very quietly Brodie got to his bare feet, stepping lightly and surely to the side of the boat and leaping to the deck of the barge, the gun held across his body while he switched on the flashlight in his other hand.

The man sprang to face him, blinking, and Brodie said, "You're up late, Joe."

Chapter 9

"Couldn't sleep," Joe said. "What the hell do you think you're doing with that gun? You scared me half to death."

"What the hell were you doing with that light?" Brodie retorted. "Talking to your friends?"

It was a moment before Joe spoke again. "Dunno what you're on about," he said. "Thing's not working properly. Keeps going out."

"Every second or so, huh? Shove it over here. Maybe I can fix it."

"Brodie…"

Brodie shifted his grip on the gun, pointing it straight at Joe. "Put the torch down on the deck and push it over here."

"Aw, hell, Brodie." Joe stooped and obeyed, and Brodie caught the flashlight with his foot.

Rogan was there now beside Brodie, also holding a rifle. "What's up?"

"Why don't you tell us, Joe?" Brodie invited him. He stooped, not taking his eyes from the other man, and put down his own light to pick up Joe's, flicking the switch. The light burned steady and bright. "Well, look at that, it works perfectly. What were you saying to your mates over there on the trawler, huh?"

"Nothing!"

"He was signaling?" Rogan queried.

"Loud and clear," Brodie answered. "Telling them to come and get it, were you, Joe?"

"You've got it all wrong," Joe protested. "Rogue—you know me."

"I thought I did. I know you've sailed pretty close to the edge of the law a couple of times, but I didn't think you'd cheat on us."

"You don't understand—"

"Damn right I don't," Rogan answered.

Brodie said, indicating his injured arm, which was throbbing anew, "Reckon I owe you for this, *mate*. Rogue, do we shoot him now and push him overboard, or wait for the tug and take him in to be charged with attempted murder?"

"You wouldn't..." Joe looked sick. "I'm not a murderer!"

"Be a lot simpler to just shove him overboard," Rogan said casually.

Brodie put down the light in his hand, straightened and moved the gun he held to his shoulder, steadying it with his bandaged arm.

Joe flung his hands up in a gesture of panicked surrender. "Bloody hell, Brodie!"

Behind him Brodie heard a tiny sound, between a gasp and a cry, the first indication that Sienna, and he supposed Camille, were watching the ugly scene.

Tilisi and the engineer now appeared on the deck of the barge, demanding to know what was happening.

Brodie lowered the rifle but kept it aimed at Joe. "Well, maybe not yet," he said. "Keep back," he warned the newcomers. And to Joe, "When are you expecting your friends, and how many of them are there?"

Joe licked his lips. "I don't know what you're talking about. Are you crazy?"

"Nope," Brodie answered. "But you are if you think you can get away with this."

Rogan said, "We're not going to get anywhere. Let the cop deal with it when he gets here."

"What cop?" Joe asked, looking apprehensive.

"The one who should be here in—" Rogan glanced at his watch "—a couple of hours. Meantime you can be our guest on board the *Sea-Rogue*."

They gave the other men a brief explanation of their suspicions, tied Joe's hands and locked him in the securest place they had—the cargo hold of the *Sea-Rogue* where they'd stowed the gold and other treasures.

"Ironic," Brodie said as he and Rogan scanned the sea with flashlights while Sienna and Camille watched.

Rogan switched off his light. "No sign of anyone. If Joe was guiding them to us they'd probably have realized something had gone wrong with the plan when they saw your light. They could even have watched the whole thing."

Brodie switched off his own flashlight. "I guess we don't want to give them any help if they try again."

"If they do, we're ready for them." The other team members had been roused, and several of them were armed with spearguns. Hunk had even produced a pistol. Everyone was awake and alert.

"Are you sure you're right?" Camille asked. "About Joe?"

"If we're not," Brodie said, "he can sue us for wrongful imprisonment. But he was definitely signaling."

"Why don't you girls go back to bed?" Rogan suggested.

Camille gave a little snort, and Sienna said, "You expect us to sleep while you men guard the ramparts?"

Brodie turned a grin to her. "I don't mind if you want to stay and keep me warm."

"We're in the tropics," she retorted. "You don't need... anyone to keep you warm."

Brodie sighed loudly and Rogan gave a quiet chuckle.

Camille said, "Can you use a speargun, Sienna?"

"No." She'd never been interested in killing the beautiful creatures she saw underwater, even suffered a pang of regret at eating those that others caught. "Maybe the men could show us."

"No," Rogan said.

Brodie added, "A couple of women who've never used them, loose with spearguns on a rocking boat? We'd be safer jumping overboard."

Camille said darkly, "I'll get you for that. Remember, I'm the cook."

Rogan laughed. Camille moved closer to her husband and he put an arm about her. They sat side by side, perched on the afterdeck above the cockpit. Brodie clambered onto the cabin roof and sat there cross-legged, the rifle resting on his thighs.

Sienna, feeling helpless and irritable, wedged herself into a corner of the cockpit. She had no intention of being sent off to bed. Dawn was still some way off.

She was almost dozing when Brodie said quietly, "Something's out there."

Her head jerked up, a shiver spiraling down her spine. Brodie and Rogan, crouching shadows against the faintly lightening sky, moved noiselessly forward to the bow.

Sienna heard a splash, somehow stealthy, then another. Too rhythmic to be fish, different from the wavelets hitting the hull of the boat.

Carefully she stood up, looking over the cabin roof.

Camille came to stand beside her. Rogan said, his voice barely audible, "Camille—you and Sienna go below."

Neither of them moved.

The splashing came closer. A gray shape appeared, and dimly Sienna made out the fat outline of a rubber dinghy, with several black-clad figures sitting in it.

Rogan called, "Stop right there!"

The splashing abruptly ceased. Then a motor roared, the dinghy leaped forward, and Brodie yelled, *"Down!"*

He and Rogan flung themselves prone, and Sienna and Camille, grabbing at each other, ducked to the floor of the cockpit. A loud, rapid chatter of gunfire—a sound she recognized with disbelief from myriad TV programs but discovered was much more terrifying in reality—sent Sienna's heart into overdrive, and she winced at the shattering of wood and glass, the motor coming closer, roaring past them.

Brodie, she thought in panic. And Rogan. Had they been hit?

Camille's hand dug into her arm. She hardly felt it.

Then Brodie was there, leaping into the cockpit almost on top of the two women, snarling, "You were told to go below! Get the hell down that companionway!"

Rogan followed him as the runabout turned back toward them.

This time Camille and Sienna obeyed, leaving the men room to maneuver the rifles from where they crouched in the cockpit.

"They mean business," Rogan muttered.

"Damn right." A submachine gun was far too businesslike for Brodie's liking. His mouth was dry, and if he hadn't been so fired-up mad at whoever these murderous thugs were he'd have been scared out of his mind.

"Try to get the rear pontoon," Rogan said, leveling his rifle and firing off a shot, but the dinghy was already turning.

Brodie nodded. The motor would be almost unusable if the rear chamber of the inflatable was punctured.

Tilisi, holding a speargun, leaped over the side rail from the barge and joined them, hunkering down just before another round of bullets tore at the top of the cabin, sending splinters of wood flying.

Brodie waited for the boat to pass before he steadied his rifle on the coaming and fired. A sputter of white foam briefly rose off the dark water. "Missed, dammit."

The attackers were concentrating on the *Sea-Rogue,* and

there was precious little cover. The men on the barge were blocked by the ketch, while the inflatable again roared by with a fresh burst of gunfire. Two more of the dive crew leaped to the *Sea-Rogue's* side deck, sheltered by the cabin structure. Hunk let off a couple of pistol shots as the dinghy came round again in a spray of white water. A quick chatter of fire answered and everyone flattened themselves to the deck.

"The hell with the air chambers," Brodie muttered. "Get the guy with the gun." He dared to poke his rifle over the coaming and loose off a shot, aiming at the man with the fire-spitting gun, not sure if he'd found his mark, not even sure he wanted to know. It was the first time he'd ever shot at a human being.

He thought about Sienna down below, and the lurid stories he'd heard about what pirates sometimes did to women. All of them sickeningly true. Setting his jaw, he raised himself to the deck, lying prone and steadying the rifle as the dinghy turned again, sending up a shower of foam. Deliberately he sighted on the figure he could dimly see near the bow, holding a long-snouted weapon, and pulled the trigger.

The man jerked and slid down in the boat; his gun fired again, this time into the air.

Tilisi whooped and leaped up onto the deck despite Rogan's sharp warning. He aimed his speargun at the boat as it roared by, and the silver point headed straight and true, the line snaking after it until the spear embedded itself in the ballooning pontoon side of the dinghy.

Tilisi jumped back into the cockpit, all grinning, cocky triumph, and began reeling in his spear. Brodie swore at him for a bloody stupid bastard and fired off another shot at the boat where there seemed now to be some confusion, someone yelling in what sounded like a foreign language. The inflatable was slowly collapsing, at the back and side.

This time it didn't return the attack, but roared off erratically into the night. With at least two holes in it, it would be almost unmanageable and half full of water, and although the occupants probably wouldn't drown before they got back to base, they and their guns would be wet.

Light was beginning to break over the horizon. The sound of the dinghy's motor faded in the distance. Hunk called, "Hey, are you guys okay?"

Rogan dared to lift his head, and then stood up. Brodie followed, and found his legs were unsteady. His injured arm was on fire with pain, and when he looked down he saw the bandage was soaked in blood.

Tilisi jumped onto the deck, waving. "All okay," he crowed. "We got them!"

"Sienna…" Brodie said, turning to the companionway, even as Rogan plunged toward it, saying hoarsely, "Camille!"

And there they were, white-faced and looking shocked but unharmed.

Rogan pulled Camille into his arms, and fear left Sienna's eyes as she saw Brodie. He wanted to follow Rogan's example and haul her close, but he had no right, and she probably wouldn't appreciate being smeared with his blood.

She saw it and her eyes widened. "You opened the wound again!" And, looking over at the barge, "Where's Hunk?"

Her anxiety gave Brodie a buzz that eclipsed the renewed pain in his arm. He grinned at her. "It's okay. No one got hurt." No one who mattered, anyway. Fleetingly he recalled the man with the machine gun, and told himself that whatever the guy got was only what he deserved.

The rest of the crew joined them, slapping him and Rogan and Tilisi on the back. Brodie winced at an overenthusiastic hug from Hunk, easing his arm out of the way as the man said, "I thought we'd be picking up bodies. How'd you get away with it?"

"It must be a bit hard to aim when you're in a speeding boat," Brodie guessed. "Lucky for us."

Rogan said, "They must have hoped they could sneak on board and hold us up. Shooting at us from the boat was a bit desperate. Let's hope that's the last we see of them."

The *Sea-Rogue* was battered but still seaworthy. "I don't suppose they wanted to sink her," Brodie said over coffee and toast in the saloon after Hunk had repaired a couple of stitches and dressed Brodie's wound again. "If they knew we had the gold aboard there'd be no sense in sending it to the bottom of the ocean again."

The excitement over, the crew had gone back to the barge to have an early breakfast and prepare for their departure. But just in case, they were taking turns to keep a lookout for any further activity from the trawler.

Rogan took breakfast to their prisoner and reported, "He still reckons he's innocent. Didn't know a thing about any attempt on the treasure."

"If we went through his stuff," Brodie said, "d'you think we'd find any evidence?"

Camille demurred. "Shouldn't we wait for the police?"

Someone thumped on the deck above, and they all looked up, Brodie leaping to his feet. Damn, but he'd got jumpy with all that had happened in the last couple of days.

Tilisi poked his head in. "The tug's in sight."

By the time the tug reached them the trawler was long gone, rapidly disappearing off the *Sea-Rogue's* radar screen. The policeman, a massively burly six-foot-six islander with legs and arms like tree trunks and a patient expression, looked a bit disapproving when they said they had a prisoner.

"What evidence do you have against this man?" he asked sternly.

"He was signaling," Brodie insisted, "to the guys who tried to kill us this morning."

"Tried to kill you?" the officer repeated skeptically. "Do you have proof of this?"

Brodie swallowed a sarcastic retort, gesturing at the splintered wood over the companionway, the shattered glass still lying about. "They fired on us with a submachine gun!"

"They came from a trawler called *Scorpio*," Rogan told the officer. "It's been hanging about here on and off since we arrived. They used an inflatable."

"Ah—you saw the boat leave the trawler?"

"No!" Brodie growled. "It was dark. But they couldn't have come from anywhere else."

"If it was dark," the policeman said, "how do you know there was no other ship in the vicinity? You see, we have to be careful to get our facts right. It wouldn't do to cause an international incident by arresting a perfectly innocent ship from some other country."

He wasn't, it was clear, convinced that Joe wasn't perfectly innocent too, as the diver continued to maintain. "Using a flashlight at night is no crime," the policeman worried. "It's not enough to detain him in custody."

"Can't you hold him for questioning at least?" Brodie demanded, exasperated. "*Someone* shot up the *Sea-Rogue*. You can at least investigate! Look through his things and find out if there's anything suspicious there."

Somewhat reluctantly the policeman agreed he could do that, but Joe had to be there when he did it.

Rogan and Brodie accompanied them. They'd untied Joe's hands and hoped the serviceable pistol the policeman wore at his waist was enough to deter any mayhem. Certainly an attempted escape was unlikely since there was nowhere to go.

The search turned up a satellite phone and a pistol, along with a clip of ammunition. Brodie wondered if they would have found some plastic explosive if they'd searched earlier. Though, presuming Joe was the safe-blower, he'd had plenty of opportunity to throw such damning evidence overboard.

"Is this licensed?" the policeman queried, holding the pistol.

Joe shrugged. "Yeah. Don't have the license with me though."

To Brodie's relief the policeman confiscated the weapon anyway. "When you prove it's legal," he said, "you can have it back."

The satellite phone, he pointed out, was not illegal, and when Rogan asked Joe why he carried such an expensive piece of technology, Joe said, "I've got a family, right? I like to keep in touch."

"A family?" Brodie queried. It was the first he'd heard of Joe being a family man.

"Parents." Joe glowered. "They're getting old. I need to keep an eye on them, okay? Brothers. And my girlfriend."

The policeman looked sympathetic. Family ties meant something to him. "I can't arrest a man for having a phone."

"Try the redial," Brodie suggested.

The policeman looked at him, and pressed the button, listened and shrugged. "No such number."

Joe smirked. "I must've dialed a wrong one."

Glumly Brodie and Rogan watched as Joe packed up his things and made ready to leave with the others.

"There will be an investigation," the policeman promised before climbing back aboard the tug. "Piracy is a serious matter, but unfortunately some countries are less vigilant than they might be about policing it."

"They could hardly be less vigilant than that!" Brodie growled in disgust as he watched Joe board the tug with the other divers for the journey back to Parakaeo. Looked like the guy was free and clear.

"The cop's got a point," Rogan admitted. "When you look at the evidence it doesn't seem all that strong. Like Granger would say, it won't hold up in court."

They stuck with the tug and the barge all the way back to the little island port. A cruise ship was tied up at the wharf where the freighter had been when they left, and along the foreshore, tents and booths had sprung up where the locals were selling handcrafts, shells, coral, pearls and hand-dyed pareus to the tourists.

Rogan handed out checks to the team, including generous bonuses and the promised gold coin. He passed Joe's envelope to him in tight-lipped silence. Joe took it, ripped it open to check the contents, turned away with a two-finger salute and shouldered his pack, and after climbing ashore to the wharf, strode toward the hotel where the divers would await the twice-weekly flight out to Rarotonga, and from there to wherever in the world their next job was.

Tu and Tilisi organized students of the dive school into a twenty-four-hour watch on the *Sea-Rogue*—fit, strong young men, who took turns to sit in pairs on the wharf and keep their eyes peeled for any strangers or suspicious activity. At the first sign of trouble they could muster most of the male population of the port within minutes.

A sleek oceangoing cabin cruiser with a blue hull and white superstructure nosed into the harbor near dusk and dropped anchor. An inflatable runabout took ashore three men, who ambled up the rise toward the hotel.

"Anyone we know?" Brodie queried Rogan.

"Don't recognize them," Rogan answered. "The boat though—I might have seen that before. At Mokohina?"

Brodie squinted at it. "Not a regular. I don't remember seeing it."

"Maybe I'm wrong. Are we going for a drink at the hotel?"

"I guess the guys expect us." A farewell drink with the team before they dispersed was normal. "What about the girls?"

"I'll ask if they want to come. It should be safe enough either way—Tu's boys will be around, and if the burglar alarm goes off we'll probably hear it from the hotel."

The bar was crowded, the locals outnumbered by tourists. Brodie looked for the three men from the motor cruiser but couldn't identify them.

It was a subdued farewell. The team occupied a couple of tables and the drinks flowed freely, paid for by Rogan, but the fact that Joe sat alone in a shadowed corner of the crowded bar, sinking glass after glass of beer, introduced a sour note.

When he got up and slouched out of the door that led to the back of the hotel the atmosphere lightened a little. Olin and Tilisi snagged some pretty female tourists from among the cruise-ship passengers soaking up local color in the bar, impressing them with tales of their diving adventures. By the time the remaining *Sea-Rogue* crew left, the celebration was developing into a real party.

Brodie held the door open for Sienna and Camille, and before he let it go a man brushed by him without thanks, wearing a white jacket over a striped shirt and wraparound sunglasses. Some rich guy off the cruise ship, Brodie guessed, used to having lesser mortals open doors for him. He grinned to himself as he caught up with the others. Rogan had his arm about Camille, and Brodie debated taking Sienna's hand in his, but decided he'd better not.

Something teased at the back of his mind about the stranger in the doorway, some memory that wouldn't come to the fore. Had he seen the man somewhere, sometime? Hard to tell with those glasses on. Maybe he was famous as well as rich, pretending he didn't want to be recognized. As if anyone on Parakaeo would care.

After the women had gone to bed, leaving the two men in the saloon, Rogan said, "Think we could persuade Camille and Sienna to take a plane back to New Zealand?"

Brodie grinned. "In case the trawler's lurking about, waiting for us to sail with the treasure on board? I don't fancy your chances. Did Camille promise to obey you?"

"You were at our wedding," Rogan reminded him. "You should know she didn't."

Brodie didn't say he'd been preoccupied with wondering if the bridesmaid was as pretty as her back view promised, not really listening to the words.

"I'll talk to Granger," Rogan said, "and see what we come up with."

Brodie was asleep in his bunk when he heard a thump at the side of the boat, bringing him out of a dream in which Sienna featured, sitting on the prow of the *Maiden's Prayer* with her hair streaming in the current, her pink-tipped breasts an invitation, that neat belly button just begging for a forefinger to explore it—and below that a few inches of smooth skin and a tail, all gleaming gold scales like coins overlapping each other, culminating in a waving silver fin…

Brodie muttered a curse and woke up. The bump came again, then something that sounded like a groan.

Flinging back the sheet, he padded out into the saloon and groped his way up the companionway.

The boys on the wharf came to their feet. The sounds had come from the seaward side of the boat where the dive ladder was. He turned toward it as the boys leaped on board.

A hand clung to the ladder. Dimly he could see an upturned face. A hoarse, slurred voice said, "Help me!"

They hauled him aboard, despite a yell of pain when they grabbed him, and he slumped onto the deck, breathing heavily, with a hitch and a groan at each inhalation. Brodie gingerly turned him over, eliciting another, louder groan, and at first didn't recognize the bruised face with puffy, half-closed eyes, a swollen nose that was probably broken, and blood mixed with water flowing from cuts over the cheekbones and on the lips. One arm was bent at a weird angle, and when Brodie touched it the man yelped, "Jeez, Brodie!"

Looking at him more closely, Brodie said, "Joe?"

"Don't…throw me overboard, 'kay?" Joe said weakly, then seemed to lapse into unconsciousness.

Brodie dug a couple of fingers into the man's neck and found a pulse still beating strongly. "Look after him," he said to the boys, and went down to fetch Rogan.

The women followed Rogan up to the deck. Joe seemed half-conscious, enough to mutter "No!" when Camille suggested taking him straight to the island's only hospital. "Not the hospital," he said. "They'll get me…"

"Who?" Brodie asked. "Who beat you up?"

Joe didn't seem to hear. "Don't tell anyone. Please, guys. Rogue…sorry…"

He drifted into unconsciousness again. Brodie poked him in the ribs, some of which he suspected had been broken, but got no reaction. "We ought to chuck him back," he said.

Sienna looked up from her horrified contemplation of Joe's injuries. "You can't do that!"

"Yeah, I know." It was hard not to feel sorry for the guy, in the circumstances. "I wonder who did this to him."

Rogan said, "Maybe he'll tell us when he wakes up again. That could be useful."

Brodie grunted. "I guess. D'you think it's safe to keep him on board?"

"Safe?" Sienna sounded scornful. "You surely don't imagine he's a danger to anyone, the condition he's in? He needs a doctor."

"We'll send for Hunk," Rogan decided, and one of the island boys was dispatched to find him while the other helped Rogan and Brodie carry Joe to the saloon, where they laid him down on a blanket on the floor. Camille fetched a pillow and lifted his head, her hand coming away smeared with blood. "He's been hit on the head too, I think."

Hunk arrived and while Joe, partially roused, groaned and muttered, he confirmed Brodie's diagnosis of cracked ribs, set the broken arm and said, "He's had a blow on the head. Keep an eye on him and wake him up now and then, make sure he doesn't slip back into unconsciousness. He's a tough nut—he'll probably fully recover in a few days."

"And when he does we'll have some questions for him," Brodie said after the medic, sworn to secrecy, had left.

The two boys were also told to keep quiet about what had happened, but Rogan said, "I wouldn't count on it."

They cleaned their uninvited guest up and put him in the second bunk in Brodie's cabin, where Brodie could keep an eye on him. Except for the several times Brodie poked him awake according to the doctor's instructions, he slept like a log—if logs gave a grunt of pain with every breath.

Chapter 10

In the morning Rogan reported, "Granger's chartering a plane to fly the treasure back to New Zealand. It'll be landed in Auckland and he'll make sure the gold's stored safely with his bank. The plane should arrive within a couple of days."

They were having breakfast in the saloon with the women when the door of Brodie's cabin opened and Joe stood there, stark naked and swaying. His face and body were a patchwork of blue and purple and red, and his right arm rested in a sling while his left arm cradled his ribs. "Sorry, ladies," he gasped. "Where the hell are my clothes?"

Camille said coolly, "We're drying them for you, but they're still damp."

Brodie said, "You can borrow some of mine." He got up and pushed the man back into the cabin. In a few minutes they both reappeared, Joe now attired in shorts and a T-shirt that were a size too small for his bulky frame.

Rogan picked up his empty plate and cup to take them to the galley. Joe staggered to the table and sat at right angles to Sienna. Camille put coffee in front of him and offered toast.

"Thanks," he said as she buttered it for him, before seating herself again beside Sienna. He cast a glance around at their wary, hostile faces, the men now standing shoulder to shoulder.

Brodie said, "What happened?"

"I got jumped."

"Yeah, we know that." His voice heavy with sarcasm, Brodie added, "Now tell us you don't know who did it."

Joe shoved toast into his mouth and bit into it, wincing. "Would you believe me?" he mumbled.

"No," Brodie assured him, "we wouldn't. And if you don't want to be thrown out on your ear you'd better start telling us what's going on."

"Look, I don't know their names. And this is…it's confidential, you know? You won't go to the cops?"

"Why not?" Rogan asked. "I'm sure they'd be interested."

"You want to know or not?" Joe began to look belligerent. "No cops, okay? D'you want to get me killed?"

"Frankly," Brodie drawled, "why should we care?"

Joe tried a weak version of his usual cocky grin, somewhat spoiled by the fact that he winced again when a cut on his lip opened. "You're the good guys," he said. "I know you're not killers."

"And the bad guys are?"

"They thought they'd got me dead last night. Musta followed me when I went to the can at the hotel bar—y'know it's outside. It was dark, and when I came out they were waiting for me. Didn't see their faces but I know who sent them. I never had a chance against three of them." He looked down at his knuckles, which were bruised and grazed, evidence that he'd put up a fight anyway, Brodie thought. "Don't remember much, but I woke up in the water. They'd knocked me out and chucked me in the harbor to drown. Or maybe they thought they'd already killed me." He grinned again, more of a painful grimace but holding a vengeful malice.

"I'm tougher than they bargained for. But if they think I'm dead I'd rather stay that way."

"And you want us to help you," Brodie said. "In return for what?"

Sienna said, "Shouldn't you go to the police, Joe? If they really tried to kill you—"

He shook his head impatiently and Brodie gave her a pitying look. After seeing how futile their own attempt to bring in the cops had been, she still had her innocent belief in the omnipotence of the long arm of the law?

Joe swallowed his mouthful of toast. "I go to the cops and I'm a dead man for real."

Brodie explained to Sienna, "Crime on Parakaeo is the odd pub fight on a Saturday night, driving a moped under the influence, growing a bit of backyard dope, maybe the occasional jealous husband taking a machete to a fence jumper. The jail is unlocked every Friday night so the prisoners can go home for the weekend, and if they don't come back the constabulary—all two of it—rounds them up. They're not equipped for the kind of thing we're up against."

"So tell us," Rogan said to Joe, "why they want to kill you."

Joe looked uneasy, picking up his cup to gulp some coffee. "They think I double-crossed them."

Brodie leaned forward. "You were working with them— the guys on the trawler?"

Joe avoided his eyes. "I didn't know what they had in mind," he muttered. "The plan was for me to tell them if you raised gold. That's all."

"And once you'd satisfied their curiosity," Rogan suggested, "they'd sail happily off into the sunset? Pull the other one, Joe."

"All right," he said grudgingly. "They were going to take it off you."

"With a please and thank-you?" Brodie inquired.

"They said if you gave it up no one would get hurt."

Brodie made a disgusted sound of disbelief. "And what were you getting out of it? A share?"

Joe looked more ill at ease than ever. "Look, I'm sorry, guys—but if I didn't agree they said they'd kill me."

"You did agree," Brodie said, "and they tried to kill you anyway."

"You were ready for them. They reckoned I'd given them away. I tried to tell them last night it wasn't my fault but they wouldn't listen." Joe hunched over his plate, shuffled in his seat. "In a way they were right."

"You blew the safe," Brodie guessed. "But not for them."

Rogan said, "Making sure of your share in case they didn't come across with the goods after all?"

"I figured if I could get hold of some of the gold—y'know, just a coupla bars or so, I could disappear once we got back to shore, get away from them. I tell you, those guys scare me." Joe rubbed the back of his head, and flinched. "I've got a headache," he mumbled.

"Too bad." Brodie was unsympathetic, mad all over again at Joe's treacherous behavior, putting them all at risk—including two innocent women. Sienna was looking big-eyed and shaken, maybe remembering how they'd been fired on at sea. Besides, his arm still ached and burned, and he was getting sick of nursing it so he didn't open up the cut again. "Did you sabotage the winch?"

Joe hesitated. "I needed a bit of time before I had to contact them and tell them we'd found the gold. Well, until the safe was open, I didn't know for sure anyway."

"And once we had all the gold on board," Rogan guessed, "you got on your satellite phone and told them they could come and help themselves."

Sienna said, "If Joe was in touch with the trawler all along why didn't they keep out of sight? Surely they knew you'd be suspicious of them hanging around?"

"That's a point." Brodie shot her a look of respect.

Joe shrugged. "To keep an eye on what was happening, I guess. And let me know they were around. They didn't trust me. I know it made you nervous…but not half as nervous as it made me!''

Brodie reluctantly took his gaze from Sienna. ''So who are these guys?''

''I told you, I don't know. Never gave me names.''

''Don't give us that,'' Brodie said wearily. ''How did they know you were working for us?''

Rogan remembered. ''You came looking for me at Rarotonga. They put you up to it?''

It wouldn't have seemed so coincidental at the time, Brodie supposed. News about new jobs coming up spread among the exclusive worldwide community of professional divers with the speed of light. Rogue wouldn't have been surprised that a veteran like Joe, one he'd worked with before, should have heard a rumor about his plans.

''Word was around at Raro,'' Joe confirmed, ''that Rogue Broderick was fitting out a barge and hiring divers. I'd just finished a job and this guy…approached me.''

''And,'' Rogan said, ''offered you a share in *our* treasure if you'd spy for him and his pals.''

''It wasn't just that,'' Joe said defensively. ''The thing is…my last job was a bit dodgy.'' His voice dropped and he looked about nervously, as if afraid of eavesdroppers. ''I didn't know what I was getting into when I took it on. They were hard men—I mean, really hard men.''

''What last job?'' Rogan asked.

Joe licked his cut lip. ''They…were bringing up something illegal. That's why I agreed to keep them in the picture about the *Sea-Rogue* job. They threatened me, and I couldn't go to the cops because of the other thing—I don't want to end up in jail.''

''Better than ending up dead,'' Brodie commented.

''You thought you'd get away with neither,'' Rogan said. ''Trouble is, Joe, you picked the wrong side.''

Brodie frowned. ''So these were the same guys you did the last job for?''

Joe shifted in his seat, and took another bite of toast. ''If you guys go to the cops—'' his eyes lifted under their swollen lids ''—I never said anything.''

Rogan regarded him thoughtfully. ''Your friends aren't the only hard men on the planet,'' he said. ''We might not murder you, but those thugs scared my wife half to death, and they could have killed us all. I'm already tempted to add a few more colors to all those pretty ones on your ugly mug.''

''I'll help,'' Brodie promptly offered.

Camille's gaze flew to her husband's face. She opened her mouth and closed it again. Sienna too looked up at Rogan's implacable expression, then caught Brodie's eyes. He gave her a concentrated stare and an infinitesimal warning shake of his head, and she bit her lip.

''I said I'm sorry,'' Joe muttered.

Rogan swept the apology aside. ''These guys were after the *Maiden's Prayer*, tried to get at it before we arrived, and you were their diver. You're the one who cleaned out the surface stuff from the site and blew that first hole in the hull—isn't that right? And later on you knifed Brodie.''

Sienna made a stifled little sound.

''Come on, Joe!'' Brodie's patience snapped. ''You want us to save you from these crooks, you've got to tell us what you know about them.'' He leaned down, his face inches from the other man's. ''Personally I'm itching to pay you back for taking a knife to me.''

''You wouldn't hit a man with a broken arm, Brodie.''

''I reckon it about makes us even, don't you think?'' Brodie thrust his bandaged one forward.

''I didn't mean to hurt you. When you came after me I panicked. I didn't know it was you.''

Brodie recalled Sienna chiding him for chasing the mysterious diver and sent her a fleeting glance as he straightened. Her expression was apprehensive rather than I-told-you-so, her skin pearl-white. Hell, she'd been through too much trauma in the last thirty-six hours. This was a far cry from her safe academic world.

Remembering he'd goaded her into accepting the job with

Pacific Treasure Salvors, Brodie found his temper rising further. Folding his arms to resist the temptation to plant a punch on Joe's already damaged nose, the very action reminding him again who he had to thank for the nasty twinge he felt, he glowered down at him and said grimly, "So tell us the rest, *mate*. Before I lose my cool altogether."

Joe threw up his good hand. "Okay, okay. It was me—and a couple of their guys—not professionals. Sport divers. We were on the trawler. Found some coins and stuff scattered round the site but we couldn't get inside the wreck. Bloody amateurs. I told them they needed better gear and better divers. They didn't have the right equipment, said they didn't have time."

"So you must have known they were poaching," Brodie interjected.

Joe didn't answer that. "I warned them blowing it would prob'ly make the timbers fall in and destroy some of the stuff. The other bloke didn't like it either. But the boss guy just said we could use the trawler winch to clear the debris and get the gold out. He reckoned the rest wasn't worth bothering with."

"What other bloke?" Rogan inquired.

Joe picked up his coffee cup and put it down again. "There were two of them—not sailors or fishermen. They told the trawler skipper what to do—guess they'd hired him."

Brodie supposed the trawler was one of the ships Drummond had used to smuggle his stolen antiques and heritage items to unscrupulous buyers around the world.

"They had this big argument," Joe went on, "about the explosion damaging the other stuff in the wreck. The boss guy…" He paused, rubbing his eyebrow, and his voice dropped. "He won. But when we started dragging out the timbers the winch broke down—that's what gave me the idea later on about disabling the winch on the barge. The boss man was fit to be tied. Sent me and the others down again but we couldn't move the rubbish off. And it was like I said it would be, impossible to get at the gold. We sailed back to Raro, and when we heard you were there already I was told to get on the team, no matter what.''

''And then they followed us. While you kept them informed.'' Brodie's tone was filled with contempt.

''You don't understand!'' Joe's voice rose. ''I said the boss guy won the fight—remember?''

Something chilled Brodie's spine. ''Yeah?''

''He killed the other guy. Took out a gun and shot him in cold blood!''

There was a silence, while the water slurped at the *Sea-Rogue's* hull and a seabird distantly screeched. Somewhere on shore a woman was singing, children called to each other and one of them laughed.

Joe was breathing fast, the sound loud and harsh, each breath accompanied by a grunt of pain. With a shaking hand he picked up his coffee and gulped down the remainder. The cup thumped to the table. ''He'd have done the same to me if I didn't do what he wanted.''

Rogan spoke finally. ''What did this guy look like?''

''A business type. Sharp clothes, medium height, brown hair. Ordinary, except he's got these cold eyes.''

''What color?''

''Color?'' Joe hesitated. ''Blue, I think. Gray, maybe.'' He shrugged. ''Sort of in between.''

Rogan said softly, ''Sounds like Drummond, all right. I always knew the guy was a killer. But he usually got someone else to do the dirty work.''

Brodie said, ''Maybe he ran out of employees. We know one's dead, one's in jail. So hard to get good help these days.''

Nobody laughed.

Joe spent the day lurking in Brodie's cabin and nursing his sore ribs. Camille offered painkillers but he shook his head, apparently afraid they'd make him sleepy, and afraid to close his eyes.

''Drummond and his henchmen have got him spooked, all

right," Brodie said quietly to Rogan as they stood on deck together.

"Yup. What are we going to do with him?"

"No use handing him over to the cops here. If we got him back to New Zealand the police there might be interested in news about Drummond."

"I don't fancy sailing all the way home with him and the women on board."

Brodie nodded. "We'll send Sienna and Camille back on the plane with the treasure."

"Alone?" Rogan frowned. "They should be okay, but I think one of us should go along."

Guessing he wanted to be with his wife and make sure no harm came to her, Brodie was silent.

"If we don't try to keep it secret that we're loading the gold onto the plane," Rogan said, "sailing the *Sea-Rogue* back home should be safe enough."

"With Joe on board?"

"All he wants to do is lie low. I don't think we'll have any more problems with him."

"Still, we don't know what Drummond's next move might be. Or if Joe's really been straight with us. He might still be holding back on some things. Suppose the *Sea-Rogue* was followed? They might not believe that everything's on the plane."

It was a dilemma. Both men wanted to protect their women—and Brodie realized that was how he'd begun to think of Sienna. Yet neither wanted the other to risk a possibly dangerous journey back to safe harbor. "You go on the plane with your wife," he said reluctantly. "I can sail the *Sea-Rogue* back."

Rogan smiled slightly in appreciation of the offer. "Thanks, but it's my boat. Toss you for it," he said.

In the end it was Rogan who stayed with the *Sea-Rogue*, recruiting Tilisi to sail with him. Camille objected to being sent off with Sienna, only slightly mollified by the news that

Brodie would be flying with them. "You can both stay at my place until Rogan gets back to port," he said.

"Brodie will look after you," Rogan said. "And there's no sense in going to a hotel when he's got a perfectly good spare bedroom."

It might have been Sienna's quickly masked dismay at the prospect of sharing a house with Brodie alone that finally swayed Camille.

All the artifacts from the wreck were carefully packed and loaded onto the plane when it arrived, and within three hours it was landing in Auckland. Granger was there to meet them, with an armored van and security guards to transport the gold to the bank, and other precious finds to secure storage at the museum where Sienna had arranged for a specialist restorer she knew to look after them.

Sienna had asked for two small crates to be kept separate. "Those are things I'd like to work on myself. None of them are worth millions—more the kind of stuff that the poachers were willing to destroy to get at the gold. And I'm paid to work for PTS, not twiddle my thumbs waiting around for something to do."

When they got to Brodie's house after dark and he'd shown them the room they were to share and unpacked the car they'd hired, the crates were stowed in a spare room that held some diving gear parked in a corner, a snooker table and nothing else.

Sienna asked Brodie, "Can I use that? Could we put a board over it or something?"

"Yeah, okay. I'll sort something out in the morning. Are you girls hungry?"

On the way from Auckland they'd bought bread, milk, butter, eggs and bacon. Brodie got to work in the kitchen and the smell of bacon and eggs and coffee wafted through the house. Sienna too found her taste buds waking up, and when he presented her and Camille with crisp bacon and barely filmed eggs plus hot buttered toast on the side, she ate all of hers.

''That was nice,'' she said sincerely, looking up at him as she pushed away her plate.

His smile was crooked. He held her eyes, a hidden message lurking in his, and she remembered she'd said the same thing about their night together on Parakaeo. Camille smiled in a puzzled way at her, and Sienna shook her head.

Next day Brodie said, ''Will you be all right if I go down to the shop to check everything's okay? I'll lock the door behind me.''

Sienna cast him a glance of amusement. ''What do you think might happen to us?'' She looked out the big window at the sunlit street, deserted but for an elderly man and the big Labrador dog trotting at his heels. A glimpse of tranquil blue-green harbor was visible at the bottom of the slope. A world away from a dark night on the deep ocean and a pack of pirates with a submachine gun.

''Can't be too careful,'' Brodie growled. ''Rogan's trusting me to look after you two. If anyone comes to the door don't open it unless you know them.''

He returned with a sheet of marine ply that more than covered the pool table, plus a couple of bar stools for Sienna and Camille to perch on while they worked on the artifacts.

''Anything else you need?'' he asked Sienna.

''Some big plastic tubs like the ones we had on the barge?''

''Sure. I'll scout around the port. And I'd better get groceries too. What else?''

''A water distiller. I'll come with you,'' Sienna said. ''I need to find someone who can sell me some sulphuric and nitric acid, and I'd like to get my hair done if there's time. Or I could go on my own later.'' The salt air had played havoc with her curls, making it impossible to keep them in any sort of order. She needed a conditioning treatment as well as a trim.

''Looks fine to me,'' Brodie said, causing Camille to send Sienna a sympathetic grimace. ''You're not having it cut, are you?''

"Just tidied up," she said, giving him a direct look that dared him to make any further comment.

"Okay, we'll go after lunch."

He'd bought fresh mussels from a boat in the harbor and cooked them for lunch, steaming them open and serving them with white wine, chives and wholemeal bread.

"You're a gem, Brodie," Camille told him when they'd finished. "I don't know why some woman didn't snap you up long ago."

He grinned at her across the low kitchen counter where he'd seated himself opposite the two women, and transferred his gaze to Sienna, lifting his eyebrows slightly. "Sienna thinks no one would have me."

Camille looked at her friend questioningly.

"I didn't mean it," Sienna said. "Brodie was teasing."

Camille shot an interested glance from her to Brodie, but said nothing.

Sienna got up, taking her plate and Camille's and walking round to the kitchen. "When are we leaving?"

"Soon as the dishes are done." Brodie stood up with his own plate in his hand.

He leaned across Sienna to slide it into the sink, and she caught a whiff of his male scent, clean skin, soap and an indefinable hint of something that made her insides go hot and fluid and sent her pulse into overdrive.

"I think I'll stay here," Camille said, "and try to raise the *Sea-Rogue* on the computer, see how they're doing."

Brodie looked uneasy. "I dunno. I promised Rogue I'd keep an eye on you."

"I'll be fine, Brodie. There's no danger here, surely."

"Okay," Brodie said dubiously. "But remember, keep the door locked and don't open it to strangers. If anything happens to you Rogue would kill me."

Sienna and Camille exchanged exasperated glances. "It's no use fighting it," Camille said. "It's in their genes."

"Haven't you ever heard of women's lib?" Sienna asked

Brodie, lifting more dishes into the sink before turning to face him.

"Yeah," he said, "and the day you can knock me cold is the day I believe a woman your size can physically beat a man like me."

She looked at his muscular arms, bared by the short sleeves of his T-shirt, and his wide chest, and said loftily, "Physical strength isn't everything. Sometimes brains are more useful than brawn."

"Sure," he said, leaning across her again to turn on a tap. "Your brain would have been just the thing to deal with those guys trying to kill us out there if they'd got on board. What would you have done? Tried to head-butt them?"

She quickly moved aside as he squirted detergent into the water and replaced the container on the sill over the sink. "I don't like violence," she said.

"Maybe you hadn't noticed," Brodie said quite gently, turning off the tap, "but those guys were already involving us in violence, whether we liked it or not." Holding her gaze with an almost stern one of his own, he asked, "What would you have thought of Rogan and me if we'd tamely let them climb aboard and get the gold—and then shoot the lot of us?"

It all seemed unreal now, with Camille stacking cups on the counter and tipping mussel shells into a bin, Brodie handing Sienna a tea towel and then plunging his hands in the sink, prosaically washing dishes.

She said, "That was extreme. I didn't mean to belittle what you and Rogan and Tilisi and the others did. And I don't have any right to criticize. I just wish it hadn't been necessary."

"So do I," Brodie said. "Believe me, I could have done without it."

He sounded so heartfelt she searched his face, but his profile was turned to her, his head down as he rinsed a plate and put it on the drying rack.

Sienna found a hairdresser who could take her immediately, and Brodie, after looking about the place as if he expected gunmen to be lurking under the wash basins, reluctantly agreed to leave her while he went hunting for suitable bins for the artifacts. "But don't go wandering about on your own if I'm not back when you're done," he told her. "Wait for me."

He was back before she was finished, taking a seat in the waiting area and picking up one of the women's magazines on the low table. When Sienna joined him he cast aside the magazine and stood up, critically inspecting her newly trimmed hair.

"Well?" she couldn't resist asking.

He grunted. "Looks good," he said, then gave her a smile that made her breath hitch for a moment. "I didn't think they could do anything to make you even prettier, but I guess I was wrong. By the way, I found someone who can sell you those acids you wanted."

The abrupt change of subject gave her a second or two to stop the butterfly that seemed to have taken up residence in her midriff from taking wing, and remind herself that compliments came naturally to men like Brodie, and this one didn't mean anything except that he appreciated women and noticed when they looked nice. It was one of his most disarming traits, one that spelled danger for her, jeopardizing her determination to retain her common sense and her autonomy.

They collected the acid, then went to the supermarket and were in the shopping center car park, packing groceries into the plastic fish bins Brodie had found for her, when a group of four young men slouched by and she straightened suddenly, saying, "That's him!"

Chapter 11

Slamming down the car back, Brodie said, "Who?"

"The boy who tried to snatch my bag. That one, in the striped beanie."

Brodie took off before she'd even finished, sprinting after the group, homing in on the one with the woolen hat pulled down over his eyebrows, who looked around a split second before Brodie reached him and broke away from his companions, running along the street.

Brodie pushed through the others, leaving them staring, then hooting encouragement to their friend. Pursued and pursuer disappeared around a corner, but reappeared moments later, Brodie with a stranglehold on the neck of the teenager's shirt, one of the boy's arms firmly held behind him, marching him toward the car park. Sienna didn't hear what he said to his captive's indignant friends who milled about yelling protests, but the look on his face was intimidating, and they fell back, following at a discreet distance until he reached Sienna.

"This him?" he asked her.

She looked carefully at the boy's sullen face and nodded. "Yes."

The boy wriggled and tried to twist around. "I didn't do nothink."

His mates huddled in a bunch, trying to look belligerent but obviously in two minds whether to stick by their friend or flee from trouble. Other people paused, staring uneasily at the tableau. One man took a cell phone from his pocket and thumbed in a number.

"You tried to take the lady's bag," Brodie said.

A woman bystander said, "That's not true—I was here and I didn't see him do anything of the kind!"

Brodie glanced at her impatiently. "Not today, lady. A while back, couple of months ago."

The boy said, "It wasn't me!"

"It was you," Sienna said. "I know it was."

The man with the cell phone said, "The cop's on his way."

The boy's head jerked, then he looked at Sienna, his brown eyes pleading. "I never took anythink!"

"You tried," she reminded him. "If I hadn't fought you off you would have."

"I didn't hurt *you,* did I?" His aggrieved tone implied he blamed her for kicking him.

"That's not the point," Brodie said. "So you admit it was you, huh?"

"Yeah, well…sorry," he muttered to Sienna. "Only it wasn't my idea."

"Your mates' then?" Brodie suggested, appraising them.

"Hey!" one said. "Give over, Dub—you can't pin it on us."

"I'm not!" Dub protested.

Brodie demanded, "Whose idea was it then?"

Again Dub twisted his head to speak to his captor. "Some old guy said he'd give me fifty bucks if I got it."

One of his friends whistled. "Fifty!"

"What old guy?" Brodie's eyes narrowed. He turned the

boy to face him, taking a tight grip on the front of his shirt. "What's his name?"

"I dunno, honest! I never saw him before. He just pointed to the lady and said she had somethink of his in her bag and it was worth fifty bucks to him to get it back."

"And you believed that?" Brodie jeered.

The boy lifted a shoulder. "It was fifty bucks," he said reasonably.

Brodie frowned. "Have you seen him since?"

Dub shook his head. "He wasn't a local, I don't think. Look, I said I'm sorry. If *she* doesn't know who he was, how'd I know? Anyway, you don't have no right to grab me like that. You're not a cop! I could do you for assault!"

A siren wailed briefly and a police car nosed in to the car park and came to a stop at the small crowd that had gathered. Brodie grinned mercilessly at the boy and said, "Here's your chance. The cavalry's arrived."

Dub didn't seem thrilled.

After a visit to the police station, where the parents of the markedly subdued Dub were called and turned up—his father looking thunderous and his mother embarrassed—and he'd been sternly questioned, Sienna said she'd just as soon not press charges, and she and Brodie returned to the house.

"You're too softhearted," he told her as he carried a bin filled with groceries inside. "The little punk deserves a short, sharp shock."

"I think he's already had enough of one. He was scared stiff by the time you and the policeman finished with him. And he seems to have law-abiding parents. They'll probably straighten him out."

Brodie grunted. "What the hell *did* you have in your bag that someone wanted that much?"

The policeman had asked the same question, and she'd told him it must be a case of mistaken identity, although Dub swore she was the woman pointed out to him by the mysterious stranger, a man he described so vaguely that the constable clearly thought it was useless to pursue the matter.

"There was nothing particularly valuable," Sienna said.

Brodie put down the bin on the kitchen counter and looked around. "Where's Camille?"

"Here!" Her voice floated from the bedroom. "Be there in a minute."

Brodie turned to Sienna. "You had a disk with notes on it about the artifacts that Rogan and Camille handed over to you."

"Nothing very exciting, just photos with possible dates and makers. And nothing that hadn't been passed on to Granger. I suppose someone might have thought I had more information about the *Maiden's Prayer* than I actually did have."

"Granger had his copy locked in a safety vault. And if they'd tried the *Sea-Rogue* the burglar alarm would have scared them off." He suddenly looked stricken, his eyebrows drawing together, his cheeks taut. "You were the one that was vulnerable—we should have realized!"

"I don't see that the information would have been much help to anyone."

"If someone—not Drummond, because he already knew—wanted to find out where the wreck was, they might have thought your notes could tell them."

"*I* didn't even know where it was. I still couldn't tell anyone, exactly!"

"They didn't know that."

Sienna was thinking. Gooseflesh rising on her arms, she said, "If the artifacts were stolen by someone who wanted proof that the pieces were from a historic wreck, and worth more than their intrinsic value…that might make sense."

"No." Brodie shook his head. "That's not enough to have gone to so much trouble for. But…it's common knowledge the *Maiden's Prayer* was a gold clipper—worth spending money hiring a ship and a professional diver and some heavies and breaking the law. Maybe even worth killing for. They wanted to know if you'd confirmed the identity of the wreck."

"And they were following me..." She shivered. "From when I left home, or even before."

"Damn!" Brodie said softly. His eyes were dark, his face tightly controlled. "I'm sorry, Sienna. We should have protected you."

"Well, it's all over now," Sienna said, shaking off the shivery feeling. "And I didn't come to any harm."

"Yeah," he agreed, beginning to relax as Camille came in. "Your hair looks great," she said to Sienna.

"I already told her that," Brodie said, on his way out to collect more things from the car. He slanted a small grin at Sienna in passing, and her heart did an alarming little flip.

Camille began helping Sienna unpack groceries. "The boat's sailing well," she said, "and the weather's fine. Joe's still nursing his injuries and not causing any problems."

They spent the rest of the day setting up Sienna's makeshift laboratory in Brodie's spare room, and converting the laundry into a space she could use for rinsing articles that needed continuous running water.

It was dark when Brodie straightened from fitting a flexible shower hose onto a tap for her and said, "Is that it? How about a celebration dinner?"

It had begun to rain, so they took Sienna's car down to the township. She had to park around the corner from the hotel because a tour bus was occupying the space in front. "Just as well I booked us a table," Brodie said.

They had wine with their meal although Sienna limited herself to one glass. Brodie had offered to drive but she said there was no need. She never drank very much and he might as well enjoy the wine.

It was a relaxed dinner, and even Sienna cleaned up her seafood basket. After his pepper steak Brodie had a generous slice of pecan pie with cream and ice cream while Sienna shared a light dessert with Camille. Brodie looked approving but her answering look dared him to comment, and he merely grinned at her, his blue eyes innocent, before digging into his pie.

Something inside her turned to a kind of warm mush. It just wasn't fair, the effect he had on her. In fact it was positively alarming, considering how totally wrong they were for each other. Him with his devil-may-care attitude and his casual charm that he exercised without thought for the devastation he could cause to a woman's life, and her with too much experience of that kind of unthinking destructiveness.

And there he was, tucking into his disgustingly sweet dessert as if it was the only thing that mattered to him.

He swallowed a mouthful of pie and looked up, his forehead creasing into quizzical inquiry at her indignant expression.

Realizing she'd been staring, Sienna hastily turned her attention to the caramel mousse between her and Camille.

When they left, the rain had stopped, the wet pavement reflecting the lights from the hotel doorway and the street lamp at the corner.

Once out of the lamp's glow it was very dark in the side street. Brodie took the women's arms and guided them to the car, where he and Camille waited by the passenger door for Sienna to unlock.

Someone started a car parked on the other side of the street a little farther down. The motor roared into life and the car leaped forward, veered toward Sienna and came to a screeching halt. The back door opened even as Brodie vaulted over the front of her car, swept her aside with one arm and pinned her against the driver's door, shielding her with his body. Behind him the other car's door slammed, and it roared off into the night.

Pressed to Brodie's hard chest, Sienna could hear his heart beating and realized she was clutching a handful of his shirt. He smelled of soap and cotton and man, and she felt utterly thankful for his strong arms about her.

Slowly he slackened his hold, and she discovered she was shaking.

"Are you okay?" he queried, his head bent to scan her face.

"Yes. Are you? Your arm…"

"Fine." He bent and pressed a hard, brief kiss on her mouth. It had the effect of stopping her trembling, a lightning bolt of sheer sensation shooting through her. Adrenaline, she thought dazedly. Something to do with danger averted.

Camille was looking at where the other car had disappeared around the corner. "What on earth just happened?" she asked.

Brodie said, "I wish I knew." He took the keys from Sienna's nerveless fingers and unlocked the doors. "Get in the back," he said. "You're in no state to drive."

"You've been drinking—"

"A couple of glasses of wine won't have put me over the limit. Get in—both of you."

Too shaken not to do as he said, Sienna climbed into the car. Camille joined her in the back seat and Brodie drove them home, throwing frowning glances at the rear-vision mirror every few seconds. "You didn't get a look at the number plate, did you?" he asked Camille.

"No. Everything happened so fast. It can't have had anything to do with the treasure, surely? Those people would know that we'd have made sure the gold and anything really valuable was safe as soon as we reached New Zealand. If they suspected anything else they'd be after the *Sea-Rogue*. Rogan said there's no sign of any other boat on the radar."

"Right," Brodie said. "It could just be that some hoons thought they saw a lone woman and it'd be fun to give her a scare. Or they had something more sinister in mind. In the dark they might not have seen you and me on the other side of the car."

He drew into the garage and escorted the women into the house. "Make sure you close your blinds, and keep your bedroom window closed tonight," he ordered.

"I don't suppose they followed us home," Sienna said. She'd willed herself to pragmatism and a determination not to see James Drummond's fell hand in every mishap or puzzling incident. "I'm sure you're right, it was nothing to do with the treasure, they were simply opportunists who saw a woman in a dark street."

"Maybe." He looked at her frowningly. "That kind of thing happened before, when I walked you to the hotel the first time. Is there something going on in your life that I don't know about? Any reason someone wants to get at you?"

Sienna shook her head. "No! And that was my fault, the first time. I stepped onto the road without looking." Because Brodie had been taking her attention, upsetting her equilibrium, making her altogether too conscious of his male charisma, to the exclusion of everything else. It hung about him like an aura, she could feel it now more strongly than ever, with the imprint of that quick, adrenaline-fuelled kiss still on her lips. "You told me off," she reminded him, "for being stupid, remember?"

"Yeah," he said. "Coincidence, I guess. But I don't like coincidences."

After he'd left the room she heard him prowling about the house, checking every door and window before tapping on the women's bedroom door and calling good-night to them. Sienna had the impression as she climbed into bed that he wasn't going to sleep. It gave her a mortifying feeling of comfort.

At breakfast Brodie announced, "I'm going to get burglar alarms installed. And just in case, we'd better leave the crates unopened until it's done."

The installer came that afternoon, hooked up a sensor in a corner of the newly converted workroom, inspected the big up-and-down windows and suggested Brodie might want some security locks on them, which he put in, then placed a couple more sensors in other parts of the house and departed.

"So," Brodie said, after showing them how the system worked, "from now on we arm it every night and whenever we're away from the house."

Camille admitted, "It's a good idea. I was relieved when we got an alarm put on the Sea-Rogue."

But Rogan and Brodie hadn't trusted the alarm to warn them about a possible boarding party. They'd kept watch— and kept the women in ignorance, something that still rankled with both Camille and Sienna.

Brodie opened the nailed lids of the crates and helped the women remove some things that Sienna had packed in wet sawdust. They went straight into a bath of distilled water.

"The other box can wait," Sienna said. "Those things aren't likely to deteriorate in the air, like these. We can start work on them tomorrow."

After breakfast next morning Brodie said, "I need to see a doctor and get these stitches out. Then I might go to the shop for a while, if you two will be okay."

"Spend the day if you like," Camille told him. "We'll be fine."

"I don't need much time. They're used to me being away. I won't be long."

He wasn't, bringing some paperwork home with him and spreading it out on the kitchen counter-cum-table while in the other room Sienna and Camille chipped patiently at a china candlestick and the remains of a ship's lantern, removing layers of seaweed and coral.

After a couple more uneventful days Brodie relaxed his vigilance a bit and began spending more time at the dive shop. Camille was in touch with the *Sea-Rogue* every day and reported the boat was making good time. Rogan hoped to be home the following week.

When they'd sorted through the first box, cleaned up the more lightly coated articles and left others to soak in acid baths for a few more days, Sienna and Camille turned to the second crate. Sienna lifted out a cardboard box.

"What's in it?" Camille asked.

"A few odd rings, watches, fob chains—stuff that didn't need a lot of cleaning but sometime we should try to check if we can get some detail on when and where they were made.

If we can find any particularly interesting information on them it could enhance their value to collectors or museums.''

''I could do that,'' Camille offered, ''while you carry on with cleaning the other stuff.''

It was her area of expertise, after all. Sienna handed over the box and said, ''Go for it.''

Sienna was gently rubbing a black film from a pewter platter with steel wool when Camille gave a sharp exclamation and said, ''Where did this come from?''

''What?'' Sienna looked up to see her friend's face white and her eyes wide with shock, holding a ring in her fingers as though it were a bomb.

Sienna reached out to take it, curious to see which of the several in the box had caused this reaction. ''Brodie found it,'' she said. ''But it could be from another wreck. Unless we find out who the owner was we may never know.''

''I know,'' Camille whispered, her eyes riveted on the ring with its black enameled background and golden urn.

''You do?'' Sienna queried, apprehension beginning to beat a tattoo in her chest.

Camille lifted troubled eyes—haunted, even. ''I don't know who the original owner was, but James used to wear a ring like that.'' She paused, touched her tongue to her lips and emphasized, ''*Exactly* like that.''

''James?'' No wonder Camille was upset. ''James Drummond?''

''Yes,'' Camille confirmed. ''James Drummond.''

Chapter 12

When they told Brodie, he looked almost as shocked as Camille had. "*Drummond's* ring? Are you sure?" Turning to Sienna, he said, "You told me these things were handed out to all and sundry after a death."

"Friends and family," she said. "Maybe only one or two, not more than a few dozen or so at most. It's hardly likely that one person in New Zealand in the twenty-first century would come across two identical ones by sheer coincidence."

He grunted. "But if this is Drummond's…" He turned it in his big fingers. "Aw, shoot."

"Could he have lost it," Sienna asked Camille, "when he was holding up you and Rogan on the *Sea-Rogue?*"

Camille shook her head. "He was still wearing it when the police took him away. He told me once he couldn't get it off anymore, it would have to be cut, and he didn't want to do that to a fine piece of jewelry." She looked up at Brodie. "*Where* did you find it?"

"I took it off a skeleton on the reef."

Sienna exclaimed, "You didn't tell me that! This was the

skeleton you told the policeman about? The one with the bullet in the skull?''

''But that means…'' Camille's voice trailed into silence.

Brodie put into words what they were all beginning to realize. ''It means Drummond's dead.''

''Well,'' Sienna said cautiously, ''I wouldn't wish anyone dead, but…he can't do any more harm to us—or anyone.''

Brodie's tone was harsh. ''He's been dead for months. Rogan and I first came across him—his bones, I mean, just before the wedding.''

''Months?'' Sienna digested that. ''You said, when you first saw him—it, there was no flesh left?''

Brodie shook his head, giving her a peculiar look.

''Then he must have already been dead *then* for two months or so.''

Brodie and Camille both stared at her. Camille said, ''How do you know that?''

''I've talked to pathologists. Sometimes we find bones, especially near beaches, when we're excavating an archaeological site. We have to check that they're historic and not recent. I've picked up all kinds of odd information. There were plenty of fish around the reef—they'd clean a body up in two months, easily. Was it whole?''

''No. Unless the bottom half was buried in the sand. But sharks…''

''Clothes?''

He shook his head. ''Whoever shot him might have stripped him. He wasn't wearing a watch, just that ring.''

''So maybe they were trying to make sure he wasn't identified,'' Sienna guessed. ''But they couldn't get the ring off—or didn't even notice it.''

Camille said thoughtfully, ''When Joe said that the man he called the boss didn't care about destroying the other artifacts to get to the gold, something seemed odd. I know James was a criminal and apparently quite willing to sanction murder, if not carry it out himself, but he had a genuine love of beautiful old things.''

Brodie said, "So we got it wrong. Drummond was there, but his partner dispensed with him when they fell out."

Sienna shivered. "He must be utterly ruthless."

"If Joe was an eyewitness and we've got this…" Brodie looked down at the ring. "Though it's probably not enough evidence to convict anyone."

"Joe swore he'd never talk to the police."

"Seems to me," Brodie said, "he'd be safer in jail than anywhere. And four witnesses can swear to what he told us."

"Why did he?" Camille wondered.

"Because," Sienna pointed out, "he'd been beaten up, concussed, almost drowned, had several broken bones—and two big, fit men were threatening some kind of repeat performance if he didn't cough up." She would have had trouble resisting their distinctly unsympathetic treatment in the circumstances. Joe, aware that his safety depended on them, had crumbled like an anthill under a couple of bulldozers. "He was caught between the devil—a couple of them, from his point of view—and, literally, the deep blue sea."

Brodie shot her a glance. "You didn't approve."

"I never approve of bullying." She added reluctantly, "But I admit the provocation was…extreme."

"Yeah." He was still fingering the ring.

Camille said, "Shouldn't we take that to the police?"

Brodie grimaced. "I reckon we hold on to it until Rogue gets back here with Joe, and the police hear his story. There's a safe at the shop."

The new alarm went off in the night, rousing the two women and sending Brodie, in the shorts he slept in, to peer out one of the front windows. Then he raced to the door and flung it open, slamming it behind him before chasing after a dark shadow that leaped into a waiting car.

The car, unlit, took off with a roar down the street, and in the dim light he couldn't read the license plate. Swearing to himself, he trudged back to the house.

Sienna and Camille, both wearing long T-shirts that bared

half their thighs, were in the lighted hallway. Camille let him in and Sienna was on the phone, talking to the police.

She hung up. "The constable will be right round."

He was, but with no description or number plate he didn't hold out much hope. "Your company seems to have a lot of trouble," he remarked, closing his notebook when he'd taken what meager information they could give.

"Yeah," Brodie said, "and maybe more to come. Rogue's bringing back a suspect with him. They should be here in a few days."

"You people," the constable said disapprovingly, "really mustn't take the law into your own hands. You can't go around detaining people at will."

"He came to us," Brodie explained, "and confessed."

"Confessed to what?" Obviously the policeman's patience was tried.

"Theft, sabotage, conspiracy, witnessing a murder. An accessory after the fact, maybe."

The constable blinked. "A murder?"

His radio crackled and he answered a call, then said, "Right, I'll be there." Putting the radio away, he told them, "There's been a car crash—I have to go. Busy night." Casting a speculative glance at Brodie, he added, "When this… witness arrives we'll see what he has to say."

"We should have told him about the ring," Camille said after he'd left.

Brodie shrugged. "It'll keep."

"I s'pose so." She yawned, and stumbled in the direction of the spare room. "I'm going back to bed."

"I need a drink," Brodie said. "Sienna?"

She hesitated, wide awake now, every nerve on full alert, precluding any chance of sleep. "Yes," she said, and followed him to the kitchen.

"What'll it be?" he asked, rummaging in a cupboard.

She supposed she ought to ask for hot chocolate or a cup of tea. Instead she said, "Baileys. Make it a double."

"Living dangerously." He reached for the Baileys.

"We seem to have been doing that lately."

"Yeah." He poured her drink, and a whiskey for himself, then led the way to the big sofa, and when she'd sat down handed her glass over and seated himself a foot away.

Sienna took a mouthful of the creamy liquid, savoring the sharp underlying tang. "You're used to it." He quirked his eyebrows at her, and she said, "Living dangerously."

"Right," he conceded. "There's a high attrition rate in diving. Only about ten percent of divers who start out in the business stick to it. Unlucky and careless ones die."

Sienna watched him take a slug of whiskey. Every movement he made emphasized his coiled strength, the command he had over his body. The light he'd switched on gleamed on the tanned skin of his chest and arms. His long, powerful legs were spread before him. He was beautiful, a perfectly formed male. No wonder she had trouble keeping her eyes from him, controlling the disturbing sensation, hot and electric, that coursed through her.

With surprise she noted her glass was already half empty, and she was feeling almost relaxed. Wonderful what a little alcohol could do in the right circumstances. "So," she said, leaning back beside Brodie and turning her head to look at him, "what's this spell that makes you go back?" If she could keep him talking, the overwhelming urge to touch him might be kept at bay.

He turned too, looking at her. She could see the dark rings around the irises of his eyes, and the incipient beard on his chin. "Just being down there," he said. "It's so different, so…rare. Plus all the interesting places I've worked, the people I've met—especially the divers, guys I know I can trust with my life. The sea's unforgiving. Knowing we need one another to survive builds a special kind of comradeship."

A shadow passed over his face, and he drank some more of his whiskey, then hunched forward and stared into his glass. "That's why it's hard to stomach that Joe would let us down. We'd worked with the guy…thought we knew him."

Without thinking, Sienna put her hand on his bare shoulder,

stroking down to his arm, a gesture of comfort. She felt a
ripple of something pass over his skin beneath her palm. He
went very, very still, and she knew she should move her hand
away, but some compulsion of her own kept it there. She
wanted to keep touching him, and no longer for comfort.
Something else—elemental, urgent—washed over her like a
hot tide.

Brodie straightened suddenly and her hand fell. His head
turned, his eyes searching her face, and she knew what he
saw there but was powerless to look away. His voice low and
almost soundless, he said, "Sienna?"

He was only inches from her. Her lips parted and she knew
she should say something—anything—to break the moment.

"Sienna," he said. His gaze dropped to her mouth, and he
closed the agonizing gap and pressed his lips to hers.

Her head resting on the sofa back, she met his kiss at first
tentatively, a small voice in her mind saying, *What are you
doing? Are you mad?* But the nagging warning was dispelled
by the magic of his mouth and she gave herself up to it.

Brodie seemed to have all the time in the world to coax
and tempt, tease and persuade. The kiss was a revelation, long
and leisurely and relentlessly, marvelously sexy. Only their
mouths were touching, yet she'd never felt such intimacy with
a man, as if he knew both her fear and her desire and was
willing to confine himself to exploring nothing more than her
mouth, until he knew it so thoroughly she could scarcely tell
where she left off and he began.

He drew back, leaving her dazed, and his thumb stroked
over her mouth, that felt full and tingling. He gave her a
crooked little grin, his eyes brilliant and very blue. Turning,
he put his whiskey glass on the floor by the sofa and then
gently removed her glass from her unresisting fingers, stoop-
ing to place it out of the way too.

Quite slowly he put an arm about her and drew her close,
holding her eyes with his. His big hand cradled her nape, a
thumb stroking her cheek. He seemed to be trying to read her

face. "Sienna," he said, a sudden doubt in his voice, "you're not drunk, are you?"

She smiled. "No." A lie—she was drunk with his kiss, with the scent of him, subtle and warm and male and wonderfully familiar, with the fact that he was almost naked and his magnificent chest was pressed against her breasts, separated only by a layer of cotton. Yielding to temptation, she touched him again, laying her hand on his arm, moving it to his shoulder, feeling the muscles tense.

He said something short and inaudible, and then his mouth was on hers again, seeking, finding, giving pleasure and taking what pleasure she gave in return.

She ran her fingers down his back and he made a throaty, inarticulate sound and returned the compliment, his hand cupping her behind as he bore her down on the wide sofa, their legs tangling together. He held her close—so close she could feel what this was doing to him, and her heart leaped and thudded with a kind of savage joy.

His lips left hers and through the cotton of her shirt he found her breast, closed his mouth over the center, making her shudder with a renewed wave of singing sensation.

He pushed the shirt up, his hands slightly rough on her thighs, and then with both hands on her breasts, he flicked his tongue into her navel.

She had never known, until the night at the beach at Parakaeo, that this was an erogenous zone. But with Brodie, every part of her seemed to be one. She burned all over with need, with passion. And so fast…

Brodie lifted his head, his teeth set in a feral smile. "I've wanted to do that again ever since the first time. I remember the little sound you made."

"You do?" She hadn't been aware of it. Her voice was slurred, her mind dimmed, but her body had never been so alive, so sensitive to every slightest touch, like the light brush of his thumb caressing her now under the shirt, until he slid it up farther and she lifted her arms to help him remove it.

She wore only the tiniest scrap of lace now. He smoothed

a hand along her thigh, over her hip, dipped his thumb for an instant into the hollow of her navel, and laid his palm over her breast. She reached up to bring him down to her again, but he shook his head. "Time we found a bed," he said. "Mine's available."

"No," she protested. She didn't want to move, didn't want to interrupt this lovely progression of feeling that swamped everything else, every doubt and rational thought.

He bent and dropped a quick kiss on her lips. "Yes," he said. "I don't have anything with me, hon. We need to go to my room, where I keep my supplies."

She ought to be grateful. He was being considerate and far more sensible than she had been. She watched him sit up and pass her shirt to her, but when he tried to take her hand she clutched the shirt over her bared breasts and swung her feet to the floor, closing her eyes tightly.

"What's the matter?" Brodie asked quietly. "Sienna?"

Her thoughts were chaotic, at war with her body that still yearned for him, heated and ultraresponsive with new awareness and yet lethargic, wanting to stretch out like a cat in the sun and be stroked and petted.

But in her mind she was appalled and angry and humiliated and guilty all at once.

The anger, she knew, wasn't reasonable. Confusedly, she knew it was rooted in her own chagrin at her lack of control. He could still keep a cool head when she'd been so carried away by...lust, she told herself cruelly, that the necessary precautions hadn't figured at all. But the guilt—that was deserved.

It wasn't fair to back out now. She opened her eyes. She'd go through with this. And deal with the aftermath later. She *wanted* to, wanted Brodie with a fierce longing.

Already they'd made love once, and the memory haunted her dreams, so that she woke unsatisfied and craving more. Why not take it now—a second time would make little difference, but give her one more memory to cherish.

Brodie was on his haunches before her, his expression troubled. "What's the problem?"

"No problem," she whispered. "Kiss me, Brodie." Surely that would help her recapture the headlong abandon that had possessed her only moments before.

He didn't move for a second or two. Then he lifted a hand to her face, laid it along her cheek. His eyes searched hers before he leaned forward and kissed her, but not as she expected. It was soft and light and almost sexless. Then he moved his mouth away and said, "Only if you really want to."

"I want to." But her voice sounded thin and indecisive. She bit her lip. "It will be all right."

He took his hand from her and rubbed it over his face, giving a short, harsh laugh. When he looked at her again his expression was rueful. "I think you've lost the mood. Pity." He stood up. "Maybe it was the Baileys talking after all. Do you want to finish it up?" He stooped, picked up both glasses and offered hers back to her.

Sienna shook her head, torn between relief and a sharp regret. Apparently she wasn't the only one who'd lost the mood.

He tipped his whiskey glass to his lips and downed the inch of liquid left in it. Lowering the glass, he said, "You'd better put that shirt back on. You're shivering."

She was—not with cold but some sort of nervous reaction. She pulled the shirt over her head and said, "I'm sorry."

He was regarding his empty glass, apparently having averted his eyes while she dressed. A bit pointless, she thought, remembering how they'd devoured her with frank, pleased appraisal when he'd pulled the garment off. "Me too," he told her. "But when I take a woman to my bed I like to be sure it's where she wants to be. What were you doing?" he asked curiously. "Setting yourself some kind of test?"

Her gaze flew to his face. "No! I just…it just seemed a good idea at the time."

"An idea you soon regretted."

She lifted a shoulder. "Sort of." The fever that had temporarily swept away all doubt, all resolution and any shred of self-preservation was rapidly receding. "I got a bit carried away. You're a very attractive man." She wasn't telling him anything he didn't know, she reflected bitterly. "And last time was...good."

That remark about taking a woman to bed, implying it was a frequent occurrence, had doused the last of her illusory hope. Belatedly she remembered all the reasons that Brodie Stanner was seriously bad news for a woman like herself. A woman who craved exclusivity, commitment, permanence in a relationship. And who knew perfectly well that she wouldn't find any of that with him.

She'd been through all this in her teens, sorted herself out and made sensible resolutions about not giving away her heart to someone who didn't want it, or cheapening her body, wasting emotion on some trivial affair for the sake of slaking a natural instinct.

Would she never stop falling for the wrong kind of man?

Chapter 13

If Camille noticed a certain strain between Sienna and Brodie in the following days, she didn't mention it.

On Thursday Camille was on the computer in the bedroom and Sienna was inspecting a lump of coral that had something in it she thought was a pipe. If it was clay she'd have to be very careful. The local hospital might be persuaded to X-ray it, she supposed. But perhaps it should wait for a specialist restorer.

Brodie had returned from a visit to the shop restless, prowling around the workroom, looking out the window.

Sienna looked up. "Is something wrong?"

"No." Turning from the window, he said, "Remember that guy who came to the *Sea-Rogue* looking for a chance to invest in Treasure Salvors, said he knew Drummond?"

"The man in the dark glasses? Fraser something."

"I think I saw him downtown today."

"Camille says there were lots of inquiries about investing when word got around about a possible treasure."

"And there's a cabin cruiser in the harbor that looks like

the one that was at Parakaeo the night Joe got beaten up.'' Brodie flexed his scarred arm as if it still irritated him, and looked at the artifacts on the table. ''Maybe we shouldn't have brought this stuff here.''

Sienna put aside the coral lump. ''Mr. Big, whoever he is, must realize by now that he doesn't have a hope of getting the gold. Surely he'd have made himself scarce, not followed us to Mokohina. What would be the point? Compared with what he was after, all this is peanuts.''

There was a knock on the door and Brodie went to it.

A man's voice said, ''I'm looking for Sienna Rivers.''

Sienna lifted her head and got up, starting toward the passageway as Brodie growled, ''Who wants her?''

Coming to his side, Sienna said in surprise, ''Aidan—what are you doing here?''

Relief flooded Aidan's face, which was thin and strained. ''Thank…heaven,'' he muttered. He cast a quick glance behind him. ''I was worried about you.''

That was why he'd come all this way? Wary of his motives—she couldn't help being touched by his concern. ''I'm fine,'' she said. ''How are you?'' He looked unwell. She felt a pang of pity. It seemed things had not improved for him.

Brodie asked her, ''Friend of yours?''

''My head of department at Rusden.''

''Oh, yeah.'' He sent an unfriendly gaze to the other man. ''What do you want?''

''I'd like to talk to Sienna,'' Aidan said. ''Privately.''

''Of course,'' she said as Brodie barked, ''Why?''

Sienna sent him a chilly glance and reached forward to take Aidan's arm. ''Come into my workroom.'' She didn't want to take him to the bedroom she shared with Camille, and nowhere else was private.

So it was Brodie's house she was inviting the other man into, but he didn't need to be so rude and unwelcoming.

''Sienna!'' he said peremptorily as she opened the workroom door. ''Is that wise?''

"Aidan allowed me to use the university lab for PTS. I don't see any point in hiding things from him now."

She opened the door and let Aidan in, closing it behind her.

"You found the treasure?" he said, walking over to the table.

"The real treasure isn't here. All the valuable stuff is stored in Auckland."

He swung round. "Where in Auckland?"

"A bank, and some at the museum."

He looked at her containers of water and diluted acid, the opened crate, a couple of smaller boxes beside it, the few things on the table. "So what do you have here?"

"Minor jewelry pieces, buttons, some everyday articles."

"I'd be interested to see them." His eyes burned with some intense emotion, making her uneasy. "May I?"

"I'm not sure—"

"Please!" The weak smile that followed hardly lessened the impression of urgency.

"Aidan," she said, "what's wrong?"

He flushed. "Nothing. I hadn't heard from you, couldn't get hold of you—not even on your cell phone."

It hadn't been any use at sea, and she'd had no reason since returning to switch it on, using Brodie's landline to talk to her mother and chat with a couple of friends. "Why did you want to get hold of me?"

"I was worried—there've been rumors. I warned you not to mix with treasure hunters. You must know, Sienna, I...I feel some concern for you."

She supposed word of the attack on the *Sea-Rogue* had leaked out. Perhaps the divers had talked about their latest adventure.

"Well, now that I'm here," he said, "are you going to show me what you've got? I might not have approved of what you were doing but I confess I'm curious."

What harm could it do? And he might have some useful advice. They went through all the pieces she had and when she asked his opinion on the best method of tackling cleaning and restoration he gave it almost absentmindedly.

"Is that all?" he asked, fingering one of the rings as she began packing things away.

"Are you disappointed? I told you there was nothing of any great value here."

"It's very interesting," he said jerkily. "What sorts of things went into storage?"

"All of the really valuable stuff." Brodie and the Brodericks wouldn't want her to detail it.

"Jewelry? More rings?" He picked another one out and studied it, then replaced it and handed her the box.

"Only a few, with precious stones in them." Sienna busied herself placing the lid on a box and asked casually, "How's your wife, and Pixie?"

She saw his Adam's apple move as he swallowed. "They're…well." He looked around him. "You don't have anything more to show me?"

If he was looking for an excuse to stay longer, it wouldn't wash. "Thank you for coming," she said. "It was kind of you to bother."

He swallowed again. "I'm…glad you're all right."

As she closed the front door behind Aidan, Brodie came from the living area, looking thunderous. "What the hell was that all about?" he asked. "How did he know you were here?"

"He probably asked around town for someone connected with Pacific Treasure." He'd gone to some trouble to find her. "He was worried about me."

"Why?"

Irked at his proprietary assumption that he had a right to ask questions about her visitor, she said, "He'd heard something about the attack on the *Sea-Rogue,* I think. Or maybe he just wondered if I was safe with people like you. I've wondered myself."

Brodie gave a harsh little laugh. "You know you're perfectly safe with me, Sienna.'' Glaring at her meaningfully, he added, ''In every way.''

He'd demonstrated it conclusively, and she flushed at the reminder. ''I have work to finish,'' she said, and returned to her workroom.

Later Brodie went out, and Sienna was relieved. His mood had been uncomfortably ominous and even Camille had looked at him askance.

When the telephone rang while they were having a break for coffee, Sienna went to pick up the receiver in the hall.

It was Aidan.

''I thought you'd left,'' she said. ''Where are you?''

''I'm at the hotel. I thought,'' he said, ''maybe we could have dinner together here tonight? Say yes!'' he added quickly. ''It's important.''

''What's important?'' Obviously something was agitating him. She hesitated. ''Is this personal?''

''No. No, it's to do with—with your work. I can't tell you now,'' he said. ''Can you come to the hotel at seven?''

''All right,'' she said slowly. ''I'll be there.''

Brodie arrived back with a package in his hand while Sienna and Camille were drinking coffee at the dining counter. ''Smoked kingfish tonight,'' he said, putting the package in the refrigerator, ''courtesy of one of my regular customers.''

Sienna put down her coffee cup. ''I'm having dinner with Aidan.''

Brodie swung round, slamming the refrigerator door. ''You're *what?*''

Sienna lifted her head. ''I'm having dinner with—''

''The hell you are!'' Brodie exploded. ''Not if I have anything to do with it.''

Sienna raised her eyebrows, trying to appear cool and in control. ''You *don't* have anything to do with it. And what makes you think you can dictate to me—''

''You're not going out of this house,'' Brodie said flatly. ''Not without me.''

''And leave Camille alone? Rogan would never forgive

you. I don't need a chaperon, Brodie. I'll drive to the hotel and back and keep the car doors locked—it's only five minutes. And I'll be with Aidan while I'm there—I'm sure he'll walk me to my car.''

Brodie snorted. ''Aidan! A bloody academic—what use would he be if anything happened?''

''Nothing's likely to happen! I know you mean well, and Rogan asked you to watch Camille and me, but you're over-doing it. Frankly, I'm tired of being cooped up with a human watchdog. A meal out will be a nice change!''

He looked infuriated. ''Well, this watchdog takes his job seriously. I'm not letting you out of my sight, so live with it, honey.''

Before Sienna, further irritated by the casual, anonymous endearment, could reply, Camille cut in. ''Why don't we all go out for dinner? The alarm can be switched through to the firm that put it in, can't it, in case anyone does try to burgle the house while we're out?''

Brodie turned to her. A slow smile lit his face. ''I like it,'' he said. ''I look forward to seeing Aidan's face when we all turn up for a date with him.''

Sienna made an outraged sound, and Camille gave him a reproving look. ''I didn't mean that. You and I could have dinner together at the Imperial, so you can keep an eye—a *distant* eye—on Sienna without intruding. If that's all right with you, Sienna?''

Reluctantly Sienna said, ''I suppose.'' Glaring again at Bro-die, she said, ''And don't you dare come near us!''

Still grinning, he looked back at her. ''Okay. But I'll be watching every minute.''

Brodie suggested they only needed one car to drive to the hotel, that it was silly for Sienna to travel the short distance separately.

''I don't want to arrive and leave with you escorting me like some Victorian father,'' she said.

''Give me your keys. I'll drive and drop you off, then park

the car, and Camille and I will come in a few minutes after you.''

It was probably the best offer she was going to get.

When she got out of the car at the hotel door, Brodie waited until she'd gone inside and then drove off.

Aidan got up from a chair in the lobby and came to meet her, his smile still holding the strain she'd noticed earlier. ''I've reserved a table for us,'' he said, leading her to the restaurant. It was busy but there were still several empty tables. The hostess ushered Aidan and Sienna to a booth in a corner. Perhaps he'd requested privacy.

They were opening their menus when Brodie and Camille came in and were given a table by the window. Brodie looked around him, caught her eye briefly without altering his expression, then turned his attention to Camille.

Aidan ordered wine, the first glass of which he gulped down before pouring himself a second. Sienna noticed his hand was unsteady. Had he already been drinking today? That wasn't like him.

He spent a long time poring over the menu, yet when the waitress asked for his order he seemed flustered and undecided. ''Oh...fish, I suppose,'' he said finally.

''Fish of the day, sir?''

''Yes, that'll do.''

Sienna asked for the chicken special, and when the waitress left said, ''What did you want to talk about, Aidan?''

He was staring across the room. ''Isn't that Brodie Stanner?''

Of course it was, but she turned her head all the same. Brodie was talking to a waitress who hovered over the table, smiling at him in a besotted way. She'd probably forget what he'd ordered and have to come back and check. Any excuse.

Aidan said, ''What is he, your bodyguard or something?''

Brodie seemed to have assumed the role. Sienna said, ''No, of course not. Camille and I are staying with him for a couple of weeks. There aren't that many places apart from the

Imperial in Mokohina where you can get a good dinner, you know, if they felt like going out.''

Aidan looked suspicious and almost hunted. "Coincidence?''

"Does it matter? They won't bother us.''

"I suppose not.'' He fiddled with the fork at his place, picking it up, putting it down.

Sienna was aware of when the waitress left Brodie and Camille's table. She couldn't stop herself from glancing over at them. Camille was looking out the window at the harbor. Brodie's blue gaze collided with Sienna's. This time he didn't look away, and she had to wrench her attention back to Aidan, who was still looking broodingly down at the table.

She supposed that eventually he'd tell her what was worrying him.

When he looked up he began to talk about the artifacts she'd shown him earlier, in a peculiarly random way. "There were some quite nice rings in that little collection you have,'' he said after their meals were put in front of them and he'd started on his fish, though with no appearance of enjoyment. "I'd have expected to see a mourning ring or two among them. At that period, you know.''

Sienna, about to lift a piece of chicken to her mouth, went suddenly cold. Even her brain seemed to freeze, her fork poised as she stared at the morsel on it, with no idea what it was. She put it down, feeling sick, and raised her eyes to Aidan, seeing him as if he were a total stranger.

His hair was damp at the roots, his forehead glistening. He was sweating, although the restaurant wasn't particularly warm. Still talking, he said quickly, "They were quite popular in Victorian times. You didn't find any?''

"No,'' she said distantly, as though someone else were using her vocal cords. "Not in the ship. Why do you want to know, Aidan?''

He blinked twice, rapidly. "Just…general interest. What do you mean, not in the ship?''

"You know what I mean." Leaning forward, her voice steely now, she repeated, *"Why do you want to know?"*

Aidan blinked again. "Someone…someone I know may be interested in buying it…I mean, one—a mourning ring."

"A particular mourning ring," Sienna suggested very quietly. "A gold ring with a snake frame and a gold urn on black enamel."

"You do have it." He grasped her hand, so hard that it hurt. "Sienna, for your own sake, give it to me!"

Something made her turn her head, an awareness that she was being watched. Across the room Brodie's blue stare was fierce, one hand clenched on a table napkin in front of him. Camille was saying something to him but he seemed to be ignoring her.

Resisting an urge to free herself and run across the room to him, she looked back at Aidan. "Tell me what's going on. How long have you have been working for these people?"

"I'm not—"

"Tell me!"

"I knew this wouldn't work," he moaned. "I told them—"

"Who's *them?*"

"I can't—Sienna, *please!* You'll be safe once they have it. And so will—" He stopped, swallowing hard.

"You?" she suggested with contempt, trying to draw away her hand, but his hold convulsively tightened. Obviously he was scared stiff of whoever these people were. "Did your masters threaten to kill you if you didn't obey them?"

To her dismayed astonishment his eyes glazed with tears. His voice was a hoarse whisper. "You don't understand! If I don't get that ring they'll hurt Pixie!"

"Pixie!" Her stomach hollowed. They'd threatened to harm his *child?*

Instinctively she put her free hand over his. "Aidan, you have to go to the police—they can protect her."

"It's too late for that. I'm in too deep—being watched—

they'd know, and then… I can't risk it. I'm begging you, Sienna. For my baby girl."

Brodie watched in outraged disbelief as the tête-à-tête in the booth seemed to get more and more intimate. First Sienna had leaned over the table, fixed her gorgeous eyes on this Aidan character and said something earnestly intense to him, and then he took her hand, making Brodie prickle all over with hostility, and mash the napkin in his hand into a creased, sorry mess. It also made his recent wound sting, further exacerbating his temper.

The conversation got real concentrated after that, until Sienna put her hand over Aidan's and Brodie could scarcely stop himself from jumping up, marching over there and demanding to know what the hell was going on between them.

Only Camille's cool voice restrained him.

"What?" he said, forcing himself to turn away from the tableau in the booth. "Sorry, Camille."

She glanced toward where Sienna was, and when she looked back at him, sympathetic amusement lurked in her green eyes. "I said, is your steak all right? I've never known you to not finish a meal before."

He looked down at his plate, half his carpetbag steak and an untouched baked potato lying neglected in the middle. Camille's was empty. He picked up his knife and attacked the meat. "It's fine," he grunted.

Camille said, "Aidan's married."

"Is that so?" Brodie didn't lift his eyes from his plate. The smarmy sod wasn't acting married. Shoving a piece of steak into his mouth, he chewed it viciously, unable to resist another quick look at the couple in the booth. Their heads were close together, but he was relieved to see they were no longer holding hands. Both their meals were practically untouched, though. Irritably he swallowed, and sawed off another piece of steak. It was thick and juicy and the oysters inside were fat and luscious-looking. But his taste buds for some reason had gone on strike. Everything seemed dry and bitter.

He got through it all and shoved away his plate. "Do you want dessert?" he asked Camille.

"Not for me. You have some."

He shook his head, and when the waitress came back ordered coffee for two. A quick look showed him Sienna's plate being taken away still half-full. Soon afterward she and Aidan were served coffee too. They were still talking. With a lift of his heart he thought they were arguing—Sienna looked quite fierce and the bloke wasn't too happy. "Maybe it's a big breakup scene. He's going back to the wife who doesn't understand him."

He scarcely realized he'd spoken the thought aloud until Camille said, "Sienna wouldn't have anything to do with a married man."

It was some comfort. If she'd never forgiven her father, she'd hardly be likely to follow his example.

Brodie wasn't married. So that theory didn't explain why she was so determined to keep him at arm's length.

When he saw Sienna slide from her seat he put down his coffee cup and said, "You ready to go?"

Camille nodded and got up. They were outside the door by the time Sienna joined them.

Back at the house Camille said good-night, but Sienna hesitated, slowly removing the jacket she wore over a short-sleeved shirt and dress jeans. Brodie took her arm and drew her into the living room. "A nightcap?" he suggested.

Her upward glance told him she remembered the last time they'd shared one. "No," she said. "Thanks."

He went to the kitchen and poured one for himself while she stood in the middle of the room, seeming undecided about something. With the counter still between them he took a sip of whiskey. "That was a pretty intense conversation you were having with whatsisname," he said.

She looked up, appearing to have difficulty focusing on him. "Aidan has...problems."

"Yeah?" Brodie wasn't really interested in Aidan's problems unless they affected Sienna. "You were lending a sympathetic ear." He winced inwardly at the unintended sneer in his tone.

Sienna didn't seem to have noticed. "Brodie…" She turned to face him properly. "Could you get me that mourning ring?"

For a moment he didn't connect, the change of subject was so complete. Then it clicked. "Drummond's ring? What the hell for?"

She threw her jacket down on the sofa and walked over to stand at the other side of the low counter. "I need it," she said tensely. "It's important."

"It's evidence. Once Rogan gets here with Joe—which should be in a day or two—"

"I know." She looked down at the counter, clasped her hands tightly together. "It's…it may be a matter of life and death."

Brodie's brain went into overdrive. This had come out of her date with Aidan. What the hell did her department head, with whom she seemed to be on intimate terms, have to do with Drummond's murder?

Gradually a series of unrelated facts started to coalesce, making some kind of pattern. The artifacts stolen from the laboratory at Rusden, where Aidan had necessarily been let in on the secret of their origin by Sienna. Drummond's antiquities-smuggling trade, his connection with the mystery man who had hired Joe—and murdered Drummond. And now Aidan turning up out of the blue and Sienna demanding the ring that would identify the killer's victim.

The pattern was incomplete—pieces missing, the shape amorphous—but it was there. "A matter of life and death?" he repeated, putting down the glass in his hand with a small thud. "Yours or your precious Aidan's?"

Sienna blinked at him. "He's not my precious Aidan."

"Then why the hell are you trying to save his skin?" Brodie demanded ferociously. He came round the counter and gripped her shoulders, giving her a furious, unblinking stare, ignoring her efforts to free herself. "That's what this is about, isn't it? Is he our Mr. X?"

"*What?*" She stopped struggling to gape at him in obvious, unfeigned astonishment. "No! Aidan's not a murderer! He's just—"

"Just what?" Brodie said between his teeth.

"He's caught up in something that's gone beyond his control. I can't tell you everything—I promised. But I made *him* promise to go to the police when—when it's safe."

"Safe?" His scowl was petrifying. "What's going to make him safe?"

"Brodie, please! Just give me the ring."

"And no questions asked? I don't think so, hon. My guess is it will conveniently disappear, and then the killer—presumably the same guy who was trying to wipe us out with a submachine gun, or his boss—will be free to kill again."

Sienna bit her lip. "I tried telling Aidan all that, but—"

"Then why," Brodie grated, giving her a small shake out of sheer frustration and anger, "are you protecting him?"

"Not him," Sienna cried. "His daughter!"

"His…daughter?" Brodie's hold slackened and Sienna wrenched herself free.

"He has a little girl," she said. "Six years old. They told Aidan that if he doesn't get the ring…he'd wish she'd never been born."

Brodie stared at her, his stomach churning, his anger turning to cold fury and disgust. "My God! They really are the scum of the earth."

"He's terrified that if he goes to the police they'll carry out their threat."

"How the hell did he get into this in the first place?"

"I promised—"

"You might as well tell me the rest."

Sienna looked at his implacable expression and reluctantly said, "Aidan was being blackmailed. Years ago, before he got his present appointment at the university, he took some Maori adzes and ornaments from an archaeological site he was working on and sold them to a dealer. At the time he was very short of money, with a new baby and his wife to support—she's a rather...well, demanding sort of woman, his wife.''

"So he's a crook." Brodie's lips curled.

"He thought he'd get away with it once. Then the dealer insisted on more. Of course if anyone had found out Aidan would have lost his job and never got another in his field. And probably his wife would have left him, taking Pixie with her.''

"Pixie?"

"That's what he calls his daughter. He adores her.''

"This dealer was Drummond?" Brodie guessed.

"No. But you know how small this country is. Everyone knows someone who knows someone... I suppose James Drummond sniffed around his contacts in the illegal trade and found out that Aidan was vulnerable to pressure, so he or someone working for him—apparently it was done by phone—persuaded Aidan to make sure I was out of the way while they burgled the laboratory.''

Brodie's eyebrows drew together. "Out of the way?"

"I was spending too much time there, working on the wreck artifacts. He put something in my coffee at work.''

Brodie swore violently. "Camille said you'd had food poisoning.''

Sienna recoiled slightly, and gave a faint, twisted smile. "It wasn't meant to kill me, just keep me home for a night or two.'' With a flash of anger she added, "He seems to think he did me a favor, maybe saved me from being knocked on the head. The thieves got the goods, but their principal wanted the notes too.''

"Proof, if you had any, that the source of the artifacts was the *Maiden's Prayer*—the gold-ship. I suppose access to the treasure was his price for helping Drummond skip the country. But once Drummond had taken his friend to the wreck site he was dispensable. So Mr. X killed Drummond and threw him overboard.'' Brodie took a breath. ''And your Aidan was aiding and abetting those bastards.''

''While I was in hospital Aidan tried to find the notes. Only they were on a disk and I'd asked Camille to keep it safe until I was better. I thought when he visited so often he was being a good friend.'' She paused there. ''It must have been frustrating for him—if he ever got the chance to look in my bag he didn't find anything.''

''So then they went after you.''

''He didn't know about any of that. Or what happened on the way here. He's not one of them, Brodie. He broke the law and he's been very stupid, but none of that is Pixie's fault.''

''It's the ring Mr. X is after now,'' Brodie said. ''Because it identifies his victim. And he thought you had it, or could get it? Joe must have told him I'd handed it over to you when I found it. That's why Mr. X sent Aidan.'' He snapped his fingers. ''Aidan—*he* must know who this guy is!''

Sienna shook her head. ''Aidan swears it was all done by phone.''

Something teased at Brodie. He recalled Rogan looking down at a business card in his hand. ''That guy who wanted to invest, he was in shipping. Fraser...Cooper? Con...Conran!''

''Aren't you jumping to conclusions?''

''He arrived just as you were showing me your dive fitness certificate. I wonder...''

''What?''

''If he thought it was notes about the *Maiden's Prayer?*''

''That's a bit of a leap of logic.''

''It's possible. They'd drawn a blank with your luggage, and why wouldn't you have been sharing your findings with us once you got to the *Sea-Rogue?*''

''Camille and I put them on the computer.''

''There was no way he could know that.''

''The thing is,'' Sienna reminded him impatiently, ''what are we going to do about Pixie?''

''I'm not letting you give that ring to Aidan.''

"Brodie! She's a *child*. A child in danger—you can't let them hurt her!"

"I won't. And I won't let them hurt you, either," he said forcefully. "She's not the only one in danger. Does Aidan know where the ring is?"

Sienna shook her head. "He knows it's not with the other things in my workroom." She bit her lip. "I...suppose I sort of let slip that it's not with the things we stored in Auckland, either."

Brodie didn't comment on that, though his eyes briefly flared. "So...he'd probably guess that we've got it somewhere here—or that we've handed it to the police. That'd make him sweat a bit."

"I should have told Aidan that's what we'd done!" Sienna exclaimed. "That would have let him off the hook."

"Not necessarily. There's no guarantee Mr. X would believe it. Okay, let's see if we can persuade this scumbag to come out of the woodwork and show his stinkin' face."

Chapter 14

On Friday morning Brodie took the mourning ring from the safe at the shop and looked at it closely—the coiled snake around the enameled center, the exquisitely pictured urn.

He tried it on the middle finger of his right hand. It wouldn't fit, and instead he slipped it on the third finger, pushing it down past the knuckle until it was firm.

Then he went to the hotel and asked that Aidan Rutherford be told he had a visitor.

The desk clerk put down the phone and said, "Mr. Rutherford will be right down, sir."

It was a few minutes before Aidan appeared, looking apprehensive, then surprised, then worried. "What are you doing here?" he blurted out.

"Were you expecting someone else?" Brodie asked.

Aidan shook his head uncertainly. "Is Sienna…is she all right?"

"*What the hell do you care?*" Brodie snarled. He couldn't help it, despite an earlier resolution that he'd conduct himself civilly with this pathetic excuse for a man. The guy had poi-

soned Sienna, lied to her, put her in danger, and now expected
her to pull him out of the hole he'd dug for himself and his
family by handing over vital evidence—making herself, Brodie supposed, an accessory to murder.

Aidan blinked, paled, and a nerve twitched under one eye.
"I care very much for Sienna," he said, drawing himself up
in an attempt at dignity. "I...would hate any harm to come
to her."

But he'd sacrifice her in an instant for his daughter. Brodie
supposed grudgingly that he couldn't be blamed for that—but
he was completely culpable for all that had gone before, leading up to this point. "Can we talk in your room?" he suggested grimly.

Aidan seemed to measure his size, and not be reassured by
it. He cast a nervous look around them, and Brodie lifted his
right hand briefly to rub at his chin.

Aidan's eyes became riveted on Brodie's fingers and he
went an even whiter shade of pale. Almost inaudibly, he said,
"You'd better come upstairs."

When Brodie returned to the house he still wore the ring.
Sienna, having coffee with Camille, noticed it immediately
and threw him an accusing glance.

He helped himself to coffee and sat down opposite them.
Camille exclaimed, "Brodie! What are you doing with that
ring?"

"Showing *to whom it may concern* that Sienna doesn't
have it," he replied.

Sienna slowly put her cup down, a simmering anger building.

Brodie continued calmly, "I hope it will bring our Mr. X
out in the open."

Sienna's heart plunged in fear. Trying not to screech at him,
she said with ominous calm, "You're setting yourself up as
a target—to protect me?"

Brodie shrugged. He looked infuriatingly relaxed and confident, a man in charge of his own fate—and hers.

Sienna pushed back her chair and stood up. "How dare you!" she said, her voice shaking with rage.

"What?" She had the satisfaction of seeing his smug self-confidence waver into wary surprise.

"You walked out this morning without telling me a thing except that I was to *stay put* and trust you! And now you're turning yourself into a walking target. What are you going to do, wave that ring around until someone jumps you like they did Joe and beats you to a pulp—or worse?"

"I won't let them do that."

"Oh, no, of course not!" Sienna tossed at him. "You're the big, tough, macho hero who's going to grind the baddies into the dust! I thought you'd given up on being invincible. Have you forgotten how you got that scar on your arm?"

He looked at her reproachfully. "I wish you'd stop harping on that. This time I'm prepared."

"And I wish *you* would stop treating like me like a child!" Reminded, she added, "How is this supposed to help Pixie?"

Camille, who'd been interestedly looking from one to the other of them, said, "Pixie? Who's—you mean Aidan's little girl?"

"Yes," Sienna confirmed, and quickly explained.

Camille's expression changed from bewilderment to horror. "Surely they wouldn't really—"

"They might," Sienna said. "And it's too big a risk to take. Aidan certainly believes them." She turned to Brodie again. "For God's sake—for *Pixie's* sake—cut out the heroics and just let Aidan hand over the damned ring!"

"That would nix the chance of nailing this guy for murder," Brodie pointed out. "And then he'd be free to kill again—maybe some other innocent child."

But *this* child was in clear and present danger. Before she could point that out he said, "It's okay, Sienna. The kid and her mother are safe. There's a plainclothes policewoman in the house posing as a visiting friend, and the cops have it under surveillance. At the first sign of trouble they'll be in there."

Sienna digested that. "You contacted the police? Does Aidan know that?"

"No. There's a chance he might do something stupid and tip off the crooks. He's told the guy I've got the ring."

Her fear and anger rising again, Sienna said, "I suppose that was your idea? Are you trying to get yourself killed?"

He slanted her a grin. "Nice to know you worry about me."

She was torn between a desire to slap the self-satisfied smirk from his face and a contradictory one to fling herself on him with a mad idea of protecting him from the harm he was inviting. "Someone has to," she retorted. "You've been so gung ho about looking after *my* safety, it might as well be me."

He grinned wider at her bitter tone, then unexpectedly reached across the counter between them and grasped her shoulders, giving her a quick, hard kiss on her mouth. "Thank you, hon."

Annoyed to find she was blushing under Camille's delighted stare, she scrubbed at her mouth with the back of her hand. "I'm not your *hon!* I've got a name."

His eyebrows rose at that. "Sien-na," he crooned. "It's a beautiful name. Like its owner. Even when she's cross with me."

"Oh, shut up! You patronizing, male chauvinist...*idiot!*"

He laughed as she stuttered into frustrated silence and simply glared at him.

The laughter died and he looked at his watch. "I have to go."

"Where?" she demanded. "Are you planning to stand in the middle of town and wave the ring until Mr. X notices?"

"I'm going to the shop. In my four-wheel drive so no one can jump me on the way. And when I get there my new assistant will be waiting for me."

"What new assistant?"

"A detective from Whangarei. The Mokohina cop got on to them early this morning. Don't you worry your purty li'l head, Miz Scarlett—everything's taken care of. You just sit tight, don't let anyone in, and wait until it's all over.''

Torn between relief, annoyance at his deliberate provocation and continuing anxiety, Sienna made an inarticulate sound of frustration.

She tried to work, to blot out what Brodie was up to. He had left the house in his big vehicle with an ostentatious roar of the engine and a couple of toots of the horn. Making sure, she supposed, that anyone who might happen to be watching knew he'd gone. He even waved his right hand out of the driver's window, so that the sun glinted momentarily on the ring. Did he know she was standing in the living area, watching his departure and praying? Or was the gesture meant to reinforce to any hidden watcher the fact that the damning ring was no longer in the house—and ensure Sienna's and Camille's safety?

About an hour after he'd left she was scraping coral with a dental tool from what might be a group of silver coins.

The telephone shrilled, and Camille said, "I'll get it. It could be Rogan. The *Sea-Rogue* should be in range of the phone system anytime now."

She came back, saying, "It's for you, Sienna. Aidan?"

Camille was right. And he sounded agitated, his voice low and hurried. "Sienna, I need you," he said. "Can you come to the hotel?"

"Why?"

"Something's happened." His voice rose briefly, then sank again to almost a whisper. "I need you. Please, Sienna. You've got to come."

"Aidan—"

"I can't explain on the phone," he said rapidly. "Sienna—I'm begging you, for Pixie's sake. And your friend Brodie's."

"Brodie?" Her voice sharpened. Was Brodie in trouble?

"Come *now!* And don't tell anyone."

The phone went down in her ear, and she lifted the receiver

away, stared at it, then dialed the number of Brodie's shop. Engaged. Slowly she replaced the receiver.

"What's up?" Camille asked.

"He wants me to go to the hotel."

"Brodie said not to leave the house."

"I know what Brodie said!" His high-handed command still rankled, no matter how sensible it was. And now her anger was mixed with a renewed anxiety for him. "Aidan said something's wrong, and not to tell anyone."

Camille said, "You're not going?"

Sienna chewed her lip. "Aidan sounded so urgent."

"Phone the police."

She dialed the number of the police station, and got an answer machine advising her to dial 111 for an emergency, or the Whangarei office for other business. She didn't suppose this would be classed as an emergency, and Whangarei was over an hour's drive away. Besides, according to Brodie they already had officers in Mokohina waiting for someone to try taking the ring from him.

"There's no one there," she said, putting down the phone.

"Try the dive shop," Camille suggested.

"I did." But she tried again. The number was still engaged. Could Brodie have slipped away without his police protection, got himself into trouble somehow? He was so damned gung ho, thinking he could outwit a master criminal who already had blood on his hands. "Do you know his cell phone number?"

Camille shook her head.

Sienna decided. "I'm going."

"Sienna…"

She was already on her way to the bedroom, picking up a jacket, and as an afterthought her cell phone, dropping it into the jacket pocket.

Camille had followed her. "Sienna, do you really think you should? If anything happens to you—"

"It's broad daylight, and there are plenty of people around

in the street and at the hotel. And I'm not the one in danger now. Brodie's wearing the ring.''

"I'll come with you," Camille said.

"No. Keep trying to reach the dive shop. And if you get hold of Brodie or the police tell them where I am."

If Brodie was in danger because of her, she wasn't going to just sit around and do nothing.

Camille looked dubious. "All right. Be careful."

On her way to the door, Sienna paused at her workroom, then walked in and picked up a smallish brown bottle. She slipped it into the other pocket of her jacket, then hurried out to her car.

At the hotel she was sent straight up to Aidan's room. Before knocking she pulled out her phone and dialed the number of Brodie's house. Engaged. She hoped Camille had got hold of someone. She dropped the phone back into her pocket, knocked, and Aidan opened the door looking as if he'd had no sleep, hadn't even shaved this morning. He quickly pulled her inside, closing the door immediately and locking it.

"Sienna," he said, "I'm sorry."

So was she. Even before he turned away from the door she'd seen the man sitting at a table near the window, seeming completely at ease, one ankle propped on his other knee, a pair of almost colorless eyes, like a wintry morning, surveying her, and a quite small but lethal-looking silver gun held casually in his hand.

If she screamed, surely someone would hear. But would the man panic and try to shoot his way out of trouble? She'd be first in the line of fire, then Aidan.

Though the man didn't look the type to panic easily. He wore an open-necked gray shirt under a darker gray suit, very respectable-looking. A pair of wraparound sunglasses lay on the table beside him. His hair was brown, slicked back from a smooth, expressionless face that, except for the cold, light eyes, had nothing memorable about it. Mr. Average.

"Mr. Conran," she said.

She made to put her hands in her jacket pockets and he said quietly, "Don't move, sweetheart."

This was ridiculous. The hotel wasn't busy at this time of the year—the long corridor had been empty with several room doors wide open, showing the lack of occupants—but there must be people about.

"What do you want?" she said. There had to be a reason for him to have forced Aidan to summon her here.

"The pleasure of your company," he mocked. "Sit down." Indicating a chair at the other side of the small table. "I want you to do something for me."

"No," she said instantly.

Conran smiled. It made her inwardly shiver. "What a brave girl." His tone changing to a peremptory command, he raised the gun and said, "Sit down."

"If you fire that thing people will come running," she pointed out. "They'll call the police, and the armed offenders' squad will surround the place."

Conran's eyelids flickered in faint surprise. "They're miles away in Whangarei. By the time they got here I'd be long gone, believe me."

She supposed he had an escape plan ready. But it seemed he didn't know there was already a larger than usual police presence in Mokohina. She hoped they were armed. Anything she knew that he didn't might give her an edge.

Conran sighed and reached a hand into his jacket pocket, bringing out something that looked like a short length of pipe that he proceeded to attach to the barrel of the pistol. "Haven't you ever heard of a silencer?" he asked. "Miss Know-it-all. Now for the third time—and my patience is getting short—*sit down!*"

Her heart going into overdrive, she walked forward slowly and took the chair. Aidan, as if afraid to attract any attention to himself, stood rock-still where he was.

There was a telephone book on the table, open at the Yellow Pages, and a phone. Conran turned the book toward her.

She looked down and saw a half-page ad for Brodie's dive shop, with the number in large bold print.

''Phone your friend,'' Conran said, ''and tell him you want him here.'' His perfect teeth showed in a crocodile smile. ''Maybe he'll think he's in for a good time.''

Sienna lifted her eyes from the page. ''No.''

He sighed again. ''Don't be difficult, darling.''

''I'm not your darling!'' she flashed at him. ''Or your sweetheart.''

He leaned over the table and grabbed at her chin, his fingers cruelly digging into her cheeks. ''You're anything I want you to be,'' he said, quite softly. ''Anything, understand? As long as I hold this.'' He lifted the gun and pressed the end of the silencer against her forehead.

Sienna reminded herself that he wanted something from her. He wouldn't give up that easily, just shoot her and be done with it. She dared to lift a hand and push the gun aside. ''Do you need that to make you feel like a real man?''

He released her chin and slapped her hard, making her ears ring, her skin sting fiercely. Aidan made a sound of protest and started forward, but Conran swung the gun in his direction and said, ''Stay there!''

Aidan stopped, with a glance of hopeless apology at Sienna. She had to clench her hands to stop herself raising one to her smarting cheek.

''Phone him,'' Conran said, looking at Sienna again.

''No.'' She looked back at him defiantly.

For a moment disbelief brought a spark of humanity to his eyes, then unexpectedly he laughed almost tolerantly. He turned to Aidan. ''You do it,'' he said, and got up from his chair, coming to stand behind Sienna. ''Go on.''

Aidan approached hesitantly. Conran tugged at Sienna's hair, painfully, forcing her head back until her neck ached. ''Dial,'' he said to Aidan. ''Tell Stanner his girlfriend's here and wants to see him.''

''He won't come,'' Sienna said, her voice strained. ''I'm not his girlfriend.''

"The phone's engaged," Aidan said.

Sienna hoped Camille had got through and was telling Brodie and the policeman where she'd gone. Conran swore and released her. "Try again," he ordered.

On the third try Aidan said, "Brodie Stanner? I have a—a message for you." He looked at Conran, his eyes dilated with fear. "Sienna's here—at the Imperial. She…she needs you. You'd better come."

There was a pause, and then Aidan said, "No, it's true—she's really here." He covered the receiver. "He wants to talk to her."

Sienna shook her head.

"Put the receiver near her," Conran said, and as Aidan held it to her, suddenly her arm was grabbed from behind and twisted viciously up her back. The pain was unexpected and agonizing, and she was unable to stifle a cry of protest. She heard the sound of Brodie's raised voice saying her name, and screamed, *"No, Brodie!"*

Then her head exploded and she thought, *This is how it feels to die,* before everything turned to blackness.

There were voices somewhere far away. They became louder. Her head hurt, and something trickled along her cheek. She seemed to be lying at an odd angle, with her head on a table. Right in front of her eyes she could see a telephone and an open telephone book.

She blinked. Brodie. One of the voices was Brodie's. *"I'll track you down,"* he was saying in a voice like a tiger's snarl, "and make you pay for this."

Someone laughed, sending a shiver of fear down her spine. *Danger*—the man who'd laughed was dangerous. She blinked her eyes, willing herself to full, alert consciousness. Her brain felt woolly, but she lay still. *Don't let him know you're awake.*

He was a few feet away with his back to her. She could see Brodie now, and Aidan, both partially obscured by Conran. By the way he was standing Conran still held the gun. He'd laughed because obviously he intended to kill them all once he'd got the ring from Brodie. He thought Joe was dead, and knew that Brodie had taken the ring from Drummond's skeleton. Once they were both gone and he disposed of the ring there'd be nothing to connect him to Drummond's murder—unless someone could locate the skeleton again and identify it.

It must have made him anxious if he'd seen—or Aidan had told him—that Brodie was flaunting the ring in public.

Sienna and Aidan too were expendable—Aidan had failed in his mission but had been useful to lure her here as bait. Conran must have been desperate, to have taken over the job himself. And now they knew who he was, he'd have to get rid of all three of them.

Damn Brodie, with his determination to protect her—why hadn't he let the police do the job instead of riding in like Zorro to rescue her, putting himself in danger? Where *were* the police? How could they let him *do* this?

Her hands lay in her lap. Very slowly she began to move one to the pocket that held the brown bottle. Brodie was saying, "You've forgotten something."

"I don't think so," Conran answered. "Give me the ring."

Sienna's fingers closed on the bottle. Her head moved slightly and she shut her eyes momentarily against a blinding pain. Inch by inch she drew the bottle out of her pocket. Conran said, "Give me the bloody ring! How did you find it, anyway?"

"Luck," Brodie said. "Sheer dumb luck—the day yours ran out."

If she swiveled her eyes she could just see Brodie's face, his eyes fixed on Conran, lit with a deep, piercing rage. As if he'd felt her looking at him, he moved his gaze momentarily, and she saw a quickly doused flare of some emotion before his face closed down to a wooden mask and he wrenched the ring off his finger and handed it over. "And I found something else. Something that could put you in jail where you belong. The bullet."

There was a strangely still little silence before Conran spoke again. "What bullet?"

"The one you put into Drummond's head. It was still there when I found his bones."

"Joe never said anything about any bullet! You're making this up."

"Nope. Think about it. Did you see any exit wound when you dumped Drummond's body overboard? I'm telling you, the bullet was still in the skull. The police were *very* interested."

"No." Conran was shaking his head. "Why would you take it to the police?"

"Why wouldn't I? Unlike you, I have no reason to fear the law. I thought they'd like to know about a murder. And in fact—" Brodie's voice hardened "—this place is surrounded by armed police right now."

"Don't make me laugh."

"It's true. They're out there, just waiting for you to make a move. Give it up, Conran. If you hire a good lawyer you might get away with killing Drummond, but you'll never get away with shooting us. You've gotten too clever for your own good. Or too nervous."

After a moment Conran laughed. "Good try," he sneered. "You haven't had time to get the police here."

"Wrong. They've been here for hours. And at Rusden. If your threat to this guy's daughter ever was real, the cops there would all be ready to nab your hired thugs the minute they make a move."

"You told them…" Conran swung the gun toward Aidan, who stepped back, looking terrified. "You stupid—"

"It wasn't me!" he said.

Brodie cut in. "If you don't believe me, look out the window. They're probably all in position by now. But be careful you don't get shot by a police marksman."

This time the silence seemed to stretch forever.

Then Conran took a step back, and another. "Don't move a muscle," he warned.

He bumped against the table, and Sienna's stomach lurched. Her hand was on the screw cap of the bottle, very carefully removing it. She closed her eyes, then slitted them open.

Conran had moved to the other side of the table, backing against the wall beside the window. He still held the gun pointed at the two men. He turned his head, took a quick look. "I don't see anything. You're lying."

"Look again. I tell you, they're out there."

"You're bluffing. Wasting my time."

Sienna lifted her head, pushing back the chair, and hurled the contents of the bottle at his hand.

Chapter 15

There was a sound between a hiss and a pop, and a lightbulb shattered. Conran dropped the gun, emitting a spine-chilling howling sound as Brodie leaped toward him.

"Be careful!" Sienna screamed. "It's acid. Get him into the bathroom."

Someone was banging on the door, shouting, "Police! Open up!"

Brodie kicked the gun across the room, then grabbed Conran from behind by his good arm and pushed him toward the bathroom, telling Aidan, "Open the door and let the cops in."

Sienna darted ahead of Brodie and turned the shower on. She wanted to throw up or faint, but instead she helped Brodie get Conran into the stall, where he writhed and swore and moaned under the force of the water. His hand was raw and red, and there were holes burned in his clothing, small peeling spots on his face. "It was all I could think of," she said. "We'll need an ambulance."

Then two men in police uniform burst in, carrying guns at the ready. Another man wearing a floral shirt and jeans also had a gun. He looked at Brodie and said, "I could charge you with obstructing the police. I told you to stay out of it. You could have got yourself killed."

"You guys took your time," Brodie retorted. "What if he'd killed Sienna while you were getting your act together? You can take over now."

"I thought he *had* killed you," Brodie said, back at the house after lengthy police interviews and a visit to the hospital. "When I saw you lying there bleeding. Then your eyelashes moved a fraction. I've never been so relieved in all my life. And when you opened your eyes I was sweating in case you let on you'd woken up."

She'd been sweating too, at first simply thankful to see him, then sick with fear and anger that he'd put himself in danger for her sake. "Thank you for coming to the rescue. But you should have waited for the police."

Camille offered coffee, and he and Sienna both gratefully accepted. They sat side by side on the big sofa, and Camille seated herself opposite them. "What on earth happened?" She looked at the dressing on Sienna's forehead. "Are you all right?"

Sienna had a huge, throbbing bruise with a nasty little cut in the center where Conran had hit her with the butt of the gun. "I'll be fine. It didn't even need stitches." At the hospital they'd suggested keeping her overnight but she'd said firmly that she wanted to go home.

"What the hell were you doing there anyway?" Brodie demanded roughly. "I told you to stay put! I thought you were safe here."

"While you were happily playing sitting duck?" Sienna inquired.

"I had police protection!"

"Which you apparently evaded. That detective was livid."

"He was rabbiting on about backup, and I could hear you screaming at the other end of the phone."

"I did not scream," Sienna said. "At least, only to tell you not to come."

Brodie's expression was taut and murderous. "The bastard was hurting you. What the hell did you expect me to do?"

So he'd jumped into his four-wheel drive, roared off leaving his police protection behind, and once at the hotel hurtled up the stairs to Aidan's room. If Conran hadn't been waiting for him and made Aidan open up immediately, he'd have broken down the door.

He'd nearly died when he saw Sienna slumped at the table, her face deathly white and a pool of blood spreading under her head. The gun wouldn't have stopped him if he hadn't seen that faint flicker of her dark lashes and realized she was still breathing, and forced his mind into some kind of rational thinking, starting to consider ways of getting her out of there without further harm.

Conran had been smarter than Brodie had bargained for. Expecting to be held up at the shop, or that the crook would wait until after dark and make his move then, he'd missed the possibility of a more devious plan. The slimy scumbag had used Sienna to make sure of a private little killing party, with all his victims conveniently in one spot—a neatly devised trap.

He'd have left behind a massacre that he must have hoped wouldn't be discovered for hours, at least. And meantime he'd have been well away from the scene. All he'd need to do was ditch the gun and the ring and there'd be nothing to link him to the crime.

"What did you think *you* were going to do, unarmed against a gun?" she asked.

"I'd have taken him," Brodie said. "Somehow. I'd have made damn sure he didn't hurt you again."

Sienna said, "And got yourself shot in the process."

Brodie shrugged. "I've been in tight spots before, learned a few dirty tricks—with blokes like him you don't stick to Queensbury Rules."

Camille smiled at him. "I gather the police got him before you did?"

"Sienna got him."

"Sienna?" Camille stared at her. "What did you do?"

Sienna told her, wincing at the memory, reminding herself that what she'd done was self-defense—and defense of Brodie. She didn't dwell on the details, instead giving a brief rundown of all that had happened between her arrival at the hotel and the advent of the police. She hated to think what she'd done to the hotel carpet and curtains.

"I suppose Aidan will be charged with something," she said. He was still at the police station, "assisting" the officers with their inquiries. "But he's cooperating fully now he knows his wife and daughter are safe."

Brodie snorted. "He could have gone to the cops in the first place."

"Oh, yes," Sienna said. "And do what they told him to, just the way you did today?"

"I can look after myself. Your Aidan is a wet fish. He had no right to put you at risk."

The phone rang and Camille jumped up. "That *must* be Rogan!"

Her subdued voice floated to them from the hallway. Brodie turned to Sienna and lightly touched the dressing on her forehead. "Does it hurt much?"

"A bit. I was lucky it wasn't worse."

"Yeah." His face darkened. "Do me a favor and don't do anything like that ever again. It's not good for my heart."

"I don't think I'm likely to be confronting a cold-blooded murderer again."

He fingered a curl that had fallen over her forehead, teased it back to tuck it in with the others. "Sienna…"

"Yes?" She reminded herself that hair didn't have nerves. But she could feel his touch all the way to her toes.

"I…oh, hell!" He leaned forward and kissed her quite fiercely, setting her pulse thrumming. Her lips parted under the pressure of his, and she kissed him back, glad to be alive, glad that he was. Glad that he wanted to kiss her, make love to her.

The phone clattered back into its cradle, and Brodie drew away.

Camille entered. "They're back. The police came on board and took Joe away for questioning, and Rogan and Tilisi are on their way here now." She paused, an inquiring smile on her lips. "Am I interrupting something?"

Brodie dropped his hand from where his finger was still tangled in Sienna's hair, and she said, "No. Do you think Joe will tell them what he told us?"

Brodie said with satisfaction, "Now they've got Conran in custody I don't think they'll have much trouble persuading Joe to talk. And they've got our evidence that Conran tried to kill us, and Aidan's story. This guy surely won't be given bail!"

Rogan and Tilisi arrived at the house shortly afterward, and Brodie poured celebratory drinks all round. Camille looked as if a light had been turned on somewhere inside her, and Rogan scarcely let go of her hand when he didn't have an arm about her. Every now and then they exchanged a glance of hidden understanding.

Maybe Brodie had been right on the day of the wedding. Sienna couldn't imagine these two ever parting.

Tilisi didn't stay long, intending to catch a bus to Whangarei where he'd arranged to visit some diving friends. Brodie saw him out of the house and came back to where Rogan and Camille sat together on one of the two-seater sofas while Sienna occupied the other.

Brodie got Camille another drink, then turned and gave Sienna one of his slow, devastatingly sexy smiles, making her heart ache with longing. She wished passionately he was a different kind of man—or she a different kind of woman, the kind who could tame an adventure-loving diver with a roving eye and a way of making women fall at his feet.

She couldn't help smiling back helplessly, as besotted as

any other woman she'd seen drawn into the magnetic field of his male attraction.

"Another drink?" he said, crossing to her, and she blinked, realizing her glass was empty.

She handed it to him, nodding. "Thanks."

He poured her some more of the fruit juice she'd been drinking in deference to medical advice, and brought the glass over for her. Then he hunkered down onto the floor, his back against Sienna's chair. She resisted a desire to touch his hair, fascinated by the light glinting on the blond streaks, tantalizingly close to her hand. Tightening her fingers about her glass to quell temptation, she sat quietly while Camille and Brodie filled in Rogan on all that had happened since they'd parted from him at the island.

Rogan whistled. "And I thought I'd got the risky job," he said. "I guess after Drummond jumped bail he persuaded Conran to get him out of New Zealand on the promise of a share in the gold. He probably planned to take his own share and disappear to some foreign country and start a new life."

"Instead," Brodie said, "he ended up at the bottom of the ocean. And his partner's on his way to jail."

There was a silence then, and Rogan stirred. "Time I got back to the *Sea-Rogue*."

Camille, nestled against his shoulder, straightened reluctantly. "I'll move back on board tomorrow. Tonight I want to keep an eye on Sienna."

Rogan looked rueful but didn't argue, giving his wife a kiss that turned lingering.

Brodie said, "I'll watch Sienna. You go with Rogue."

"It's okay," Rogan said regretfully, still looking at Camille. They smiled at each other as though there were no one else in the room.

The ache around Sienna's heart increased. "I'm all right," she insisted. "Really."

After a bit more argument Camille gave in. "If you're sure you don't need me," she said. And to Brodie, "Call me if you're at all worried about her."

"If I'm worried," he said, "I'll call an ambulance. I won't let anything happen to her."

Closing the door after Camille and Rogan had left, Brodie turned to Sienna. "Alone at last." His grin teased. Then it faded, and he reached out to touch the dressing over her bruise again. "You'd better go to bed," he said. "It's been a long, tough day."

For him too. "Mmm," she said, not moving, reluctant to leave him although she knew she had to.

He touched the backs of his fingers to her cheek. "Are you okay?"

Impulse took over. Without thinking, she turned her head and kissed his fingers, tasting his skin against her lips.

"Sienna?"

She lifted her head and stood staring at him, drinking in the sight of him—so big, so vital, so tough, and yet capable of amazing tenderness. A man that a woman could lean on forever.

He'd dropped his hand from her, a frown creasing his forehead. Waking from her trance, she stepped back, then quickly made for her bedroom, ignoring the slight dizziness that attacked her.

He caught up with her in the doorway. "Sienna!" His hand closed on her arm. Turning her to face him, he stared down at her, his eyes incredulous, then softening to something else. "You're dead on your feet," he said. "You don't know what you're doing." He bent his head and kissed her, long and tender and appallingly sexy. She swayed into his arms and he held her close until at last he lifted his mouth from hers and said, "Good night, Sienna."

Then his arms fell from her and she was standing alone, watching him stride back to the lighted living area.

She slept late and didn't remember being woken during the night, although Brodie told her next morning that he had done so, following the doctor's instructions.

But she had dreamed about his voice, his kisses. Dreamed

that they were swimming together under the sea, hand in hand among the coral and the fishes, skimming the white sand at the bottom, and then rising through crystal water into the dazzling sun and a blue sky the color of his eyes.

She didn't tell him that as she nibbled her way through hot buttered toast under his disapproving eyes, after turning down his offer of bacon and egg.

"We're invited to lunch on the *Sea-Rogue*," he told her. "Camille phoned earlier but didn't want to wake you. First I'll take you back to the hospital. They said they wanted to check you over this morning."

He drove her there and they waited in the outpatients clinic for some time before a doctor pronounced himself satisfied and told her to come back if she experienced any problems, though he didn't expect any long-term effects.

They went to the wharf and Brodie jumped to the deck and lifted her down, keeping his hands on her waist while she steadied herself.

Camille looked radiant and Rogan's eyes rested on her with lazy appreciation and a glint of something more elemental. She refused to let Sienna help with the meal, telling her to relax in the wintry sunshine on deck.

Suppressing a pang of envy for her friend, Sienna obeyed, leaving the cramped galley space to Camille.

The men joined her in the cockpit, cracking open cans of beer while they engaged in a discussion about the next steps in getting their treasure hoard onto the market and satisfying their investors. Sienna declined the offer of a drink, and with her feet up on the seat leaned back against the bulkhead, slipping into a doze.

When she woke, Rogan wasn't there anymore and Brodie, sitting opposite with his feet resting against the bulkhead, was watching her intently. The sun glinted on his hair, but someone had rigged the awning to shade Sienna's face.

"Hi, Sleeping Beauty," he greeted her as she blinked at him. "I was wondering whether I should wake you...in the time-honored fashion."

Sienna straightened and swung her feet to the deck. "Did I miss lunch?"

"No, we waited for you. Rogue went to pour the wine."

Rogan appeared. "Ready to eat, Sienna? Stay there, we'll have it on deck."

Camille and Rogan brought food and wine up to the cockpit and took their accustomed seat while Brodie shifted over to Sienna's side.

She recalled all the times they'd sat together like this on the voyage to the *Maiden's Prayer,* and the time they'd watched the sun rise over the ocean together.

Now that the treasure hoard had been recovered, none of the other three would need to worry about money. Brodie would be free to roam the world if he liked, visit exotic dive sites without having to take professional work to pay for it or play shopkeeper in between times.

Lunch was leisurely, and afterward they finished a second bottle of wine and talked in desultory fashion. All of them felt lazy and replete and content.

It was late afternoon when Brodie finally said, "I guess we should be getting back." He stood up, stretching, and turned to take Sienna's hand, pulling her to her feet.

"We ought to show Rogan what Sienna's done with the artifacts we brought to Mokohina," Camille said. "I didn't think of it last night."

Last night they'd been unwinding from a particularly stressful day.

"Come with us now," Brodie suggested. "We can all have dinner at my place."

They piled into his vehicle and he drove to the house, where Sienna and Camille spread out the cleaned articles on the big table and Rogan inspected them. "You've done a great job," he told Sienna, picking up a pewter platter that glowed softly after being cleaned and polished.

"Camille helped."

"I just did what you told me to," Camille said.

"There are still some things that need to soak in acid baths a bit longer to get rid of the coral.'' Sienna indicated the row of tubs against one wall.

They returned to the living room for dinner, and after a last cup of coffee Rogan and Camille left, walking down the darkened street hand in hand.

Brodie closed the door and Sienna said, ''I should put away those things in the workroom.''

''Can't it wait until tomorrow? We'll arm the burglar alarm just in case, but we don't need to worry about Conran and his gang now.''

''I might as well do it before I go to bed.''

She turned to go to the workroom and he followed.

''Don't shut the door on me again, Sienna,'' he said softly.

''What?'' She turned to face him, surprised. She'd never closed the door while she was working.

''Last night,'' he said, ''you kissed me as though you meant it.''

Of course she'd meant it. ''I don't go in for meaningless kisses,'' she said. ''Or meaningless sex.''

He frowned. ''You think I do?''

''I think you're open to offers.''

''From you,'' he said promptly, ''sure. And it wouldn't have been meaningless for me. If you thought Parakaeo was, you're dead wrong. It meant a lot to me, still does. But last night wasn't the right time.''

''The thing is,'' she said steadily, ''there isn't a right time for us, Brodie. For me.'' She hesitated. ''I'm not your kind of woman.''

Brodie realized he needed to tread carefully. This conversation was important. ''And what kind of woman would that be?'' he asked. ''I know you're not the one-night-stand sort, Sienna. That isn't what I'm looking for.'' He wanted her for much longer than that—wanted to make love to her, sure, but also to laugh with her, look after her, and chase away the shadows he saw in her eyes. For a long, long time—maybe for the rest of their lives.

The thought welled up from his subconscious and hit him

like a hammer-blow, right between the eyes. It snatched the breath right out of his body.

But this wasn't about him, it was about her. "What you really mean is, I'm not your kind of man," he said. "Is it because I'm just a dumb diver? You want someone with a string of letters after his name? Sorry, I should have thought of that."

"No!" She looked horrified. "I'd never have thought *you'd* suffer from an inferiority complex!"

"I don't," he said. "But if that isn't what's bothering you, what is?"

"A relationship between us—wouldn't be healthy."

"Not healthy?" Bewildered for a moment, he said, "You don't mean that literally, do you? You don't have some incurable disease? I certainly don't."

"I mean, emotionally healthy." She lifted a hand in a helpless gesture, and he caught it in his own, stilling her fluttering fingers in a firm grip.

"*Make me understand,*" he said fiercely. "*Talk* to me!"

"It's not you," she said, avoiding his eyes. "It's me. I can't trust myself."

Already prepared to assure her that she could trust *him,* Brodie was thrown. "What do you mean by that?"

"You'd regret it," she said. "Believe me."

"Why?" he demanded, unable to imagine it.

He could see the effort it took for her to meet his eyes again. "Because," she said, "I'd cling."

Sheer astonishment kept him silent while he digested that. Then he laughed in disbelief. "Cling? *You?* You're the most bloody-mindedly independent female I've ever met! Honey, if I could get you to cling to me I'd be in seventh heaven!"

Sienna closed her eyes momentarily, then opened them again. "*Don't,* Brodie," she said. "Can't you recognize a defense mechanism when you see one?"

He stared at her. In the distance a siren wailed but he barely heard it. "A defense mechanism," he repeated slowly. It was a bloody good one. "Why do you need it?"

She bit her lip and shook her head slightly.

The telephone rang, and Sienna jumped.

He muttered a swearword under his breath but didn't take his eyes from hers, ignoring the shrill summons.

She said, "The phone—"

"Never mind the damn phone." But he knew the moment had passed.

"It might be important," she said.

"*This* is important!" But the phone didn't stop, and at last he turned and strode to the hallway, picked up the receiver and barked, "What?"

Sienna stood in the workroom where Brodie had left her, drawing a deep breath.

A reprieve. She'd been about to tell him of the humiliation, despair and misery that still made her cringe with remembered shame and heartbreak, vowing never to let herself get into that morass of futile emotion again. Never to leave herself open to it.

And then Brodie had come along and threatened to smash through all the barriers she'd built against men like him. All her hard-fought-for protective self-knowledge.

She heard him say, "I'll be there." Then the phone was banged down and he turned to her. "I have to go. There's a fire at the shop."

She started forward at that, and was in the doorway of the workroom when he flung open the outer door, looking back for an instant to say, "Don't go anywhere!" before he plunged into the night, slamming the door.

Typical, Sienna thought, half laughing and half crying, to shout a command at her on his way out.

She heard the four-wheel-drive start with a roar and then depart fast, the noise fading as it raced down the hill. His shop was on fire. There wouldn't be staff members there at this time of night, would there? He wouldn't be tempted to rush in and rescue anyone, surely? Or stupid enough to try to save his stock? Was he insured?

He had a share in the *Maiden's Prayer* treasure. Soon he'd be a rich man. She wondered if he was emotionally attached to his business.

She wanted to follow him, be at his side. But she'd only be one of a crowd of onlookers getting in the way of the firefighters, not doing anything useful.

Going to the front door, she walked as far as the gate and peered down the street. The dive shop was hidden around curves and behind the black shapes of houses and trees, but a faint orange glow lit a thick column of smoke studded with sparks. Another siren sounded.

She stood worrying a thumbnail with her teeth, praying that Brodie was all right, that the damage wasn't going to be as great as that ominous cloud suggested, fighting the urge to run down the hill, all the way to the blaze, and be with him. A gust of cold wind made her shiver, and reluctantly she turned to go back inside. Light streamed onto the path. The door was still wide open.

Slowly she went inside and closed it behind her.

The light in the workroom was on too. She went into the room where the artifacts were spread out on the table, the softly gleaming silver, pewter and copper reflected in the darkened window at the other side of the room, along with her own reflection. She walked forward and her heart lurched, then she opened her mouth in a choked, almost silent scream as she saw another reflection just behind hers, a male shape standing beside the open door.

She whirled even as he slammed the door closed and barred her way out. Her eyes widened in horror.

This wasn't possible. It was a nightmare.

"Good evening," Fraser Conran said.

Chapter 16

The icy, colorless eyes were uncovered, naked with malice and cold purpose. He wore some kind of overall, and a white bandage covered his right hand.

He was terrifyingly real.

Sienna opened her mouth to scream in earnest and Conran leaped forward, his left hand slapping painfully over her mouth, then he was behind her, his right arm going about her throat as she attempted to dodge away, unbalancing her. "Shut up!" he hissed in her ear.

She tried to bite the hand that almost suffocated her, lifted her own hands to grasp the arm locked about her throat, managed to find her feet and hooked one of them backward around his ankle, giving a sharp pull forward.

He gave an exclamation and staggered, his hold loosening, and she wrenched herself away, took a breath and screamed, heading for the door.

Before she reached it he slammed into her back and she fell to the floor.

As she scrambled to her hands and knees he grabbed her

hair, pulling her head back painfully and shoving her again to the floor. "Another sound and I'll kill you," he threatened in her ear.

He was probably going to kill her anyway, but maybe she could give herself some extra time—time to outwit him and escape. His knee was on her back, pinning her down. Her spine arched, and she wondered if it was possible to break a person's back this way.

"Thanks for leaving the door open," he said. "I thought I'd have to break in somehow, but you made it easy. Are you easy, my little red-haired hellcat?" He leaned so close she could feel his breath stirring her hair.

A new fear added to the terror she already felt. "What do you want?" she gasped. "The gold isn't here."

"I know that. What I want, before I catch my ride out of this place, is payback for *this*." He thrust his bandaged hand in front of her eyes. "You might have crippled me for life," he said. "I'll certainly be scarred. Nobody does that to me and gets away with it."

Sienna closed her eyes. "I'm sorry." As soon as the words left her lips she thought it was a stupid thing to say. He'd been about to kill Brodie, and herself, and Aidan. There was no doubt in her mind about that.

"Sorry isn't good enough, *sweetheart*." The sneering endearment nauseated her. "You're going to be *really* sorry by the time I've finished with you."

The weight was removed from her back and he hauled her upright by her hair. "No more tricks," he warned.

"The police will catch you," she panted. "Why make things worse for yourself than they already are? Brodie's due back any minute," she added desperately.

"Your boyfriend's busy," Conran said. "Watching his precious business go up in smoke. And when I've finished with you, dear girl, I'm leaving these shores forever. My transport's waiting in the harbor right now. By the time anyone finds you I'll be gone. Unfortunately I don't have a lot of time, but while you were mooning about after your boyfriend,

I had a look around here, and I've thought of a most appropriate punishment. You'll be suffering long after I've left. Now, let's get on with it, shall we?''

Brodie stood watching as flames shot out of the roof of his dive shop, the place he'd saved for, over years of hard work. That he'd made his own, something to come home to after a dive job, something he was proud of.

A crowd had gathered before he got here, and while the volunteer fire brigade busied themselves pumping water from the dive pool adjacent to the building and directed their hoses onto the seat of the fire, the local policeman was telling people to stand clear.

Through the windows Brodie could see the front part of the place was still intact, but the fire was advancing, roaring and crackling and greedy for more fuel.

The policeman, having checked the sightseers, came to stand with him, and the fire chief came over, removing his helmet to wipe sweat from his forehead. "Sorry, Brodie," he said. "We're doing our best but it took hold pretty fast. Could be there's an accelerant involved."

Brodie turned to him. "Arson?"

The constable said, "Heck, we've got a bloody crime wave in Mokohina. Most of it," he added to Brodie as though it were his fault, "connected with you. By the way, they've lost Conran."

"What?" Brodie snapped. "What do you mean, lost him?"

"He kicked up a fuss at the station in Whangarei, reckoned his hand hadn't been properly treated here, he was in pain and insisted he needed medical attention. They took him to the hospital. He slipped away somehow when they were waiting for him to come out of the toilet."

"When?" A hole opened up in Brodie's stomach, black and dreadful.

"Not sure. I only heard about it just before I got called out to this. They'll get him back, don't worry."

Don't worry? When Conran was on the loose again and Sienna…

Sienna. Brodie swore explosively and wheeled, running to where he'd parked, leaped into the driving seat and spent precious moments finding his keys before he started the engine and took off with a screech of tires, pulling his cell phone from his pocket, but he couldn't see to dial his own number, find out if Sienna was answering, if she was all right.

Sienna…

She twisted and fought against Conran's hold, tried to scream again. Once she managed to kick out, felt her foot connect with bone and flesh, and he grunted, kicked her back, a blinding pain in her shin. She sagged, reached out with her hands, scratched at his face.

He reared back, releasing his hold on her hair, and momentarily she was free, grabbing a heavy brass candlestick from the table, raising it high, but he swung up his hand, shoved her back to the table, smashing her wrist down on the edge of it, and she yelped with pain as the candlestick rolled away.

Then he had her again, her arm yanked behind her back, making her cry out, furious with herself that she'd let him know he'd hurt her. Even with one hand he was stronger than she was. And murderously angry, bent on revenge.

"Those bins," he said, urging her toward the plastic containers along the wall. "Full of acid, aren't they? Maybe not as strong as what you used on me—you dilute it—but strong enough to melt coral away, and to spoil that pretty face of yours. You'll be disfigured for life, just like me."

She tried to tell herself that at least she'd be alive, that being murdered would be the worst fate, but at this moment it didn't seem so. And ridiculously, she thought that if Brodie found her ugly, an object of pity, she'd rather be dead.

Conran had her by the hair again, his other arm pinning hers to her body, holding her obscenely close, dragging, pushing her from behind until they stood before one of the bins and he kicked at the back of her knees, making her kneel in front of it. "Now," he said, "say goodbye to your good looks, sweetheart." He forced her head down and she closed her eyes, then was choking on liquid that bubbled in her ears, and felt the skin of her face contracting as she struggled to breathe.

Brodie slid to a screaming halt outside the house and went racing along the path, sorting his keys as he went, thrusting one into the front door with hardly a pause. The light in the workroom was still on. *"Sienna?"* In half a second he was in the doorway, scanning the room, finding the figure bent over one of the tubs, turning now to face him, astonished chagrin written on the nondescript features, cold fury in the light eyes. And before him, kneeling on the floor, his hand holding her hair, Sienna, with her face—oh God!—her face in the tub.

With an inarticulate sound of rage and pain, Brodie launched himself across the room, his fist a sledgehammer that went straight to Conran's face. The other man flew halfway across the room, his head hit the edge of the table and he slumped to the floor.

Sienna was on the floor too, curled up, coughing water—and...

Brodie scooped her up, ran to the laundry, held her with her head under the shower fitting and played it over her face. "It's all right, hon," he said. "It's all right. I'll get you to the hospital." He released her to haul out his cell phone again and dial the emergency number while still spraying her with water. "Ambulance," he said, "and police, if you can get the stupid cop."

Sienna pushed away the showerhead and said something he didn't hear, busy as he was giving directions to the operator. "Tell them to get their rears into gear." He turned to Sienna and directed the shower at her again. "We need to keep this up," he said, "until the ambulance gets here."

"I don't need an ambulance!" she spluttered, pushing away

the nozzle again, dousing him in the process. "Unless you drown me with this thing."

"You don't want to be scarred," he said. "Sienna, for God's sake—"

"Would it stop you wanting me?" she asked, turning away her face, both her hands staying his as he tried to direct the spray at her again.

"What the hell does that matter?" he snapped. "It's *you* I'm worried about. You'll still be the woman I fell in love with."

"In love?" she said faintly, then sputtered as he sprayed her once more.

"Yes, in love," he said impatiently. "I think I've loved you since I first saw you, and I know I'm going to love you forever—marry you, give you my children, if you'll have me. And I don't care what the hell you look like. Now let me do this, Sienna! It might not be too late to prevent some of the damage."

"There's no need," she said, forcing his hands away again. "Brodie, *look at me!* Do you see any damage?"

A siren sounded outside, coming closer, stopping. Brodie blinked at her. Her cheeks were flushed, her hair dripping over her forehead in little wet ringlets, the front of her T-shirt soaked, but she looked otherwise normal.

Someone was thundering on the door.

"He chose the wrong tub," Sienna said, and bit her lip to stop a hysterical giggle. "He doesn't know as much as he thinks. There was no acid in there—only pure distilled cold water. Very g-good for the complexion."

Then she burst into tears.

After the ambulance staff had inspected Conran's wound and, at Brodie's insistence checked Sienna over, the police-man took a handcuffed and groggy Conran away again, with Brodie's blistering assessment of the force's competence fol-lowing him out the door.

Brodie came back into the living room where Sienna lay

on the couch, wrapped in a blanket with a cup of hot cocoa in her hands. Camille was perched on the side of the sofa, watching her anxiously. She and Rogan had taken a little time to realize it was Brodie's shop that was blazing, and arrived in time to see his vehicle disappear at speed and to urge the policeman to leave the fire and get to Brodie's house, with him and Camille piled into the back seat.

Brodie said, "They'd better not let Conran get away a second time."

"They wouldn't dare," Camille said, "after what you threatened them with." She turned to Sienna. "I could stay with you tonight if you like. Rogan too—he can sleep here on the couch."

Brodie scowled. "You think I can't look after her?" Then he allowed bitterly, "Maybe you're right. I didn't do a very good job of it tonight."

Sienna said, "You did wonderfully! I've never been so glad to see anyone. It was only a matter of time before that man realized his mistake and got the right tub." She shivered.

"I shouldn't have left you," he said.

"Your shop was on fire! And all of us thought Conran was safely locked up. How bad is the damage?"

He looked blank, as if he didn't know what she was talking about. Then he said, "The shop? That doesn't matter. All that matters is you didn't come to any permanent harm." He came closer and hunkered down beside her, fingering one of her curls that had fallen across her forehead again. "If I hadn't been in such a hurry to get you under some running water I think I'd have killed him. I'll never let you out of my sight again."

Camille exchanged a glance with her husband. "On second thought, maybe our presence isn't required."

Brodie said, without looking away from Sienna's troubled gaze, "Stay as long as you like, if Sienna wants you to."

"Sienna?" Rogan queried. "If it would make you feel better...?"

She looked up at him and Camille, now standing side by side. "You can trust Brodie to look after me," she said.

Brodie saw them to the door, then returned and sat where Camille had, beside her. "Thank you for that," he said seriously.

"For what?"

"Trusting me, even though I stuffed up."

"You didn't, the police did—and no one expected that."

"I should have realized that the shop being fired couldn't be coincidence. From now on I'll be right by you, night and day. If you'll let me."

Sienna looked down at the now-empty cup she still held. "You'd soon get tired of it."

"Never," he said fervently. "Not on your life."

"People do," she warned. "Men."

Brodie took her hand. "Men?" He turned her palm to his cheek, then dropped a kiss into her hand and twined his fingers about hers. "I should put you to bed and let you sleep. But one question—what did you mean when you said you didn't trust yourself not to cling?" He took the cup from her and captured her other hand. "We'd started to talk before everything went haywire. You opened the door a crack, and I don't want it slammed in my face again. If you can't tell me tonight, can we talk tomorrow or in a few days—when you've had time to get over what's happened?"

She was looking at their joined hands. "It won't get any easier," she said. "The thing is…you don't know what I'm like."

"I know enough to be sure that I want to spend the rest of my life getting to know more. Marry me," he said. "And let me keep you safe for the rest of your life."

"Oh, Brodie!" She was looking at him with less joy than trepidation. Ineffectually she tugged at her captured hands. "I can't do that to you."

"You mean you don't love me," he said, dropping her hands. He'd been taking too much for granted. She might be tempted to have sex with him, but marriage, permanence, wasn't on her agenda. His heart sinking, he said, "Is there a chance you might, one day?"

"A chance?" She gave a strange little laugh that seemed to verge on tears. "You don't know what you're asking for!"

"I'm asking for you," he said. "All of you, forever. Because you have all of me, and whatever happens, wherever you go, you'll carry my heart and soul with you."

"And you'll have mine," she whispered, her eyes luminous. "But—"

His heart seemed to leap right out of his chest. She was saying she loved him! Almost angrily he asked, "Then why can't you just say, 'Yes, Brodie, I'll marry you!'"

"Because," she said, "I could never let you go. Not you— it would be worse than before."

"I wouldn't want you to! Before? Before what?" He reached out and grasped her shoulders. "Talk to me, Sienna, dammit! We can sort anything out if you really love me. I won't *let* you crawl back into your blasted clam shell now!"

She closed her eyes. He watched her take a couple of deep breaths, her mouth taut. Then with obvious effort she spoke, forcing her eyes to meet his. "When…after my father left, my mother was so bewildered and upset she hardly noticed what my brother and I were up to. And what I was up to was trying to find the love I felt my dad had taken away from me. Boys…I expected too much, was ready to give so much in return. But they were young and selfish, which I was too young myself to recognize, and I was available."

Brodie said, "I'm not shocked so far."

"I don't mean I was sleeping around with a different boy every weekend. But I was lost and lonely and looking for something they couldn't give me. All of them let me down, one way or another."

"So you decided all men were the same?"

"I knew they weren't. I still hoped… And I met someone a few years older than me, who seemed to genuinely love me, and we were together for six months…until I discovered he'd been seeing my best friend." She tried to smile, a pathetic attempt. "Such an old cliché. My boyfriend and my best friend. I was shattered. So I withdrew from a social life, until I was in my second year at university and then my professor—"

"Your professor? Some old goat of an academic?"

"He wasn't all that old—older than me, of course, in his thirties. But he flattered me, encouraged me, told me I had a great future. Looking back, I realize how patronizing he was in a subtle way, but at the time I thought he was wonderful. He was my mentor, I looked up to him, and he was kind, made me feel special. Loved... When we were on a dig and it started raining heavily he gave me his coat, insisted I take it while he got wet himself." This time she did smile, with a wry grimace. "He looked great in a wet shirt. I was young and naive, and...I'd have done anything for him."

"And did you?" Brodie asked.

"Yes. We were lovers for a whole semester."

"Was he married?"

"No, divorced. Twice. That should have told me something, but I wasn't even twenty and not very clever outside of the classroom."

"So what happened at the end of the semester?"

"He dumped me. I couldn't believe it was over, didn't understand why. I made a fool of myself—begging, crying, and taking all the blame for the breakup, asking what I'd done, how I could make things right." Her voice had sunk so low Brodie could hardly hear. "Eventually he said the only thing I could do was leave him alone. He was sick of me and my neediness, I was a clinging vine, a leech, needed a psychiatrist, and he didn't have the time or inclination to deal with my insecurities. Women in general, and me in particular, were incapable of rational thought, they always let emotion get in the way—oh, and a lot more. The next semester I heard he was sleeping with one of his new students."

"He made a habit of it?" Brodie was outraged.

"I don't know. Maybe. The thing is, he was right about me. I was an easy target for any man who offered me affection and security and protection. It wasn't the sex that mattered to me. It was all those other things I was missing since my father left and my mother withdrew from life. Pathetic, isn't it? A classic psychological case. Once I worked that out I steered well clear of men who reminded me of my father in any way, especially men who promised to look after me. By then I knew my fatal weakness. I learned to look after myself, not to ever expect someone else to do it. And then you came along, and the danger signals started flashing.''

"I remind you of your father?'' Something tasted sour in his mouth.

"He was very good-looking.''

"Do I say thank-you?''

She shook her head. "Women liked him. And he liked them—too much, as my mother discovered.''

"I've never cheated on a woman,'' Brodie said, swallowing indignation. "And I certainly wouldn't cheat on my wife.''

"I know you wouldn't. You're not the kind of man my father was. But you might regret marrying a wife who made you feel trapped, smothered you—if she leaned on you, depended on you, asked too much…you might stop loving her in the end.''

"You could never ask too much of me, Sienna.''

Her eyes glittered with tears. Almost whispering, she said, "You don't realize how desperately I want to believe that. You're taking such a risk.''

"I'm used to risks, thrive on them. Sure I want to protect you, but heck, do you think I don't know you're able to look after yourself in most circumstances? When you threw that stuff at Conran I was still trying to figure out when and how I could take him before he took us both—and Aidan—out. You saved us all.''

"You saved me tonight.''

"My turn.'' He grinned. "Makes us about even. If you feel like leaning on me, feel free. And I might even lean on you occasionally…I know you're strong enough to take it.''

"Strong?'' It was a novel thought. Doubtful, even suspicious, she inquired, "When would you ever need to lean on anyone?" She could scarcely imagine it.

"Underwater," he said. "You know how buddies depend on each other if there's a problem, trust each other literally with their lives. It's a two-way thing—like a marriage should be. And maybe—" his eyes clouded "—when someone takes it into his head to burn down my business."

"You said it didn't matter."

"Alongside your safety it's nothing. But I've spent years getting it set up and improving it, and I'm pretty damn cheesed off about losing it and having to start over."

"You'll have the money from PTS."

"That'll help," he admitted. "And it was insured. But I was sort of attached to the old place. Like I am to this house. I got a buzz out of coming home to them both."

She held out her arms, and he went into them, his own going around her, pulling her close. His lips nuzzled her neck. "You realize this was a ploy to get you back here where you belong?"

She gave a little laugh, shaking against him. "Do *you* realize you've just invited a clinging vine to twine herself around you? I warned you, I might never be able to let go." She took a breath, said something she'd sworn never to say again, laying herself open to hurt and betrayal. Brodie wouldn't do that to her. "I love you…"

"Tell me that again," he said. "I never intend to let you go, either. So don't even think about leaving me—ever."

Three weeks later they were married in the chapel at Mokohina. Camille took her place as Sienna's bridal attendant, and Rogan stood with his friend as Sienna made her way down the aisle to Brodie's side on her brother's arm. As an engagement ring, Brodie had presented her with one of the precious finds from the *Maiden's Prayer,* a gold band with a single garnet flanked by diamonds. But the ring he slipped on her finger during the ceremony was brand new, a plain gold band.

At the reception in the Imperial Hotel's private bar, Rogan wore a slightly knowing smile as Brodie came in for some ribbing from his diving friends. There were remarks about him being caught at last, hook, line and sinker, and some mention of balls and chains.

"Don't take any notice of them," Granger advised Sienna. "They're jealous."

Mollie Edwards, her defiantly golden curls newly permed, gave both bride and groom exuberant hugs. "I'm so glad you took my advice." She beamed at Sienna, who looked slightly puzzled. "To join the boys' company and help them raise Barney's treasure," Mollie reminded her.

"I'm glad too." Brodie hooked his arm about his new wife's waist.

"Although I suppose," Mollie went on, "when that horrible man attacked you, you must have had some second thoughts. At least you know now you're safe, with him in jail, and his henchmen rounded up too. As for that Joe! All I can say is, crown witness or not, he deserves to rot! How could he betray the boys like that?"

"He was afraid for his own life," Sienna said.

"Idiot," Brodie commented. "As if telling Conran he had the ring would ensure Conran wouldn't kill him." Instead, he'd sent his henchmen to beat Joe into giving it up. And he'd finally crumbled, admitting he'd never had it, but Sienna did. Joe had told the police everything in the end. "He should have come straight to us, we'd have seen him right if he'd just been honest about the whole thing."

"Well, all's well that ends well," Mollie said. "And just think—you two might never have met if it wasn't for Barney's treasure! Brodie's a good lad," she told Sienna. "Mind you look after him!"

She looked bewildered but indulgent when they turned to each other and laughed.

"I will," Sienna promised her. "All my life."

* * *

Days later she and Brodie were swimming together in the clear, silken water off a secluded beach at Parakaeo, wearing only swimsuits, unencumbered by flippers, snorkels or tanks.

Brodie dived to the sandy bottom, and she followed him down, skimming the seafloor that was crowded with shells, spotted sea slugs and starfish.

Sienna surfaced first, and Brodie came up moments later, his hair sleeked and darkened by the water. Sienna turned to float on her back as he trod water beside her. "Enjoying your honeymoon?" he asked her.

"Mmm…" She closed her eyes, felt the sun caress her lids, the water lap around her. Something touched her lips, warm and salty, and she smiled. Brodie kissed her again, and she kissed him back as his arms came about her and she sank with him into the sea's cool embrace, their legs tangling about each other, bodies close.

The kiss was necessarily brief, and they emerged sputtering and laughing. Brodie pulled her close again and planted another brief kiss on her mouth. His eyes brilliant with desire, he said softly, "Want to go back to the beach?"

Sienna nodded, silently answering the message in his eyes. They swam to the white strip of sand and the rug spread under the shadow of the palms that overhung the tiny, secret beach. There they went into each other's arms again, their bodies slick and wet as they lay on the rug and shared a long, satisfying kiss, their hands discovering planes and hollows, hardness and softness.

Brodie drew back and shucked his swim briefs, then with her eager cooperation dispensed with Sienna's bikini. Leaning his head on his hand, he surveyed her with lazy appreciation.

"I've put on weight," she said, "with all this island food."

"I look forward to the day you're a real armful—fair, fat and forty…"

She gave him a shove, and he fell onto his back, but grabbed at her wrist and took her with him, lying half over him as he grinned up at her. "…and all of it mine," he said. He carried her hand to his mouth and kissed it.

She snuggled closer, laid her cheek against his chest.

"Don't let me ball and chain you," she said. "You must tell me if I ever try."

"Honey, do you really think you could if I didn't want you to? Your professor was a bastard, he preyed on your need and made you believe it was your fault. You're strong and smart, and the fact is you don't need anybody. Not even me. But I hope you want me, and will for the rest of your life."

"I want you!" She lifted her head. "I've always wanted you. I fought it as long as I could, but—"

"You can't fight love," he said. "We were meant to be."

She bent and kissed his chest, teasing little kisses that wandered over his salty skin while his hands explored her back, and their breathing mutually quickened. Her mouth moved lower on his body and he stifled an exclamation. "No, honey, not now." He hauled her upward, and she smiled down at him and lowered her head to his kiss, straddled him and felt him glide inside her, filling her, sending her soaring, weightless, spinning into another dimension where space and time ceased to exist and only this closeness, this mystery of two in one flesh, this ecstasy in each other's arms, this rapture of the deep, was real.

When the last of the rippling aftershocks subsided, she lay against him, spent and replete, and his fingers tangled in her hair. "It's better every time with you," he said, his voice muffled. "I never realized sex could be this good."

"Me, neither," Sienna said. "I told you when we first met I knew what it was to be in love. I lied. It was never like this."

Brodie shifted, turned them over, so that he was looking down at her. Overhead the palm trees made small clacking sounds, and tiny shards of sunlight peeking through the moving fronds danced like jewels on the beads of seawater trapped in Sienna's hair. "I've caught me a mermaid," he said. "A sea creature."

"Like you," she said, remembering he'd told her that the sea threw back those who didn't belong there. "Let's go in the water again."

He traced her lips with a finger, then stood up and tugged her after him, kissed her lingeringly one more time, and took her hand, led her to the edge of the lagoon and into the slow, rippling waves until the water reached their waists, and then they swam, hand in hand, together into that magical, mysterious world under the sea. Into their future.

* * * * *

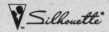

INTIMATE MOMENTS™

An Order of Protection

(Silhouette Intimate Moments #1292)

by

KATHLEEN CREIGHTON

A brand-new book in her bestselling series

STARRS OF THE WEST

Jo Lynn Starr's best friend is missing but no one will believe her. No one except police officer Scott Cavanaugh—and even he has his doubts. But as they work together to unravel the mystery, one thing becomes perilously clear—their growing attraction for each other!

Available May 2004 at your favorite retail outlet.

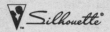

If you enjoyed what you just read,
then we've got an offer you can't resist!

Take 2 bestselling
love stories FREE!
Plus get a FREE surprise gift!

Clip this page and mail it to Silhouette Reader Service™

IN U.S.A.	IN CANADA
3010 Walden Ave.	P.O. Box 609
P.O. Box 1867	Fort Erie, Ontario
Buffalo, N.Y. 14240-1867	L2A 5X3

YES! Please send me 2 free Silhouette Intimate Moments® novels and my free surprise gift. After receiving them, if I don't wish to receive anymore, I can return the shipping statement marked cancel. If I don't cancel, I will receive 6 brand-new novels every month, before they're available in stores! In the U.S.A., bill me at the bargain price of $3.99 plus 25¢ shipping and handling per book and applicable sales tax, if any*. In Canada, bill me at the bargain price of $4.74 plus 25¢ shipping and handling per book and applicable taxes**. That's the complete price and a savings of at least 10% off the cover prices—what a great deal! I understand that accepting the 2 free books and gift places me under no obligation ever to buy any books. I can always return a shipment and cancel at any time. Even if I never buy another book from Silhouette, the 2 free books and gift are mine to keep forever.

245 SDN DNUV
345 SDN DNUW

Name	(PLEASE PRINT)	
Address	Apt.#	
City	State/Prov.	Zip/Postal Code

* Terms and prices subject to change without notice. Sales tax applicable in N.Y.
** Canadian residents will be charged applicable provincial taxes and GST.
   All orders subject to approval. Offer limited to one per household and not valid to
   current Silhouette Intimate Moments® subscribers.
   ® are registered trademarks of Harlequin Books S.A., used under license.

INMOM02   ©1998 Harlequin Enterprises Limited

A sensual, sizzling tale of love on the run
from one of romance's leading ladies!

New York Times bestselling author

LINDA LAEL MILLER

Caught in the cross fire in Cabriz, Kristin Meyers
must rely on her childhood friend—and ex-lover—
Zach Harmon to get her out alive. But who will save
her heart from being broken by him one more time?

Available in April.

Escape
FROM CABRIZ

Silhouette®
Where love comes alive™

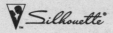

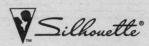

COMING NEXT MONTH

INTIMATE MOMENTS®

#1291 WANTED—Ruth Langan
Devil's Cove

Landscape designer Hannah Brennan was falling fast for her mysterious boss, Ethan Harrison. She'd been hired to turn around the gardens of his Devil's Cove mansion, and instead she found herself planting smiles on the face of this grieving widower. Yet when unexplained accidents threaten Hannah's life, would she trust him to tell her the truth about his past—and their future?

#1292 AN ORDER OF PROTECTION—Kathleen Creighton
Starrs of the West

Policeman Scott Cavanaugh couldn't help but be the hero to his partner's sister Joy Lynn Starr. Even though he had plenty of reasons not to trust this damsel-in-distress, he found himself believing her story that something terrible had befallen her roommate. Now in a desperate search for the truth, Scott must stop a kidnapper from grabbing the one woman he's come to cherish above all others.

#1293 JOINT FORCES—Catherine Mann
Wingmen Warriors

After being held prisoner in a war-torn country, Sergeant J. T. "Tag" Price returned home to find his marriage nearly over—until his wife, Rena, dropped a bomb of her own. She was pregnant! As he set out to romance his wife again, sudden danger loomed—someone wanted him and his family dead. Now he had to fight against this perilous foe to save his wife and unborn child…

#1294 MANHUNT—Carla Cassidy
Cherokee Corners

FBI agent Nick Mead sensed his witness Alyssa Whitefeather wasn't telling him everything she knew about the serial killer he was trying to catch. He needed to convince this Native American beauty that she could trust him with her life—and her secrets. Alyssa wanted to tell Nick about her visions of the murderer, but what would he say when he learned the next victim was *him?*

#1295 AGAINST THE WALL—Lyn Stone
Special Ops

There was something about Maggie Mann that made scientist Rick Dornier stand up and take notice. She wasn't strictly beautiful, but she stirred his blood and proved to be a real challenge. Rick had been determined to find out what Maggie knew about his missing sister, but would his feelings for her prove to be the deadliest distraction of all…?

#1296 DEAD AIM—Anne Woodard

One minute Dr. Solange Micheaux was tending to injured patients. The next, she was on the run with Special Agent Jack Mercier in a deadly race against time. She'd been in the wrong place at the wrong time, and Jack had no choice but to take her with him. But as the hours ticked down, Solange became critical to his success—even though each passion-filled moment they shared could be their last.

SIMCNM0404